MALFUNCTION

DARK DESIRES ORIGINS BOOK 1

MALFUNCTION

DARK DESIRES ORIGINS BOOK 1

NINA CROFT

Entangled Publishing, LLC
10940 S Parker Rd
Suite 327
Parker, CO 80134
rights@entangledpublishing.com

Amara is an imprint of Entangled Publishing, LLC.

Edited by Liz Pelletier and Lydia Sharp
Cover design by Covers by Juan
Cover photography by Daz 3d
lithian, glamour, Arthur-studio10, Amelia Fox, Vadim Sadovski, Space
creator, muratart, and Jub-Job/Shutterstock

Manufactured in the United States of America

First Edition January 2020

To my mother, who passed on her wonderful love of books to me.

Prologue

He came awake suddenly, his eyes flashing open, and he lay in the utter darkness, breathing quietly.

Don't panic.

There was nothing to worry about. Soon someone would come, and the lid would open. He'd been through the simulations. Though it had been light then. Now there was total, impenetrable blackness.

And the first flickers of fear stirred in his gut.

He stretched out his finger, which was all he could move, searching for the manual release switch. He pressed it. Nothing happened. He stabbed it again and again and still nothing. Fear crawled up his gorge, sour and bitter in the back of his throat.

Time passed.

He opened his mouth, but no sound came out, and he swallowed and licked his lips, tried again. "Is anyone there?"

His voice sounded hoarse and too quiet in the darkness. And no one answered. "Help!"

More time.

No sense of movement. No sounds except his ragged breathing. No heat. No cold.

How long had he been awake? A headache nagged at the back of his skull, and nausea churned in his stomach. He recognized the first signs of oxygen depletion and rising carbon dioxide levels. How long did he have left?

Panic took over, and he fought mindlessly against the restraints, spine arching, hands clawing at his sides until the sharp metallic scent of blood clogged his nostrils. Finally, exhausted, he collapsed back and lay panting, trying to get sufficient oxygen into his lungs.

He couldn't die like this, trapped and alone in the dark.

Maybe it was divine retribution, from a God he hadn't believed in for a long time.

Or had someone discovered his secret?

His heart hammered, and his breath was coming hard and fast now. He had to keep calm; the air would last longer, but he couldn't stop himself gasping for each breath.

Help!

The word screamed through his mind as a convulsion racked his body.

Was this the end?

For him?

Or for the whole human race?

Chapter One

Logan blinked his eyes open.

Where the hell am I?

He was lying on his back, in what resembled a coffin, and his heart rate kicked up.

Balls!

He tried to move, to roll over, to sit up, but something held him in place, and panic clawed at his guts. He forced himself to breathe slowly. The walls were gray, but the ceiling was some clear material through which filtered a dim light.

And it came back to him. He was in a cryotube on board the *Trakis One*.

With the knowledge, his heart rate slowed. It felt like only moments since he had closed his eyes and drifted off into what he had suspected would be an eternal sleep. He knew the odds that this trip would succeed were not good. There was too much that could go wrong. He hadn't expected to wake up.

And that did beg the question…

Why the fuck am I awake?

Were they still on Earth? *Had* something gone wrong? Had they aborted the mission?

Through the glass above him, he made out a movement. Looked like he was going to find out. He shook his head as much as the restraints would allow, blinking to clear his vision as the glass door of the cryotube was opened from the outside. The restraints popped free, and his pulse returned to normal.

"On your feet, sergeant."

He recognized the voice, though it sounded different—a little rougher. And the face that came into focus above him was familiar but also different. Older. Considerably older.

Fuck me.

He opened his mouth, but no words came out, and he swallowed, cleared his throat, and tried again. "How long?"

"Since we left Earth? Four hundred and ninety-nine years, three hundred and sixty-one days."

Logan pushed himself up, swiping off the monitors attached to his chest. An alarm screeched to life then cut out immediately. He swung his legs around so he sat on the edge of the cryotube, eyes closed, taking stock. His body felt heavy, his mind sluggish. Maybe that's what happened when you slept for five hundred years.

Five hundred fucking years.

He shook his head again, trying to grasp that reality. Had they made it? They must have if they were waking him up. His heart was pounding again, but in a good way this time.

Although he'd never admitted it, even to himself, deep down he'd wanted this with a desperation he hadn't experienced since he was a five-year-old kid at the orphanage, praying for someone to pick him. To take him home. That had never worked out, and he'd thought he had put those particular dreams behind him. Until the world had nearly come to an end. And with that had come the unexpected chance of a new life, a fresh start away from the old prejudice and intolerance. Maybe a chance to finally belong, not to pretend, but to actually be part of something big.

"Are we there?" Though he had no clue where "there" was. When they'd set off from a dying Earth, they'd had no destination in mind, just seeking out a world that could sustain life. Twenty-four ships. Each carrying ten thousand humans, the Chosen Ones, who would ensure the continuation of humanity. But how likely was that in the vastness of space?

"No."

No? The anticipation oozed out of him. That didn't sound good. So why was he awake?

He studied the man. Major Travis Pryce. He'd known him vaguely back on Earth. Hadn't liked him too much, but then they hadn't moved in the same circles—the major was English. And while Logan didn't hold that against him, he was also a pretentious prick born with a silver spoon shoved up his ass. An officer who considered enlisted men as some sort of second-class citizens. They were near enough the same age—that was their only similarity—or they had been. Now the major had deep lines around his mouth, wrinkles at the corners of his eyes, and his dark hair was streaked with gray. He'd also put on a few pounds. Not a good look in the tight-fitting uniform; the yellow shirt outlined an impressive paunch.

Most of the Chosen Ones were selected by a lottery. All fair and above board. Everyone had an equal chance. Well, that was the theory, though he was sure some people had more of an "equal chance" than others. But in addition to the Chosen Ones, the ships also carried crews, enough to cover ten rotations or approximately five hundred years.

And an army.

Apparently, the powers that be had decided some sort of military force would be needed once they got to wherever they were going. Maybe they were expecting hostile aliens. Little green men with laser guns. But aliens or not, soldiers were always needed. And who was he to complain? The army had been his way on board—otherwise he would have been left behind and long dead by now, even without the end of the world.

And the army was his life, had been since he joined when he was seventeen. It had given him the first home and security he had ever known. Though still not the acceptance he'd craved back then, before he'd finally realized that he would never fit in.

"Come on," Pryce snapped. "Captain Stevens wants to talk to you."

"What's going on?" he asked, searching his mind for a reason he might have been woken early and coming up blank.

"Get up, get dressed, and I'll brief you on the way."

He nodded, but as he jumped to his feet, his legs buckled under him.

"Balls," he muttered and grabbed the side of the tube.

Pryce snickered. "Don't worry. You'll be okay. Unlike the rest of us, all military personnel were allocated priority one tubes with regular muscle stimulation so you could come out fighting."

Maybe that was it. Could they have been boarded by those hostile aliens? But if they had, they were being very quiet about it—maybe it was an alien thing. Plus, he appeared to be the only one who'd been awakened. "Is there someone to fight?"

"Hopefully not."

Again—so why was he awake? Probably no point in asking the major. Likely it was need-to-know only—the army loved that phrase—and a lowly sergeant was unlikely to need to know.

He breathed deeply, his legs steadying beneath him. The light was dim, and he looked out across the cavernous chamber, rows and rows of cryotubes, each with a green light indicating the occupant was still alive. So at least that equipment had functioned as hoped.

There had been huge leaps in technology soon after it had become clear humanity needed to get away if they had any hope of surviving. The ships were built fast and were far more advanced than anything previously manufactured on Earth. No one on the outside knew where the technology came from. Some had suggested alien intervention. If so, the aliens had kept out of sight.

Logan turned around—he was almost feeling normal now—and reached beneath the cryotube for his bag. They had each been allocated a weight limit for the items they could bring with them, but Logan didn't have a lot in the way of mementos. No family photos, no souvenirs of loved ones. He liked it that way. All he had with him were his uniforms, a couple of sets of civvies, and a well-read copy of the *Count of Monte Cristo.*

As he dressed, the lights flickered off, then on, then off again. He went still, the darkness only lit by the green glow from the tubes.

"What's going on?" he asked.

"Power supply is on the blink. It happens. The cryotubes and main life-support systems have a backup power source, which is just as well, because the ship is falling apart."

That wasn't good. In theory, the ship could keep going indefinitely. The fuel was self-regenerating, the water reclaimed, as was everything else that could be recycled. But nothing lasted forever. Including the crews.

He dressed in the dark, was pulling on his boots when the lights flashed back on.

"Bloody hell, you look…young," Pryce said.

The major had to be sixty-plus years. He also sounded a little bitter. Back in the day, everyone had wanted to be a member of the crew. Except Logan. He didn't like the idea of spending fifty-plus years in the company of the same thirty people. He wasn't that…friendly. Maybe Pryce was realizing if they ever got to their brave new world, he would be too worn out to appreciate it. Or maybe he'd given up believing that they would ever get there. That they'd literally fall apart before they found anywhere capable of sustaining life.

"You ready?" Pryce asked, and Logan nodded. "Then let's go."

Logan followed him out, down the long line of cryotubes. The air was cool with a faint musky scent, as if it had been breathed too many times. Through the glass panels, he could see the faces of the occupants sleeping peacefully. He'd had no dreams in five hundred years. Or if he had, he'd forgotten them. He'd learned at an early age that dreams were a waste of energy. Better to come to terms with real life than to fantasize about a better one. Finally, they reached a set of double doors. Pryce placed his hand on the scanner pad, and the doors slid open, leading into a wide corridor with gray curved walls and flickering strip lighting.

"So why am I awake?" he asked as the doors slid shut.

"We have a job for you."

"Doing what?"

"What you've been trained for."

That could mean a lot of things. Mainly he'd been trained to follow orders. Then to blow crap up and to stop the other side's crap blowing up—but he hoped nothing was going to blow. An explosion in space sounded like a bad idea. But for the last five years—okay, maybe not the last five, but the last five he'd actually been conscious—Logan had been assigned to the military police. He'd been an assistant investigator for his unit—as high as a non-commissioned officer could go, which wasn't very high. But what could they possibly have to investigate on a ship with only thirty people? Well, thirty conscious people.

"A couple of days ago, our security officer, Major Stuart Caldwell—you might remember him"—Logan did, the man had been a total fuckwit—"was on a routine investigation to the *Trakis Two*. His shuttle exploded on the return journey. He was killed. Which leaves us without a security officer and also with an open investigation."

"What was Caldwell investigating?" Logan asked.

"Three cryotubes had malfunctioned. We do get that occasionally, but normally the alarms are triggered and we get the repairs done before anything bad happens. But in this case, the alarm malfunctioned as well. We got no warning, and the occupants were long dead when they were found. It looked like they'd woken up and couldn't get out. They died of asphyxiation when the life support failed."

"Christ." He could definitely imagine what that must have been like. Trapped in a cryotube, not being able to move, to breathe.

"It's unlikely there was any foul play, but we need to be seen to prove that."

Yeah, the army was all about being seen to do stuff. "How did you discover them, if the alarms failed?"

"Pure chance. The ships run random diagnostic checks on one another's systems. This particular one just happened to cover those tubes. But following that, we did an overall check on all the tubes and found that this wasn't the first instance. There had been similar incidences on other ships."

"Going back how long?"

"The first was five years ago on the *Trakis Three*. The last on the *Trakis Seven* a few weeks ago. The one picked up by the random audit was on the *Trakis Two* and had actually occurred somewhere in the middle of that time period."

"Caldwell believed it was sabotage?"

"He thought it unlikely." Pryce ran a hand through his hair. "Bloody hell, it's amazing we haven't lost more—we're falling apart. But we have to be seen to cover all possibilities."

"And that's where I come in?"

"I suggested to the captain that you might be up for the job."

Probably thought they would at least give the appearance of investigating, with no hope of actually stirring up anything controversial. Pryce had tunnel vision where enlisted men were concerned.

"Thanks."

Pryce halted beside another set of double doors identical to the last. He turned to Logan with a slightly malicious grin. "My pleasure. Hey, why should I have all the bloody fun?" Then he pressed his palm to the panel, and the doors slid open.

Logan went still and stared into the room. This was obviously the bridge. Large and circular, the curved walls lined with giant screens. Screens that reflected a 360-degree view around the ship. He walked slowly forward, stopped in the center of the room, turned around.

He'd never given it much thought, because if he was totally honest, he'd never believed he would get to see it. But each screen showed a vast expanse of darkness filled with infinite pinpricks of light.

"Holy crap."

It hadn't really sunk in until now. He was actually in space.

Chapter Two

Something woke her.

Katia didn't want to be woken, and she ignored the loud banging. "Piss off," she mumbled.

"Come on, Sleeping Beauty, wakey, wakey. Rise and shine."

She thought about rolling over, had the idea of pulling her pillow over her head to block out the noise. But something was wrong with this picture. While she occasionally brought men back to her place, they never slept over. Besides, even that hadn't happened in years. Somewhere along the way, she'd lost the urge for casual sex, and anything more was not an option. She didn't allow people close. It never worked out.

So who the hell was in her bedroom? Trouble was she recognized that voice. Low and dark. Despite the cheerful words, it stirred a mixture of fear and morbid curiosity.

She opened her eyes, blinked in the dim light. A shadowy form loomed above her. She tried to sit up and couldn't move. Tight bands restrained her chest and forehead, and panic churned in her stomach. Then the bands pinged open and she was free. She bolted upright, a growl escaping her throat.

"Hey, cool down, kitten," he said. "You're fine. Well, at least for the moment."

She slowed her breathing as her eyes adjusted to the low light, and it came back to her. Where she was. In a cryotube on the *Trakis Two*. Waiting to go into space. What had gone wrong? Had they been discovered? But if that was the case, then it was unlikely to be Rico waking her up. He would have been long gone. Because if Ricardo Sanchez was good for one thing, it was looking after himself.

It seemed like no time ago that the lid had closed on her. She'd hated that, but then she'd hated the idea of dying even more. So she'd run a calming mantra through her mind until the drugs kicked in and she'd drifted off into sleep.

She pushed herself up so she was sitting on the edge then to her feet; she preferred to be able to run when she was dealing with Rico. Unfortunately, her legs gave way and hard hands grasped her shoulders and held her upright.

"Hey, take a moment. No need to move so fast."

She went completely still in his arms, fear sending her heart rate ratcheting until she could feel her pulse throbbing in her throat. Her nostrils filled with the dark, musky scent of him.

He'd gone still as well, and she forced her gaze up—a long way up, he was at least a foot taller than she was—to meet his dark-eyed stare. His nostrils flared, and inside, her alter ego awoke and flexed her claws.

"Let me go," she snarled.

He dropped his hold immediately, stepped back, and held up his hands, a mocking smile on his face. "*Dios*, don't get your panties in a twist, kitten. Just trying to help."

"And don't freaking call me kitten." She rubbed her arms as if she could erase the feel of him. Strength was returning to her limbs, her brain starting to function again. Glancing around, she could make out the cryotubes. They filled the vast room, the occupants all sleeping peacefully. Looked like she was the only one awake. Had she been double-crossed? She'd paid dearly for this place, but maybe Rico had found someone willing to pay more.

Finally, she turned her attention back to him. He was leaning against the cryotube behind him, arms folded across his chest. Dressed all in black, black pants, a black shirt—he was such a goddamn poser. His midnight black hair was pulled into a ponytail, showing off the olive skin and sharp cheekbones. He was probably the most stunning man she had ever seen. Except he wasn't actually a man. And thankfully, she had never been attracted to him. She'd have to have a death wish. The mocking smile still curved his lips, and her eyes narrowed.

"What's going on?" she asked.

As he pushed himself away from the cryotube, she had to fight the urge to take a step back. Best not to ever show fear.

"You know," he said, "I was sure your first question would be 'how long?'"

"I thought—" Obviously, her brain wasn't quite functioning at full capacity yet. She pressed her fingers to her skull then forced the question out. "How long?"

"Five hundred years, give or take a few days."

Five hundred years? Holy freaking moly.

"Are we there?" She could hear the hope in her voice, and she realized she'd never actually imagined this would work. While she had never spelled it out to herself, she'd gone into this not expecting to survive. That it would be a final sleep and she would never wake up. They would crash into an asteroid, or the ship would lose power and they'd drift for eternity. There was so much that could go wrong. Still, she hadn't been able to resist. The chance to go into space, to visit new worlds and alien civilizations. She'd dreamed of space as a kid. Her favorite film had been *The Empire Strikes Back*. Her first crush had been Han Solo.

"If by 'there' you mean our brave new world, then unfortunately not."

"So why am I awake?" When everyone else was clearly still asleep.

"Because we have a situation."

"A situation?" She remembered now; Rico could be really freaking annoying.

"A situation you are in a unique position to assist with, *querida*."

She blew out her breath. "Please will you tell me what the hell is going on?"

"Okay, but let's go somewhere more comfortable. This place gives me the creeps."

She did smile at that. She hadn't known anything was capable of making Rico uncomfortable.

"And put some clothes on," he added. "You're too distracting."

She glanced down at herself; she was wearing a white tank top and panties, the length of her legs bare. He was such a lech. Crouching down, she pulled her duffel bag from the storage space beneath the cryotube. She found a pair of jeans, a flannel shirt, and boots and dressed quickly. "Let's go."

She glanced around as she followed Rico, first through a set of double doors, which he opened by pressing his palm to a panel on the wall, and then along a corridor with curved gray walls and strip lighting. Coming in, she'd been too on edge to take in much of the ship, and there hadn't been a lot to see. But then he halted beside a second set of doors, and as they slid open, she gasped.

Wow.

"This is the bridge," Rico said.

The room was large, circular, and looked like something

from the set of *Star Trek*.

Rico leaned closer and murmured in her ear, "Space. The final frontier…"

She flinched. His breath was cold against her skin, and she moved away and into the room, halting in the center and turning slowly. Screens filled the walls all around her, showing views into space. Darkness and light. She walked toward one, reached out, and stroked her fingers over a speck of light.

A grin tugged at her lips. It was all worth it, just for this one moment of touching the stars.

Rico cleared his throat behind her, and she turned. Off to the side was a seating area, where he lounged, his long legs stretched out, his booted feet up on the table, hands behind his head, watching her with that lazy smile on his face. "On a schedule here, kitten."

She scowled at the name, but with one last look at the vastness of space, she wandered over to him, her footsteps slowing as she crossed the room. The place was amazing. Consoles beneath the screens flashed with intriguing lights. She wanted to know what everything did, how it all worked, how far they had come, where they were going…

Rico cleared his throat again, and she gave herself a little shake and hurried across. He removed his feet from the table, held up a flask, and she nodded then sat down opposite him.

"How are you feeling?" he asked.

Aw—he actually sounded as though he cared. Her eyes narrowed on him suspiciously. "Why?"

"Just checking. Coming out of cryo can have some… interesting side effects. But you're okay?"

She did a quick internal check. "I think so."

"Good." He poured amber liquid into two crystal glasses on the table in front of him then shoved one across to her.

She picked it up and sniffed. "How the hell have you managed to still have whiskey after five hundred years?"

"I make my own."

"Impressive." She took a sip and choked. "Jesus."

He grinned. "It's amazing the things you can learn if you have the time."

She studied him, her head cocked to one side. He looked exactly as he had the last time she'd seen him. Five hundred years ago. "Have you been awake since we left Earth?"

"Time to sleep when you're dead, baby."

"Yeah, except you're already dead." She took another sip, felt the glow in her stomach. Time to move things on, find out what was happening. "So this…situation. What is it and how do you think I can help?"

"You're a detective, and I need you to detect."

She'd been a homicide detective for the last nine years of her life on Earth, with the Metropolitan Police in London. She'd been good at her job, the best conviction rate on the force, with the uncanny ability to get into the heads of the worst people on the planet. It was a gift. Or a curse. But she'd enjoyed her work. She wasn't sure what that made her, but definitely not squeamish. Had someone been murdered? There didn't seem a lot of potential in such a closed environment, where the vast majority of people were asleep.

She was quite aware that Rico had killed more than a few in his time, the number probably ran into the thousands, but he was hardly likely to get her to investigate a murder he had committed.

"Tell me," she said.

"It appears that someone has been going around murdering the Chosen Ones. Some of the cryotubes have malfunctioned. The occupants woke up and then died when the life support systems failed."

"And you're sure it's murder? Not a glitch in the system? Five hundred years is a long time."

"Maybe. The tubes malfunctioning I'd believe could be

down to systems failure. But there are safeguards, alarms, backup life support… That it should all fail simultaneously is a little too much of a coincidence for my liking."

It did sound unlikely, and she felt the first stirrings of curiosity. "But why are you interested? Why do you care if a few humans are murdered? I take it they were humans?"

"You take it right. And I care because three of the deaths happened right here on the *Trakis Two*. We wouldn't have known—but they were picked up on a random systems audit. After that, they did a fleet-wide check and found other similar instances. Ten cases over a period of five years. Looks like someone is systematically picking off selected Chosen Ones."

"What are they doing about it?" she asked. Presumably someone else would also be investigating this.

"The security officer on the *Trakis One* was heading the investigation—it was their audit that picked up the anomaly. As we were the first case to surface, he paid us a visit. Yesterday, in fact."

He picked up the flask, and she held out her glass so he could top it off. He swirled the liquid in his own glass, staring at the ceiling, one hand tapping against his thigh, not returning her look. Hmm. Something else had happened. He was looking distinctly shifty. If she'd considered him capable of guilt, then she would have said that there was a definite hint of guilt lurking around him. "What did you do?" she asked.

"Me?" Wow—he appeared so innocent. "Why do you think I did anything?"

"Come on, Rico, you look guilty as shit. You did something, and if you want me to take on the case, then you'd better tell me what."

His eyes turned cold. A shiver ran through her, but she refused to back down.

"You'll take the case because I'm asking you…nicely." He sort of smiled. Actually, it was more of a snarl, the corner of his mouth lifting to reveal the tip of a sharp white fang. "That could change," he added.

She swallowed her whiskey and slammed her glass on the table. Then she leaned in closer, stared him in the eye, and a low growl rumbled from her throat. She was pretty sure she couldn't take Rico—couldn't take him when they'd last met, so no way could she now, five hundred years later; a vampire's strength increased with age. That was beside the point. He held her gaze for a long time, then he sat back, breaking the contact. Tension oozed from the room. "I always liked you," he said with a grin.

"Ugh."

He chuckled. And she allowed her muscles to relax. One thing she did know about Rico—he liked his women willing. Thank God.

"So?" she said.

"It might just be that the security officer from the *Trakis One* and I had a little...altercation."

"You killed him? Jesus, Rico, we're supposed to be keeping a low profile."

Rico shrugged. "He pissed me off."

"Really?" she asked, injecting as much sarcasm into her voice as she could.

"Honestly? The guy was a total fucking dickhead. Kept on and on about how he'd known all the captains back on Earth during training, and he didn't remember me, blah, blah, blah. Like a dog with a fucking bone. I didn't have a choice." He had another drink, this time straight from the flask. "But we're okay. I shoved his body back on his shuttle, programmed it for the return trip, added a bomb, and bang! It exploded halfway back. No evidence of foul play at all."

She was betting that someone was going to be suspicious. But maybe they'd think it was something to do with the investigation. Because how likely was it that anyone would come anywhere even close to the truth of what was going on here on the *Trakis Two*?

"Anyway," Rico continued, "I was thinking it over. Fact one: the investigation isn't going to go away—we have dead people, and the powers that be will want to know why. Fact two: sadly, the *Trakis One* is without a security officer since the tragic demise of Major Dickhead Caldwell. Fact three: it occurred to me that I have my very own detective on board. Apparently, the best there is at solving murder cases."

"Me?" *Of course, me.*

"You. I'm offering your services."

She kept her expression blank, because it wouldn't do to appear too enthusiastic. But in truth, she was intrigued and couldn't wait to get started. "You think they'll accept?"

"We'll have to use all our persuasive skills." His expression turned serious. "We've got to be in control of this investigation. If they start sniffing around here, looking at things too closely, then we're well and truly fucked, kitten."

"Don't call me..." She gave up. Telling Rico not to do something was a sure-fire way of making him do it. "When do I start?"

"Now is as good a time as any. There's a shuttle ready and waiting to take you to the *Trakis One*. I'll let them know you're coming. One thing—make sure you steer the investigation away from this ship—plenty of other dead people to keep you busy. I'm not sure we'll stand up to a close scrutiny."

He was right. If anyone looked at the *Trakis Two* too closely, it was likely a few alarm bells would ring. Rico had done an amazing job of keeping them away for five hundred years—she'd hate to mess that up. "This shuttle—it's not going to blow up on the way, is it?"

He smiled. "Well, not through any bomb of mine. But who knows? On the bright side, while I'm sure you've made a lot of enemies in your time, they're all either asleep or dead, so you should be safe. Until you make a few more with that charming disposition of yours."

She snarled. "Gee, thanks."

"Just telling it like it is." He studied her for a moment. "I think it's the contrast that gets people. You look so...young and innocent and pretty, and then you open your mouth..."

"Piss off, Rico."

"Just like that." He stood up and stretched then reached down and picked up a black satchel from the floor. "All the info we have is in here," he said, handing her the bag. "Catch up on the flight."

She pushed herself to her feet and stood for a moment, swaying slightly. The whiskey? But it was more than that. Something was wrong. A shiver prickled across her skin as her eyesight sharpened.

"Look at me," Rico said, moving to stand in front of her.

She looked up.

"*Mierda,*" he muttered.

That didn't sound good. "What's happening?"

"Nothing to worry your pretty little head over." He studied her for a moment then pulled a pair of dark glasses out of his pocket and slipped them on her face. "There. No problem."

No problem? "Rico...?" she growled.

"I'll explain en route to the shuttle. But right now, we need to get you on your way before they find someone else to take over their investigation. Come along. No time to waste."

The bones in her fingers tingled, and she clenched her fists then opened her mouth to argue some more. But Rico was already striding away, and she hurried after him.

Tosser.

Chapter Three

Logan was finding it hard to believe; he was on a ship, five hundred years from Earth. A sense of excitement tightened his gut. Space. The final fucking frontier.

"Sergeant Farrell?"

Logan dragged his attention from the vastness of the universe and turned, went still.

A woman walked toward him, leaning heavily on a metal stick. He'd known Captain Stevens by sight back on Earth, but if it wasn't for the captain's uniform of black pants and a green shirt, he would never have recognized her now. She looked like someone's great-great-grandmother on her way to a costume party.

He kept his expression blank as she halted in front of him then drew himself to attention and saluted. "Ma'am."

Stevens had originally been a colonel in the British Air Force before she'd joined the Federation's Security Force and volunteered for duty aboard the colony ships. Many had volunteered, and then their numbers had been whittled down by a rigorous vetting process—the volunteers had outnumbered the places a hundred to one. What the captain probably wasn't aware of was that it had been Logan's department who had processed the applications and overseen the background checks. Logan had reviewed many of the files, including the captain's; he likely knew more about the woman than anyone else alive. Or awake, at least.

In his opinion, most of those who had succeeded were bland and boring and had the character of a pile of horse shit.

When the news had come out that Earth was failing, all the countries of the world had joined together to form the Federation of Nations, under the presidency of Max Beauchamp. Though Logan was convinced that if old Max had had to undergo the vetting process then his feet would never have left the ground. The man was a fuckwit. But that was politicians for you.

The lights blinked off, leaving the room in near darkness, the only illumination the stars on the screens all around them. It lasted only seconds before they came back on.

Pryce hadn't been lying—the ship was falling apart around them. What was the chance of finding a planet capable of sustaining life before it disintegrated totally, spilling its precious cargo—and him—into space? Not a happy thought.

"At ease, sergeant." The captain waved him to a table where Pryce sat reading something on a laptop in front of him. He glanced up as they approached and rose to his feet before sinking down again and sliding the laptop across to Logan, along with a weapons belt and a comm unit. Logan fastened the belt at his waist and slid the comm unit onto his wrist, clicking it shut. Then he took the chair opposite and scanned the report on the laptop.

Ten lots of Chosen Ones had died in their cryotubes over a period of five years. And the frequency was escalating. He got to the end and looked up. "So the shuttle bringing Caldwell back exploded? Any sign of any foul play?"

"None we can find," Pryce replied. "But then the shuttle disintegrated, so there was no evidence to examine."

"Did we get his report from the *Trakis Two* before he blew up?"

"No. He was planning to debrief us when he got back."

It looked like a trip to the *Trakis Two* was first on his to-do list. See what Caldwell had discovered.

The captain nudged him with her stick. "Are you up to this, son?" She was still standing—probably scared if she sat down she would never get up again.

And Christ, he hated it when officers called him son. He wasn't anyone's son. "I'll do my best, ma'am."

"Good. I have no doubt that you'll find there's nothing untoward occurring. That the deaths are due to a malfunction and nothing more." Was there a not-so-subtle hint there? Was Logan expected to bring a result in of malfunction and not rock the boat? "It's inconceivable that we would have a traitor in the fleet," the captain continued. "It would be drastic for morale."

Yeah, so that meant it couldn't be true. There was definitely a warning in there—the captain was telling him she didn't want a traitor found in the fleet, whether there was one or not.

He felt a brief stab of disappointment. He'd hoped the old crap had been left behind. But what choice did he have? If he didn't give them what they wanted, likely he'd be straight back in cryo. And he suspected, considering the state of the ship, this time there would be no waking up. And on balance—he'd rather not die in a cryotube.

On the other hand, maybe it was a malfunction. Logan didn't know enough yet to make any sort of guess as to the cause of the deaths. And he had to admit a traitor was unlikely. The vetting process had been intense. He gave her his most sincere smile. "I'll get to the bottom of it, ma'am."

"I'm sure you will. Are you a member of the Church, Sergeant?"

"No, ma'am." By Church, he presumed she meant the Church of Everlasting Life. He knew from her file that Stevens was a designated member. All the crew rotations had one—to look after their spiritual well-being.

In the years leading up to the exodus, the old religions had all but disappeared, overtaken in popularity by a new faith, the Church of Everlasting Life, which also happened to be the chosen religion of their great leader, President Max Beauchamp—the fuckwit. Their members were zealots, who believed that a divine hand was guiding the faithful to a new and better world.

"Even so, you must let God guide you in your investigation."

"I'll do that, ma'am." *Not.* The captain's comm unit buzzed, and she raised it to face level, peered at it, a line forming between her brows. "I have to take a call," she said. "I'll be right back." She walked to the other side of the bridge and turned away.

Logan finished reading the report. "Do you have any thoughts on the matter, sir?" he asked Pryce. "Any ideas you want to share?"

"None."

Pryce sounded almost happy about it. Maybe he didn't want Logan to succeed—he'd probably already settled his mind on the captain's malfunction scenario. Ass kisser. "I'll need files on the active crew members."

"Keep the laptop," Pryce said. "I'll send the files over to you."

"Thank you."

Stevens came back, the frown still between her eyes. "That was the captain of the *Trakis Two.* Apparently, he's sending someone over to help with the investigation. A

Detective Mendoza—some hotshot homicide detective back on Earth. I said they weren't needed, we had our own man on the job, but he'd already woken them up and they're on a shuttle heading here."

"So we tell him to turn back," Pryce said. "We don't need some bloody civilian poking his nose where it's not wanted."

"I'm afraid it's too late. They're approaching the docking bay now. Besides, a second set of eyes might give the investigation more credibility. People need to see us working together on this, setting an example. And I'm sure Sergeant Farrell will steer them in the right direction."

"Of course, ma'am."

"Good. We'll head over there now."

As they stepped off the bridge, a shudder ran through the ship, and a grating of metal on metal came from somewhere above them. Logan stumbled against the wall then found his footing. What the—

A soothing voice spoke over the ship's comm system.

Do not panic. Do not leave your stations. This is a minor malfunction of the primary stabilizers and will be resolved shortly.

The vibration stopped just as the captain's comm unit buzzed. She glanced at it then tapped something in and frowned.

"I'm afraid we're needed in the engine room," she said. "But I've asked our Scientific Officer to take over. She'll be along shortly to show you to the docking bay and then answer any questions you have."

Without waiting for a response, she turned and walked away, Pryce behind her. Logan stood staring after them, waiting for something else to go wrong, and wondering how long he had left to live.

At the sound of footsteps, he turned. A woman strode toward him, wearing the crew uniform of black pants, boots, and a red shirt. The uniform suited her a hell of a lot better than it did the captain or Pryce. Somewhere in her mid-thirties, she was tall, with blond hair that reached her shoulders, and dark blue eyes.

She came to a halt in front of him and smiled—the first genuine smile he'd seen on anyone since he'd woken. "Sergeant Farrell?" He nodded, and she held out her hand. "I'm Scientific Officer Langdon. Layla. I understand you're taking over the investigation into the cryotube malfunctions."

That was interesting. Did everyone think it was a malfunction—or was this more wishful thinking? "So you don't think it's murder?" he asked.

She actually chuckled. "Good heavens, no. Why would anyone kill the Chosen Ones?"

Excellent question. He was damned if he could come up with a motive.

"And to be honest," she continued, "I'm surprised we haven't had more incidents."

He could feel his enthusiasm draining away fast. He'd thought he'd been woken to do something useful, to find a killer. Instead, it was just going through the motions and coming up with an answer he'd already been handed.

They walked side by side down another identical corridor. The lights flashed off and on again. It didn't fill him with a lot of confidence. If something as simple as the lighting system was failing, it didn't bode well for the rest of the ship.

"Is this usual?" he asked, waving a hand toward the lights above them.

"For the last year or so," Layla replied. "The engineers do a wonderful job, but we've almost run out of spare parts."

That didn't sound good. "What about the other ships? Are they in the same situation?"

"Out of the ships left, yes, we're pretty much all in the same state. The *Trakis Two* is the only one that never seems to request assistance. No malfunctions as yet."

"Except for the cryotubes." If he remembered rightly. "Wasn't that where the audit picked up the first dead people?"

"Of course. You're right. But otherwise we never seem to hear from them, so everything must be going well. The others call us every now and then and ask for backup, spares, engineering help, supplies. Not that we're in much of a position to help. We're out of nearly everything ourselves."

That sounded grim. Though she appeared optimistic. Maybe she hadn't been around long enough for her enthusiasm to be tested. "How long have you been out of cryo?" he asked.

"Ten years. I was the last crew member to be woken up. Before that, it was Caldwell."

"The exploding security officer?"

She gave him a look of reproach but nodded. "And before that, Travis—Major Pryce."

That sucked for her. She must be considerably younger than the rest of the crew.

"What's the story with the captain?" he asked. "She looks like a walking corpse. How come she's so old?" They'd estimated an average fifty-year stint for each crew member. Though that wasn't set in stone. Stevens had been thirty-five at the time the ships had set off. She looked way past eighty-five now.

"There was an unexpected death. An accident involving the ninth captain—one of the power cells exploded. He'd only been awake a few years. It messed things up a little. Stevens has been captain for over eighty years."

That was cutting things close. The average lifespan was around a hundred and twenty—it had increased in the last decades before they left Earth, due to advances in medicine. But maybe the captain didn't want to go back into cryo, even if she could find a replacement. After all, she knew how bad the situation was and must be aware she'd likely never wake up. Climbing into that cryotube would be like climbing into a coffin while you were still alive.

Layla gave a weak smile. "She's still an excellent captain, though a little...forgetful at times. All the same, we're going to be in trouble if she dies without training a replacement."

"Though likely not for very long," Logan said as the lights flickered again.

"Do you have family in the fleet?" she asked.

"No. But I'm part of the military selection, so we didn't get the option to bring family." Even if he'd had any to bring. Which he didn't. "How about you?"

"No. I'm alone in the world as well." She touched his arm briefly. "I'm glad they woke you up. It will be good to have someone younger to talk to, to bounce ideas off. The others...they're good people, but they're so set in their ways."

Yeah, he could imagine that would happen, stuck in an enclosed place with the same people for years on end. He'd probably go off his head.

Finally, they halted in front of a set of wide double doors. Layla pressed her hand to the panel, and nothing happened. She cast him an apologetic smile then gritted her teeth and thumped the panel with her fist. The doors creaked open to reveal a huge, cavernous room, crammed from floor to ceiling with stuff. Boxes and crates, piles of things they would need to set up home on a new planet.

They wound their way between the heaps of machinery, metalwork, cases of...weapons. Even a couple of goddamn tanks. He liked tanks.

At the far side of the room was a big empty space where Layla came to a halt. Logan looked around, trying to work out how the shuttle would enter. He was about to ask when the wall in front of him slowly lifted, and there it was. Small, sleek, and shiny silver, a spaceship in miniature.

Damn, she was pretty.

It was love at first sight.

Oh, hell yeah. In that moment, he decided he would give them their malfunction result, if that's what they wanted, but only after he'd flown in that shuttle.

She glided into the room and landed gently on the docking bay floor as the wall slid closed behind her. For a minute, nothing happened. Then the shuttle doors slid open, and a figure emerged at the top of the ramp.

Detective Mendoza?

He grinned.

Not what he'd been expecting. And clearly, from her appearance, someone who didn't give a damn what anyone else thought of her. He liked that.

The detective was small and scruffy and cute as hell. She was dressed in a ripped flannel shirt and jeans, with a cloud of black hair around a heart-shaped face and dark glasses propped on a small, straight nose. Her fists were clenched at her sides and her lips clamped in a tight line. She looked like a tiny, angry kitten.

Maybe the investigation might turn out interesting after all.

Chapter Four

Nothing to worry my pretty little head over?

Katia ground her teeth as Rico's words echoed in her mind. She was going to kill the vampire. Rip his heart out and bite off his goddamn head.

He'd told her the side effect was minor, just a little control issue, that it would pass in a matter of minutes…

Instead, she'd spent the whole trip here pacing the small space, wrestling the change that clawed at her insides. She couldn't remember the last time she'd had control problems. Not since the early years.

Now her cat wanted out, and she was scrabbling and yowling for freedom. Not happening. What if she shifted and then couldn't shift back? What if she arrived at the *Trakis One* and they opened the shuttle and found a goddamn cat instead of a detective?

That would make an excellent first impression.

And she was ravenous. Hunger was tying knots in her empty stomach. But then she had a fast metabolism and she hadn't eaten in five hundred years.

Even so, she'd managed to retain a modicum of control, had succeeded in not shifting completely, but body parts kept getting away from her. Right now, claws poked into the palms of her clenched fists and her fingers were furry. And she knew, behind the stupid dark glasses, her eyes would be feral. Which meant she didn't dare take them off, and she must look a complete ass—who wore freaking shades on a spaceship? Rico, obviously. But who else?

She stood at the top of the ramp, bag slung over her shoulder, and squinted down at the welcoming committee below her. Between the glasses and the dim lighting, she could hardly see a thing. Two people. A man and a woman. The woman wore black pants tucked into black boots and a red fitted shirt. The man wore an army uniform, sergeant's stripes on his arm. They both looked cool and immaculate, and she glanced down at her own outfit. A growl trickled from her throat; at some point, she'd shredded the right side of her shirt, so it hung in tatters.

Maybe she should back up into the shuttle and lock the doors. If she'd had any clue how to fly the freaking thing, she might have done just that, flown straight back to the *Trakis Two,* and told Rico where he could stuff his investigation. But she didn't know how to fly—the shuttle had been programmed to come here, and she'd been ordered not to touch anything. Right now, she hadn't a clue how to even switch the thing on, so she wasn't going anywhere.

Which meant she would have to suck it up and hope nobody noticed the furry finger thing—no shaking hands. Why couldn't Rico have given her some goddamn gloves? She ran her tongue over her teeth and felt the sharp prick of a fang. No smiling, either. Somehow, she didn't think *that* was going to be a problem.

She rolled her shoulders and blew out her breath. She could do this.

But as she stepped down the ramp, claws raked down her insides, and she stumbled. Then the lights flickered and died, leaving her in complete darkness. The ship shuddered and the ramp shook beneath her feet, and she was falling, hitting the ramp hard and then sliding. She eventually skidded to a halt at the bottom and lay there, winded.

How to make an impressive entrance.

If the lights stayed off, maybe she could crawl away and hide...wait until Rico's "minor" side effect wore off. She could say she got lost in the dark. Except at that moment, the lights flickered back on.

She was lying on her back at the bottom of the ramp, a hand reaching out to her. She glared then realized the expression was wasted behind the dark glasses. Ignoring the helping hand, she scrambled to her feet, fumbled the glasses back into place, and shoved her claws into her pockets. Then she raised her gaze and stared into the prettiest eyes she'd ever seen. A gray shading to mauve, almost purple. Unusual enough to make her pause and hold her attention. They held a mixture of interest, concern, and amusement.

Yeah, she was so funny.

Someone cleared their throat, and Katia tore her gaze away and blinked.

The woman in the red shirt stepped forward, a somewhat forced smile on her face. "Detective Mendoza?" Her tone was dubious.

Katia guessed she wasn't what they'd been expecting, but then she was used to totally underwhelming the people she met. Even at the best of times, she didn't look like a typical homicide detective. As Rico had pointed out, she was too petite, too young-looking. And sometimes just too damn furry. "Yes, ma'am."

"I'm Scientific Officer Langdon. Layla. Welcome to the *Trakis One*."

The woman was tall. Blonde and beautiful. And she smelled so good. Like warm flesh and fresh blood. *Yum.* Saliva flooded her mouth, and she leaned in…sniffing in the scent, licking her lips.

Oh God, she was almost drooling. Not good. She snapped upright and took a step back. "Thanks," she muttered.

"And this is Sergeant Farrell, who will be heading up the investigation."

So they had already appointed someone—the sergeant with the pretty eyes. She was tempted to tell them to piss off. If she wasn't needed, she didn't want to waste her time. Though it wasn't as if she had anything better to do. And she didn't want to go back to sleep. Rico had told her a little of the situation on the walk to the shuttle, and things weren't going well for the fleet. They hadn't found anywhere even vaguely capable of supporting human life. They were running out of time, and most of the fleet was falling apart. Except for the *Trakis Two*, which still had supplies and spare parts for a while to come. Probably mainly due to the fact that most of the crews had never been awakened. Rico kept the conscious staff to a minimum and, by all accounts, did most of the work himself. She supposed it prevented him from getting bored, and it wasn't as if he needed to sleep. Or eat…much. She didn't want to contemplate what—or rather who—Rico had been eating.

The sergeant was holding out his hand toward her. Again. But she kept her distance—he looked pretty tasty, too, and she could do without the temptation—and shoved her claws deeper into her pockets, her mind scrambling for something intelligent to say. "Sorry, Sergeant, I have a skin condition. I'd hate you to catch something." Totally lame.

He dropped his hand to his side and grinned. "No worries. And call me Logan if we're going to be partners."

"Katia."

He was tall, long and lean, just the way she'd always liked them. Before she'd decided men were more trouble than they were worth. With dark blond hair cut military short, high cheekbones, and a big nose. Nice lips that were smiling at her. All in all, a very agreeable package.

But it took more than a pretty face to impress her.

Didn't it?

He cocked his head to one side and looked her up and down—okay, mostly down; she was well over a foot shorter than he was—his lips twitching. "You know," he said, "you're not quite what I was expecting."

She snorted. "Don't tell me—you thought I'd be bigger."

"Something like that."

She looked around. Rico hadn't given her any time to explore the *Trakis Two*, just taken her straight to the place where they kept the shuttles—the docking bay. She needed to get used to the spaceship terminology. Even so, compared to the *Trakis Two,* which had positively sparkled, this place had a...shabby tone.

The lights flickered off and on again. What was with that?

"Is there a problem?" she asked. Something she should be worried about, like the ship was going to implode on them any moment?

"A glitch," Layla said. "Nothing to worry about. I'm *so* glad you're here to help Logan. We really need to clear this up, though I'm sure you'll find out that it's nothing bad."

Thirty dead people sounded pretty bad to her. She reckoned Layla was something of an optimist. But she was saved from answering as her cat chose that moment to make another bid for freedom. Scratching and clawing.

"Shit, that freaking hurts," she muttered, rubbing at her belly.

"Are you all right?" Layla touched her arm, and she had to bite back a growl.

Taking a few deep breaths, she forced a tight smile. "I'm fine. Just a minor side effect from the cryo."

"Oh, you poor thing. They can be horrible. I was the same."

Somehow, Katia doubted that. She couldn't imagine the beautiful Layla with anything so ugly as furry fingers and fangs.

"Have you had something to eat?" Layla asked. "That usually helps."

At the mention of food, her stomach rumbled, and she eyed up Layla, hungrily. But no, she didn't eat people—it was one of her personal rules. And it would hardly get the investigation of to a good start. All the same, eating *something* sounded like an excellent idea. "Lead the way."

She let them walk ahead, both tall, both good looking, and both perfectly groomed. It was a good thing she'd given up comparing herself to others years ago; otherwise she might be feeling a little inadequate right now. It had taken her a long time to feel comfortable in her own skin, but she'd finally gotten there.

She took the opportunity to take a peek at her hands— still furry. She shoved them back in her pockets.

They finally stopped at an open door, and Layla waved her into a large room mostly filled by a big metal table with seating for about thirty. The galley, she presumed.

Logan nodded to the table and held out a chair for her. A gentleman. She sat down and waited while he took the seat opposite. She studied him; he was very easy on the eyes. He looked to be somewhere in his thirties. And while he appeared quite pleasant, she couldn't get a feel for him. He wasn't giving anything away.

He returned her gaze. "So what sort of detective are you, Katia?"

"Nine years in homicide with the London Metropolitan

Police."

"You don't look old enough."

She didn't take offense, because he was right. She'd stopped aging when she was nineteen. And that was a long time ago; she had a few years on Sergeant Farrell, she was guessing. But really, she was hardly going to get into explanations about *that*. "Believe me, I'm old enough. Good genes."

"Mexican?" he asked.

"How did you guess? My father was from Mexico City, but my mother is half English, half Russian. What about you?"

"I grew up in the States. Other than that, I have no clue."

"And what sort of detective are you, sergeant?"

"Not a detective at all. I spent five years in the Investigator's Unit in the military police."

A soldier rather than a detective—hence the uniform. But maybe he was the best they could do.

Layla placed a bowl of some sort of stew and a spoon in front of her then took the chair next to Logan, and they both sat watching her. The smell wafted up, and her stomach rumbled again. She curled her hands into her thighs under the table, felt the prick of claws, and stared at the spoon then the food. So near and yet so far.

Not fair.

How the hell was this supposed to work?

"Dig in," Layla said.

Her mouth flooded with saliva. Oh God, she wanted that food. Inside her, her cat screeched—she wanted the food as well.

Then the lights went out.

Yay.

She scrabbled for the spoon, her claws clumsy, picked it up, dropped it so it clattered onto the floor.

Agh!

What the hell? The lights could come on any moment. No time to waste. Needs must…

She plunged her face to the bowl and sucked up the stew, swallowing without chewing. Until the bowl was empty. She licked it clean. Inside, her cat sighed and went quiet.

She was wiping her face on her sleeve as the lights came back on.

Logan looked at her then at the empty bowl, one eyebrow raised. "You have stew on your nose," he said.

Without thinking, she raised her hand then stopped halfway to her face. But the hand was back to normal, fur and claws gone. Katia slumped into her seat, the tension oozing from her muscles. *Whew.*

"More stew?" Layla asked.

"Yes, please."

Layla took the empty bowl and replaced it with a full one and a new spoon.

Katia picked it up and ate the second bowl slowly, and delicately, while Logan looked on from across the table, an amused smile on his face.

Then she sat back, replete.

She felt almost human. Just not quite.

Chapter Five

Time to get herself up to speed. Katia hadn't had a chance to look at the information Rico had given her relating to the case. She'd been too busy trying to hold it together on the way over here.

Now she delved into the black satchel Rico had handed her. It contained a file and a laptop and a comm unit that she strapped to her wrist. She dug a little deeper and found a silver flask—more whiskey? That might come in useful. And a handful of some sort of protein bars. Maybe Rico had known that food helped with the side effects but had forgotten to mention it.

She pulled out the file, laid it on the table, and opened it to the first page. She was still wearing the dark glasses, but she was pretty sure her eyes had returned to normal, and she was fed up of the semi-darkness, so she took them off. No one screamed, so she guessed she was okay.

"Paper," Layla said. "How quaint."

"The captain is an old-fashioned guy." She bit back a smile at the thought of how Rico would react to that comment.

"Just give me a moment to catch up."

She scanned the contents quickly. There wasn't a lot of information there, though it was immediately clear that this wasn't going to be a typical homicide investigation. Even without the happening-in-space side of things.

It was more like a cold case. But she'd solved a few of those in her time.

She pulled out the laptop and opened it up. She needed to set up a murder book to record what they knew and what they needed to know.

Victims would be a good place to start, but Rico's file didn't even have names, only cryotube numbers. That would be the first thing. Who were the victims? She made a note.

She glanced up to find them still watching her. "I don't suppose there's coffee?"

"I'm sorry," Layla replied. "We haven't had coffee in centuries."

That was a bummer. Maybe Rico had coffee. "Right, so the facts. Four days ago, a routine systems audit was carried out by the engineers on the *Trakis One*. Fleet wide, which I gather is something that happens regularly."

"Yes," Layla said. "The ships take it in turns. Once a year."

"So not a one-off but not that often. What sort of proportion of the cryotubes are checked?"

"About 5 percent."

"So just good luck that the malfunctions were picked up."

"Or bad luck," Logan said.

"Or bad luck." If someone was trying to hide a murder. But she was finding it hard to get her head around the idea of foul play. What was the motive? What would anyone get out of killing a group of people in cryotubes? Nothing she could see. Though she'd covered enough serial killer cases to be aware that their minds hardly worked the same as normal people. "So three tubes were found. Not only had the tubes malfunctioned, but also the alarm and the emergency life support systems. How likely is that?" She addressed the question to Layla.

"Unlikely. Or so we believed." She gave a small shrug. "But the systems are getting old. So who knows?"

"The victims apparently awoke then died of asphyxiation when they couldn't get out and the life support systems failed." Not nice.

"Isn't there supposed to be a release mechanism in the cryotubes?" Logan asked. "I'm sure I remember from the orientation. They can be opened from the inside."

"The release mechanisms malfunctioned as well," Layla said.

Yet another coincidence? Katia didn't believe in coincidences. Certainly not this many all happening at once. "According to the report, the tubes were grouped together." In the file, there was a plan of the cryotube room on the *Trakis Two*. Three tubes marked with red crosses showed the locations. She studied the plan, found where her own cryotube had been positioned. On the opposite side of the room. "They're consecutive numbers, but I don't have any names next to them."

"You should be able to pull that from the central database," Layla said. "I'll contact the tech guys and let them know you want to talk to them."

"Thank you."

"So do we start by visiting the *Trakis Two*?" Logan asked.

Rico had said keep them away from the *Trakis Two*. And she could see his point. Though she didn't want to be too obvious about that. "No," she said.

"No?"

"I think we should start at the beginning."

Time to look at the timeline. She flicked to the next page.

It listed out the other malfunctions they had identified since the first had come to light. There was nothing listed for the *Trakis One*. Was that significant? "The deaths on the *Trakis Two* were actually the fifth 'malfunction' to occur. That was two years ago. Chronologically speaking, the first was on the *Trakis Three*. Again, three tubes, consecutive numbers. Happened a little over five years ago." She stabbed her finger onto the page. "I think we should start there." She looked up to see how the other two were reacting.

Logan shrugged. "If you think that's best. You're the expert."

She was starting to warm to Logan. He'd clearly had a lot of training in following orders. Probably institutionalized and used to taking the route of least resistance.

Layla, on the other hand, was frowning... Trouble coming. "Why not go to the most recent first?"

That was the *Trakis Seven*. The deaths there happened only weeks ago. She could live with that, but she'd prefer to see where it all started first.

"Because, in my experience with serial killers, the first victim, or group of victims, is often the most significant. Almost always, there is some link with the murderer. The victim is someone they knew. Maybe even someone they saw on a daily basis."

"Hardly likely to be the case in this instance," Logan drawled. "The victims were fast asleep, locked in their cryotubes for nearly five hundred years before they died."

Good point. But she didn't want him to get big-headed.

"You really think this is a serial killer?" Layla asked, her tone reeking of disbelief. "I don't think the captain is going to like that."

Like I give a toss. "Perhaps not, but we have to be sure." Right now, she was on the fence. She couldn't see a motive, but there were way too many coincidences. Hopefully, once they identified the victims, it might cast some light on what the motive could be. "And until we prove otherwise, I think we need to assume foul play." She smiled. Best not to give them too much chance to disagree. "That's decided, then. We start on the *Trakis Three*."

"I'm afraid I won't be coming with you," Layla said. "I've been ordered to assist but only on board the *Trakis One*. While you're here, I'll give you any help I can, and if you have any questions on the working of the ship or my research, then feel free to call on me. Otherwise I have my own duties. Which I must get back to now." She got to her feet, hesitated, then gave Logan a smile and patted his arm. "Keep me informed. And I hope I see you before you leave for the *Trakis Three*. Comm me if you have a spare moment. I'd love to talk some more."

Katia waited until Layla had left the room and then turned her attention to the man opposite. "I think she likes you," she said. "And you know, you could do worse. She's beautiful, intelligent, *and* nice."

He raised a brow. "She is a very nice lady." Then he gave her a wink. "But not my type."

Katia rolled her eyes. He was flirting with her. Obviously, she was supposed to ask what his type was and he would say—a grumpy werecat with terrible table manners and furry fingers.

Yeah right. Never going to happen.

Maybe it was time to set out a few ground rules. "Well, just so we're clear, *I* don't mix business with pleasure." Actually, she didn't mix anything with pleasure. Sort of sad. When had she turned into such a miserable bitch?

He smirked, and she had the weirdest feeling she had issued him with something of a challenge.

"Noted," he said.

"Good. Then let's go solve a murder…or thirty."

Chapter Six

Logan stood in the center of the cabin and looked around. The place was pathologically neat. The bed perfectly made. Nothing on the desk that might give a hint as to Caldwell's thoughts prior to exploding.

Detective Mendoza had suggested they inspect the security officer's cabin. In case he'd actually discovered anything useful during his investigation and left notes about it conveniently waiting for them to find.

But so far, she was letting him do the work, while she leaned against the open doorway, eating some sort of protein bar she had pulled out of her bag. She caught him watching her and pulled a face. "Hey, I like to eat."

He had no clue where she put it, then. She was tiny, though if he looked closer, she was nicely shaped, with full breasts pushing at the tank top she wore beneath the torn flannel shirt. What the hell had happened there? He wasn't sure whether it was a fashion statement or the result of a scuffle with a lion.

"Eyes up, soldier," she snapped.

He shifted his gaze to her face and gave her a wink.

She rolled her eyes.

She was pretty rather than beautiful, with a small, heart-shaped face, full lips, high cheekbones, and dark, arched brows. Her eyes, now she'd taken off the dark glasses, were her most striking feature, bright green and fringed with thick black lashes. She raised an eyebrow.

"Just wondering where you put all that food," he said.

"I have a fast metabolism. If I don't eat, I get snarky. Or so I've been told."

The lights flashed off, then on again, and she blinked. "You know, I'm glad they woke me up before the ships fell apart."

So was he. He felt curiously optimistic. And he was going to fly in a goddamned shuttle with a pretty woman. Even if she'd categorically said she was not having sex with him—it wasn't as though he had asked.

She strolled into the cabin. "Stand aside, soldier."

He moved to the side—there wasn't a lot of room. She stood for a moment, a small frown pulling her brows together, then started to systematically search. She stripped the bed, ran her hands under the mattress, opened the wardrobe. Caldwell didn't have too many clothes, but she rifled through all the pockets then knelt down, examined the floor. A door opposite where he stood opened into a small bathroom, and she checked there next. As she came out, she gave a small shake of her head. "Absolutely nothing. Not that I expected anything, but you never know."

It looked like if Caldwell had made any notes, then they'd blown up with him.

"Okay. We can cross that off the list." She headed for the door, and he followed. "Let's go find the captain and put in a request of transport to the *Trakis Three*."

"Sounds like a plan." Though he had an idea that the captain wasn't going to think it a particularly good one.

They found Captain Stevens on the bridge, talking with Pryce. They both turned as they entered, and they both frowned as they took in Katia at his side, her hands thrust into her pockets.

As they came to a halt in front of the captain, Logan saluted—he was guessing the captain was into that sort of stuff. "Ma'am. Allow me to introduce you to Detective Mendoza."

The captain's frown deepened, but she finally nodded, gave a forced smile, and waved a hand at Pryce. "And this is Major Pryce, my second-in-command."

Pryce didn't even attempt to hide his expression of disbelief as he stared down at Katia. Clearly, he was unimpressed. Was it her size, her ripped shirt, or maybe just the fact that she was a woman when he'd been expecting a man? The major spent a long time staring at her breasts, no doubt to make sure she really was a woman, and Logan had to fight back the urge to punch the asshole on the nose.

It didn't seem to bother the detective at all; she stood with a serene smile on her face.

"Scientific Officer Langdon has already spoken to us," the captain said. "She expressed some concern as to your plan to visit the *Trakis Three*."

Logan opened his mouth to answer, but Katia beat him to it. "That's so sweet. But as you appointed us to investigate this case, captain, you must allow us to use our expertise, and I believe we might find some answers on the *Trakis Three*."

"What if there are no answers?"

"Then we'll be sure to include that in our reports."

The captain was frowning again. Logan was guessing she hadn't had to deal with anyone like Katia since she'd woken up on the *Trakis One*. People got too used to everyone agreeing with them just because they wore a green shirt.

"I was presuming you'd look over the incident logs and come to the right conclusion."

"And that would be?" Katia asked.

"That this was a one off—"

"Ten, actually," she interrupted.

Logan tightened his lips to stop himself smiling. Katia was fearless. He liked that.

"It was a system malfunction," Pryce ground out. "Everything has been checked, and it is highly unlikely to happen again."

"Then no harm in us asking a few questions."

The captain turned to Logan. He was going to be put on the spot, and he didn't want to be on the spot. He didn't want to make waves.

"And you, sergeant?" she asked. "Do you think this trip to the *Trakis Three* holds any merit?"

Obviously, they were expecting a negative, and it hovered on his lips. But he hesitated. Both the captain and Pryce were staring at him as though they could will the correct answer from his lips. He flashed a glance at Katia, and she raised a brow as if in challenge. Still, he hesitated.

Balls.

The army was his life. It had given him his first real home. His first feeling of belonging. But he didn't belong. He'd known that for a long time, he'd just gotten good at pretending. Maybe he didn't belong anywhere. So he'd kept his head down and his thoughts to himself, because it was the only home he had. And he'd never been much of an investigator, because most of the time he knew the answer he was expected to come up with and didn't look any further. That was the way things were if you wanted to fit in.

Now, if he sided with Detective Mendoza, he'd be going against the captain's and Pryce's obvious wishes, no doubt gaining himself a black mark.

But they were on a spaceship in the middle of nowhere. A spaceship rapidly disintegrating around them. Soon there would likely be nothing left and nowhere to belong. So why should he give a shit?

Besides, he really wanted to ride in that pretty little shuttle, and this might be his one chance. How to do that without pissing off the people that mattered? Because he wasn't quite ready to burn all his bridges just yet. He wondered whether he could get away with saying God had told him to visit the *Trakis Three*. Maybe not.

He set his face into a serious, investigator expression and gave a solemn nod. "I believe that if we want to show the rest of the fleet that we've covered all the bases, done everything we can to ensure the safety of the Chosen Ones, then we need to visit the place this all began. The *Trakis Three*." He glanced sideways at Katia and gave her a wink. And received another eye roll.

"That's all very well, but it will take up valuable resources. We need to keep the shuttles for emergency use only."

What sort of an emergency would a shuttle solve millions of miles from nowhere?

"That's no problem, ma'am," Katia said. "The captain on the *Trakis Two* has said the shuttle I arrived on is at my disposal for the duration of the investigation. Though I will need someone to reprogram it for a flight to the *Trakis Three*." She smiled, gracious in victory.

The captain swallowed, her eyes shifting around the room as if searching for some other reason to say no. Finally, her shoulders slumped. "Major Pryce, would you see that the shuttle is reprogrammed?"

"Yes, ma'am."

He sounded like the words would choke him.

• • •

Katia was impressed. She'd thought the investigation was over and there was no way they were getting to the *Trakis Three*. Then Logan had given his covering all bases and safety of the Chosen Ones speech. "I've got to say, you're pretty good at this," she said.

While Pryce prepped the shuttle, they were heading over to talk to the systems analyst who had discovered the malfunction on the *Trakis Two* during the routine audit. And to the ship's systems specialist who had been running the investigation into the malfunctions and could hopefully access the central database and get them information on the victims.

Logan glanced at her, one eyebrow raised. She'd always been impressed by people who could do that. She'd had to practice for years before her eyebrows obeyed. "*This*?" he asked.

"Kissing ass. Saying what they want to hear."

"I've been in the military for fifteen years. It took me a while, but I got there in the end. And actually, it's not that hard. Especially officers. They're usually easy. They just want to cover their asses. The secret is, never let them know what you're really thinking."

Yeah, Logan was definitely good at that. She had no clue what he was *really* thinking. She wondered who he was when he forgot to act the textbook soldier. She reckoned he'd perfected his act. The big tough soldier. Worked hard and played hard and always did his duty.

"You don't sound like you have a very high opinion of officers. Or the military in general. Why did you stay?"

He shrugged. "Nowhere else to go."

"Aw, that's sort of sad."

"Yeah, a total tragedy. But," he continued, "it's as good

as anywhere else. And it got me a place on the ship, so it saved my life. In some ways, it's not a bad life. And maybe it will be better if we ever get to that new world. Hopefully, we'll have left a lot of the old crap behind."

She snorted. "You really believe that?"

He glanced at her. "Why not?"

"You can come out of that meeting with Captain Antiquated and Major Creepy Misogynist and say we left the shit behind? Hell, we're taking it with us. Probably in a more concentrated form. Actually, we're not even taking it—it's leading us."

"You're a cynic."

"Oh, yeah. And you're not, Mr. Tell-them-what-they-want-to-hear? Except you didn't. Because I'm guessing what they wanted to hear was: yes sir, it was definitely a system malfunction, sir, and it's been fixed, and it won't happen again, sir."

"Ah, that's where the problems arise. When what you want is at obvious odds with what *they* want. In this case, they don't want us to visit the *Trakis Three*, but I want to ride in a shuttle. The thing is to understand what they want more than that. And in this case, it's being seen to do everything they can before they admit it's nothing but a malfunction that they've fixed. I'm guessing morale throughout the fleet is low."

"We'll no doubt find out once we start talking to people," she said.

They arrived at the Tech Center. Logan placed his palm on the panel. He'd been given the freedom of the ship. She hadn't. God knew what havoc a civilian would cause if given the freedom to go anywhere. She might see something she shouldn't. Though she doubted it. They were so by-the-book it was unbelievable.

She was hungry again. It was making her grumpy. And deep inside, she could sense her cat stretching. Sometime soon, she needed to shift, and she wasn't sure how that was going to work. She reached into her bag and pulled out another protein bar.

Jake, the analyst, was an African American, slightly overweight, and wearing a blue shirt. Anna, the systems specialist, was a white woman in her fifties or sixties, also in blue. They were both very helpful, probably happy to talk to someone new.

"So right now," Katia said, taking a seat opposite them while Logan wandered around the room, inspecting all the instruments and flashing lights, "we only have the cryotube numbers of the victims. We were told you could give us the corresponding names and any information available on them."

Jake shook his head. "Not possible."

"Why is that?"

"Well, there should be a central database here on the *Trakis One,* but it's—"

"Malfunctioned?" Katia suggested. She was seeing a pattern here.

"Yes. Among other things, that was the information Caldwell was going to get when he visited the *Trakis Two.* While the central database can't be accessed because of the malfunction, the individual ships should be able to access their own data from their backup files."

Katia made a note to ask Rico to get the information on the victims from the *Trakis Two* and put in a request to the other ships to send their information. They could get the names and details of those who had died on the *Trakis Three* when they visited.

"There seem to be a lot of malfunctions on the ships," she said. "Is that…normal?"

"Considering the fleet is five hundred years old, yes, I think a few malfunctions are expected." Anna sounded defensive. Probably thought they were trying to pin the blame on someone.

"How's morale?" Katia asked when they finished the questions.

"Morale?" The woman looked surprised. "As good as can be expected when you have thirty or so people shut up together in a confined space for years on end. But I've not noticed anyone so bad that they're at the point of murdering people for entertainment."

"Hah," Katia said. "I've only been on board a couple of hours, and I've already got a list of people *I* wouldn't mind bumping off." But that was the people who were awake. Not the sleeping ones. And she'd never been known for her tolerance. But how much could someone in cryo piss anyone off? Certainly not enough to want to murder them. Did that mean whoever had killed them knew them from before, from back on Earth?

"We all have family with the fleet," Anna said. "That's a strong motivation to keep going."

"Your families are on the *Trakis One*?"

"No, all crew families were positioned on different ships than where the crew member would serve."

Interesting. Perhaps that was done so there would be more unity among the fleet. The crew would look out for all the ships.

"Mine are on the *Trakis Two*," Anna said.

Were they? Katia didn't know whether Rico had included crew members in the people he had replaced. But she thought not. She glanced at Jake, but he didn't add anything. And she looked back at Anna.

"Jake's are on the *Trakis Three*," she said. "I hear you're heading over there."

"We are. We'll make sure to say hi." She pushed herself to her feet. Time to go.

"Well, that was no use at all," Logan murmured as she

passed him.

He was right.

Maybe it was a technical glitch after all.

Everyone, including Rico, would likely be glad if she came up with that conclusion. Maybe she should give them what they wanted. Though that went against every detective cell in her body. And certainly not until she'd done a bit more whizzing about in space. And after that, then what? Would she go back to sleep? Not without a fight. The trip was clearly doomed. It had always been a long shot. Heading out into the unknown. No destination, just the hope that they would hit somewhere that could offer a home to humanity in all the enormity of space. So no way was she spending the last years of her life fast asleep. Rico would have to live with her decision. Or force her back into cryo. But why would he? The ship was big enough that she could avoid Rico. There were books, movies, virtual reality games. She could keep herself occupied.

As she reached the door, something beeped.

"Lunch time," Anna said.

She turned back. "Really?"

"We maintain a twenty-four hour daily routine, similar to Earth, across the fleet," Anna said. "Obviously, there's no night and day, but the daily cycle is considered the healthiest for humans."

Made sense. Though she doubted Rico bothered with anything so mundane as a daily routine.

Katia glanced at the comm unit on her wrist. They still had an hour before the shuttle would be ready. All right, then. Time to eat. She turned to Logan. "Lunch?"

"Are you asking me on a date?"

"Hell, no."

"Lunch it is, then."

Chapter Seven

God, the woman could eat.

Logan cast her a sideways glance. She seemed a little happier since she'd had more food. Positively jaunty.

As if sensing his gaze, she glanced up at him. "What?"

"Just impressed with your stamina." She'd eaten twice as much as him and she was half the size.

"I told you—I have a fast metabolism."

Layla had been at lunch, though they hadn't had a chance to talk and she had left before him, giving him a nod as she walked out.

Now they were heading back to the docking bay. They'd had word from Pryce that the shuttle was ready. Logan's gut was churning. He wasn't sure whether it was excitement, fear, or the result of his first meal in five hundred years. Probably a little of all three.

He was heading into space. On a five-hundred-year-old shuttle. No doubt similar to the one Caldwell had been in when it exploded. Not a comforting thought, but also not enough to dampen his anticipation.

And he was going with a woman he didn't 100 percent trust, and he had no clue why.

There was something not quite right about her, but he couldn't put his finger on it.

Logan usually had a feel for people; he could sense whether they were good or bad, whether they were telling the truth or lying. It was something he never spoke about, had tried to banish. As a young child, desperately trying to fit in—and usually failing—he hadn't wanted some stupid sixth sense, so he'd learned to ignore it, to mute the information that fed to his mind. Then, as a teenager, he'd had a therapist who'd suggested he was some sort of empath—able to read other people's emotions. But so what? Now he'd gotten to the point where only the most obvious of emotions got through. Layla, for instance, was transmitting clear as a comm. She was…nice. She wanted to help.

But from Detective Mendoza, he was picking up zero. As though she was a blank screen, with nothing behind it. And he couldn't shake the idea that she was, if not outright lying, at the least hiding something from him.

He just couldn't work out what.

He was certain she was telling the truth about just waking up. Everything was clearly new to her. She had no clue how anything worked and asked endless questions. Unless she was a good actor. Though he didn't think she would have the self-control.

She had an issue with authority and no worries about showing it.

In fact, all in all, she was quite refreshing.

No doubt he'd have time on the shuttle to ask a few questions, find out more about his new partner. The trip would take a little over thirty minutes to travel the hundred miles between the ships. The fleet was relatively close together at the moment, but apparently this was the nearest the ships ever got to one another. They were vast and unwieldy, so it was considered dangerous to get any closer. The head engineer had explained it to him over lunch. The crew all seemed eager to help. Or maybe they were bored and happy to have someone different to talk to.

When they reached the docking bay doors, he pressed his palm to the panel. Nothing happened. *Balls.* He drew back his fist and punched the panel. The door opened a little bit, enough to pry his fingers into the gap and pull them apart.

"That's sort of worrying," Katia said as she stepped through.

"I'm trying not to think about it."

They retraced their steps from earlier and finally came to a halt in front of the shuttle. "Beautiful, isn't she?" Katia said with a sigh.

He was about to answer when the shuttle door slid open and Pryce appeared. He wasn't alone. Layla was beside him, their heads close together, talking quietly. They walked down the ramp side by side, stopped talking as they caught sight of the two of them. Layla sent him an easy smile as they came to a halt at the foot of the ramp.

"It's programmed to lock into the *Trakis Three*'s signal," Pryce said. "It's all on autopilot, so you don't need to do anything."

Just as well. They hadn't included shuttle flying in his training, but then he wasn't supposed to have been awakened until they reached their new home, either.

"Report in when you arrive."

"Yes, sir."

Katia just nodded. She clearly didn't like Major Creepy Misogynist, as she'd referred to him. Obviously, a good judge of character.

Pryce strode across the docking bay, disappearing behind a pile of stuff. Layla had stayed where she was.

"Could I talk to you for a moment?" she said.

"Of course."

"Alone?"

He cast a glance at Katia, giving her a silent plea for help, but she only raised a brow. "I'll be waiting in the shuttle. Just don't take too long."

She headed up the ramp. At the top, the doors slid open, and she went inside. Logan turned his attention to Layla, trying to hide his impatience. "What is it?"

"I don't think you should go."

He didn't know what he'd been expecting, but it wasn't that. Had Katia been right and Layla "liked" him? He hadn't been getting those sorts of vibes from her at all. "I was woken up to do a job. I don't think the captain would be too impressed if I decided I'd rather stay here."

"I can put in a good word for you with the captain. See to it that she doesn't put you back in cryo." She reached out, resting a hand on his arm. "Let Detective Mendoza visit the *Trakis Three*. She's perfectly competent and will share her findings. Everyone knows there's nothing to find anyway. We're merely going through the motions. It's a better use of your time to study the system's logs. Identify the source of the malfunctions. I can help you with that." She smiled, her eyes warm and inviting.

Someone cleared their throat from the top of the ramp. He glanced up to find Katia watching him. He caught her gaze, and she rolled her eyes. "If you're coming, then get your ass on board. If you're not, you might want to get a safe distance. Wheels rolling in one minute."

He glanced from her to Layla, gave a shrug. "Sorry, but I have to do my duty."

Behind him, Katia made a choking sound, probably some sort of expression of her disbelief, but he ignored her. "I'll see you when we get back," he said to Layla then turned and headed up the ramp, brushing past Katia, stepping inside, and coming to a halt.

A grin tugged at his lips. Inside, the shuttle was a single room, circular, about ten feet in diameter. A clear screen at the front—looked like he was going to get a great view of space—with a console beneath and lots of buttons and interesting stuff. Four seats, two sets of two.

Katia entered behind him, and the doors slid shut with a *whoosh*. A red light flashed on the console at the front, and beneath his feet, he felt a faint vibration as the engines fired.

And then they were slowly rising… A thrill shot through him. He just hoped his first ride in a shuttle wouldn't also be his last.

Chapter Eight

"Sit down and strap yourself in. We're going for a ride."

Logan headed for what was clearly the pilot's chair. Katia opened her mouth to tell him that seat was taken and then shut it again. She could be magnanimous and let him have the best seat…this time. From the goofy grin on his face, he was pretty excited about the whole thing.

She'd overheard most of the conversation between him and Layla—her hearing was more sensitive than humans. Poor Layla hadn't stood a chance.

For a moment back there, she'd thought she was going to get lucky and Logan would choose to stay behind. Katia had nothing against him, but she worked better alone. Always had. She'd periodically worked with partners as a homicide detective, but only when her captain had insisted and she couldn't get out of it.

She had a feeling Logan was just going through the motions. Whether that was because he really did believe the deaths were due to some sort of systems malfunction or whether he didn't care and was happy to give the people in charge what they so clearly wanted, she wasn't sure.

Perhaps from Rico's point of view that would be the best result all around. Just close the case quickly, and everyone would be happy.

Except the dead Chosen Ones, of course.

And if this was some sort of serial killer, then there would be more victims. But did that matter if they were all going to die anyway? It was enough to do her head in.

She took the chair next to Logan and fastened the harness then set the alarm on her comm unit to thirty-two minutes, the length of the flight.

Something beeped and the screen came to life, showing the docking bay. They hovered above the floor, then the engines revved, sending a vibration though the shuttle.

Her heart rate sped up. She cast a sideways glance at Logan—he still had the grin plastered on his face. As if sensing her regard, he turned. "Fucking amazeballs."

Then they were gliding forward. Ahead of them was what appeared to be a solid wall. Her hands tightened on the arms of her chair, but the wall lifted as they approached, and they flew slowly through the opening. She couldn't see, but she presumed the doors closed behind them because they were in darkness. Then another set of doors opened, and the vastness of space lay before them. For a second, they hovered, then the shuttle shot forward, pressing her back into her seat, forcing the air from her lungs, and they were free of the ship and flying through space.

Beside her, Logan punched the air, and she found herself smiling at his enthusiasm.

As they settled to a steady speed, the pressure decreased, and she leaned forward and pressed a button on the console— the one button Rico had grudgingly said she could press. It changed the screen view, showed the rear of the shuttle and the huge bulk of the *Trakis One* behind them. She switched back to forward view. Better to see where you were going than where you'd been.

She unfastened the harness, stood up and stretched, turned to find Logan's gaze on her, lazily perusing her body, lingering on her breasts.

The worrying thing was they were responding, her nipples tightening. Who would have thought it? Probably another side effect of coming out of cryo. No way would her nipples have the bad taste to respond to Logan, who, while quite pretty—okay, stunningly gorgeous—was a bit of a dick.

"Get that grin off your face, soldier." But she couldn't get upset about it. She felt good. Her belly was full of food, she was flying on a space shuttle, her cat was snoozing, and she had an interesting case to solve. Life didn't get much better.

He unfastened his harness and pushed himself up, wandered around, hands shoved in his pockets as though, if he didn't, he might give in to temptation and press a few buttons. "Do you know how any of this works? What it does?"

"No. Though Rico promised to teach me if I solve the case."

"Rico?"

"The captain of the *Trakis Two*."

"You sound like you know him…personally."

Did he sound suspicious? Perhaps the less she talked about Rico the better. "I met him a few times before we left. I was one of the…civilian liaisons on the *Trakis Two*. Working with the Chosen Ones, preparing them. I had some training for that, and I met all the captains." Gosh, she was a good liar.

"You're lucky. I can't see Captain Stevens or the major offering to teach me to fly. But then, I'm not a pretty girl."

"Neither am I."

He grinned. "All right, a beautiful woman."

She shook her head and returned to her chair then reached into her bag and found the flask. She unscrewed the top and took a gulp, choked, then felt the warmth right down to her belly.

She handed the flask to Logan, and he lifted it to his mouth then took a swallow. "Balls," he croaked, sinking to his seat. "What is that stuff?"

"Whiskey. Rico makes it on the *Trakis Two*."

He took another gulp. "Do you think I could get a transfer?"

"Not a chance. You don't have what it takes." She studied him for a moment. "You know, I got the impression you'd already decided to go along with the whole"—she waved it off, such an implausible theory—"this is a systems malfunction scenario."

"Maybe. That doesn't mean I don't want to know the truth. I'm a nosy bastard, and something isn't quite right about this."

"Is that why you joined the military police?" she asked. "Because you're a nosy bastard?"

"A little. I was in bomb disposal before that. They tend to rotate you after a while."

Before the ships had left Earth, there had been a time of upheaval. The last ten years, from when the government had announced the program and set up the lottery process, there had been a slow—at first, then speeding up—descent into chaos. As a homicide detective, she had been kept super busy. The army even more so. Various terrorist organizations had flourished, some wanting to take over the program, others just wanting to derail it; if they were going to die, then so was everyone else sort of attitude.

Maybe one of those terrorist groups could have infiltrated the Trakis program. The deaths might have been an act of terrorism. But why so few? She would have expected mass murder. Also, as far as she was aware, no one else had been woken up, and the crews had been vetted. But she supposed it wasn't an impossible idea. For Christ's sake, look at the *Trakis Two*. If they could do it, so could others. She made a mental note to add it to the investigation.

"I could have gone back to my unit," Logan continued, "but I've learned the hard way that I...don't fit in."

"You don't?" She studied him some more. It was no hardship. "You certainly look the part."

"That bit's easy. It's playing the part that gets to be hard work in the end. And I lost the urge to bother. So I asked for a transfer to the military police—they're always looked on as outsiders anyway. I got assigned to the investigator's office and found I was good at it. That's the nosy bastard bit. And I have a...sense about people." He shook his head. "I can't believe I'm telling you this. I don't talk about myself. Not ever." He regarded her suspiciously.

Probably the whiskey loosening his tongue.

He looked away then took a deep breath. "So this case. We get to the *Trakis Three* and then what?"

Looked like she wasn't going to get any more information about him. Back to work. "Crime scene first. Go take a look at the cryo tubes. Then see if we can get some names and information on the victims from the backup files. That might give us some idea of the motive. Then we can get some witness statements—talk to the crew, find out if anything unusual happened around that time. Any visitors from other ships. It's a long time ago, but I'm betting nothing much usually happens and people will remember anything out of the ordinary. And hopefully, we can examine the bodies, if they kept them."

"Sounds like fun. So how did you become a homicide detective?" he asked.

"What? You don't think it's a suitable job for a 'pretty girl'?"

He held up his hands in mock surrender. "Hey, I never

said that."

She shrugged. "Just lucky, I guess. I always wanted to join the police. My dad was a cop. He was killed…murdered, actually. Along with my mom."

"I'm sorry."

"Don't be. It was a long time ago." Nearly a hundred years before they'd left Earth. They'd been murdered in the attack that had changed her. A rogue shifter. "They never caught the murderer. I wanted to do a better job. I wanted to give the dead a voice. It took me a while; I did a few other things first. I wasn't very settled when I was younger." That was putting it mildly. The first years after the change had been a nightmare. Not knowing what was happening to her, almost totally lacking any form of control. It was a wonder she had survived. Unlike werewolves, her kind were loners. She'd eventually found others like herself—thanks to Rico. She'd learned how to exist among humans, how to hide what she was, how to control her…appetites. "Then I joined up fifteen years ago. I did my time on the beat, and when I got the opportunity, I moved to homicide."

He shook his head. "You really don't look old enough."

No way was she telling him her actual age. That would take a lot of explanation.

"Healthy living," she said, taking a swig of whiskey, and he laughed.

She handed him the flask. He leaned across and took it, but his brow puckered, then he caught her hand, turned it over.

"What?" she asked.

"You said you had a skin condition when we first met. You wouldn't shake hands." He rubbed his thumb over the palm, and a shiver ran through her. "It seems to have cleared up."

Busted.

She gave what she hoped was a casual shrug. "Maybe I just didn't want to get touchy-feely with you."

His lips curled up into a slow smile. "And now?" He looked at her, as if trying to decide something. "You know, I've never kissed a homicide detective."

"Well, this is not the time to start." She tugged her hand free.

"When will there be a better time? This is as good as it gets. We're on a goddamn shuttle shooting across space. Seems like the perfect time to me. Come on. Haven't you been curious? I know I am."

Was she? Maybe a little. It had been so long for her. She didn't do relationships. They never worked, and she found it hard to be with someone and have to lie about the fundamental things in her life. And telling the truth had never seemed like an option, either. For a while, she'd gone through a one-night stand stage, but then she'd lost the taste for it. Which meant nothing but her vibrator for longer than she could remember.

And really, what harm could it do? Chances were they would only be together for a short time. They'd either solve the case or hit a brick wall. Either way, they would go their separate ways. Her to the *Trakis Two*, Logan to the *Trakis One*, with an impassable expanse of space between them.

When she didn't speak, he pushed himself to his feet and crossed to stand over her chair, turning it slightly to give him more room.

Resting his hands on the arms, he lowered his head. She thought about swiping his legs out from under him, knocking him on his ass, but she had to admit—she *was* curious. Curious about what he would taste like, feel like.

She held herself very still as his lips touched hers. There was nothing tentative about the kiss. Logan had clearly had a lot of practice. Heat washed through her as his lips parted hers and his tongue pushed inside. He didn't touch her anywhere else. And she gave herself up to the sensations moving through her, warmth in her belly, a tingling along her nerves.

Holy freaking moly, he could kiss.

Finally, he raised his head. His eyes were amazing, unusual, filled with heat. "That was...interesting," he murmured.

She reached up and slid a hand around the back of his neck, tugged him down, parted her lips—

Her comm unit buzzed, and she went still. They must be coming up on the *Trakis Three*. "Time's up," she said. *Pity.*

Logan straightened and turned to look at the screen. "Shouldn't we be able to see the ship by now?" he asked.

She peered around him, turning her chair so she faced the front once more. A frown pulled her brows together. He was right, the screen showed nothing but space. She reached across and pressed the button to change the screen view. Behind them was more space. No sign of either the *Trakis One* or the *Trakis Three*.

"I think we might be in trouble."

Chapter Nine

"What sort of trouble?" But Logan had an inkling. "Don't tell me—a system malfunction. There seem to be a lot of those going around."

"We appear to be heading into empty space," Katia said. "There's no sign of the fleet."

"Can you stop us? Turn us around."

She was staring at the console, a scowl on her face. "I have absolutely no clue how any of this works."

He wished he could go back to kissing her. That was much more fun than contemplating the immensity of space. And being lost in it. He stared at the screen but could make out absolutely nothing of any help. Certainly not a spaceship.

"What would Han Solo do?" she muttered.

He'd fly the fucking ship. Except between the two of them, they had not a single clue how to do that.

Katia smashed her fist down on the console, and he jumped. "I don't think that's going to help," he said.

A low growl trickled from her throat. "I am not going to freaking die in this freaking tin can." She pressed her fingers to her forehead, took a couple of deep breaths. "See if you can contact the *Trakis One*," she said.

He pressed the button on his comm unit. Nothing happened. "Anyone there?" He tapped it again. Still nothing. "Fucking stupid piece of crap."

"Why am I not surprised?" She stared at her own comm unit for a moment then stabbed her finger on the button. "Rico, are you there?" Then louder. "Rico, if you're there, answer the goddamn comm."

Nothing.

"Rico, we're in big trouble here. Answer the comm unit, pretty please." She ground her teeth, glared at the comm unit on her wrist. "He wakes me up, sends me off, and the lazy bastard can't even be freaking bothered to answer his freaking comm unit."

The comm unit buzzed, and a voice came over. "Hey, I heard that, kitten."

"Don't call me freaking kitten," she snarled.

He laughed. "What's the problem? Solved the case yet?"

"No, I haven't solved your case. We're on a shuttle, supposedly flying to the *Trakis Three*. Except, instead, we seem to be heading into space. No sign of any ships anywhere. Tell me you can get us back."

"You mean pull you in with my super-powered tractor beam."

Her expression brightened. "You can do that?"

"No, I can't do that. You've been watching too many science fiction films."

"Rico. This is no time to try and be freaking funny. Focus on the problem here."

"You're not alone?"

"No. I'm with Sergeant Logan Farrell. He's the detective the *Trakis One* assigned to the case. We're working together. Or, right now, we're heading into space together, and he doesn't look any happier about it than I am."

"Okay," Rico said, "let's see if we can work out exactly how much trouble you're in. Go to the console."

"I'm already there," she said.

"Right in the middle, there's a small screen. That should be your flight plan and estimated length of journey. Does it say anything?"

"It's blank."

"No problem. There's a switch to the left—flick it over."

She flicked, and the screen came to life. Logan stared at it. He read the words and the numbers. They made no sense. Actually, that wasn't true—maybe he didn't want them to make sense. *Balls.*

"What does it say?" Rico asked.

"It says: Earth. Estimated travel time: nine hundred years, two days, and three hours."

There was silence for a moment. "You're kidding?"

"No, I'm not kidding. Why the hell would I kid about this? This is not a freaking kidding matter. So what's happened?"

"Looks like the shuttle's programmed to head back to Earth and it's going to take a long time. Except you would never make it. You'd run out of power. These shuttles aren't made for long distances, only for transport between the fleet. Or down to a planet's surface."

"Could it be a systems malfunction?" Logan asked.

"I suppose it could be." Rico sounded dubious, though. "Who programmed the shuttle?"

"Major Pryce," Katia said. "Second in command on the *Trakis One.*"

"Did you upset him, kitten? Give him any reason to get rid of you?"

"No."

"You sure?"

"Piss off, Rico."

Could Pryce have deliberately sabotaged the trip? Logan couldn't think why. It had been the major's idea to wake him up in the first place. Why would he do that and then get rid of him? Maybe it was a genuine malfunction. He was trying to persuade himself.

"Okay," Rico said. "You're going to have to override the automatic pilot and take control. There's a switch on the far right of the console. Press it twice."

Logan's fingers twitched with the need to go press the switch, but he held himself still as Katia reached out and stabbed her finger to the yellow switch.

"Nothing's happening." She stabbed again and growled. Then she thumped her fist down on it. "Stupid machine. Stupid freaking machine."

"Hey," Logan murmured, putting his hand over hers. "Calm down."

He heard a snort come over the comm unit. "Good luck with that."

She snarled, and something flashed in her green eyes, her nostrils flaring. Then she visibly pulled herself together. "Okay, that's not working." She took a deep breath. "What next?"

"You okay there, kitten? You don't want to be losing it in front of your new friend."

She flashed Logan a look, but he decided to keep quiet.

"I'm fine. Now what's next?" There was an ominous silence from the other end of the comm unit. "Rico?"

"Give me five minutes."

Then the comm went dead.

Katia glared at her wrist then looked up, blew out her breath, plastered a completely fake smile on her face. "Well, how are you enjoying your first shuttle ride?"

A short laugh escaped him. "It's like a dream come true."

He crossed to stand beside her. Pressed the yellow button.

Twice. Nothing happened. Well, that was fucked up.

"Any of that whiskey left?" he asked.

She pulled the flask out of her pocket and handed it to him. He unscrewed the top, took a deep swallow, and passed it to her. She swigged, sighed, and handed it back.

He shook it. There wasn't a lot left. Not enough. "I suppose things could be worse."

"They could? How?"

He had another drink. "At least you're awake."

"There is that. Yeah, dying awake is much better than dying asleep."

"And from the looks of it, the fleet's about to fall apart. We probably wouldn't have lasted long anyway."

"Go on. You've almost convinced me."

He stared at the screen, willing a ship to appear, then rubbed a hand over his scalp. "Good company?" He looked down at her. She was seriously pretty—he was sure it wasn't just the whiskey affecting his brain. Maybe they should kiss some more, take their minds off the whole nine-hundred-year trip heading back to Earth scenario. He opened his mouth to suggest it when her comm unit crackled to life.

"Thank God," she muttered. "What's happening, Rico? Give me some good news."

"Sorry, kitten. I had to hunt down Sardi. Someone's got to fly this thing while I'm off rescuing you."

"You're kidding me? Sardi is awake?"

Another voice came on the comm unit, low and gravely. "Sure am, sweetheart. So get yourself back here and we can have a reunion."

"I'll look forward to it," she said drily. "So what's the plan?"

"I'm coming to get you," Rico replied. "Just prepping the second shuttle now."

"You can't come on the *Trakis Two*?" Logan asked.

"Unfortunately not. She's locked into the fleet's flight path, which is controlled from the *Trakis One*. We need to be released from that end, and right now no one is answering."

"Bastards."

"Maybe. Maybe not. The communications system is as old as everything else. We've had periodical black outs at regular intervals over the last few years. Don't take it personal."

"Hey, you're not the one heading into nowhere fast," she said. "How long?"

"Well, there's a little problem we need to solve first."

"Meaning what?" She was almost growling again.

"Right now, you're moving away from the fleet at maximum speed. So if I come after you, I'm not going to catch you. Until you run out of power, and by then, even if I catch up, we won't have enough power to get back to the fleet."

That didn't sound good.

"So what do we do?"

"You can't override the autopilot. You're going to have to find another way to slow her down. Or preferably stop her."

"How...?" She ground her teeth and rolled her eyes.

"Either of you got a weapon?"

"I've got a pistol," Logan said.

"Then there you go."

"Where?" she asked. "Where do we go?"

"Shoot out the autopilot."

"How do I do that?"

"You're being a little slow here, kitten. The yellow button. Shoot it."

Logan looked from Katia to the yellow button and back to Katia.

"You're sure about this?" Katia asked.

"Sure, I'm sure. Think of it as an order from your captain."

She shrugged then nodded at Logan. He drew the pistol,

his finger tightening on the trigger.

"Just try not to hit anything important," Rico said.

Balls. He released the trigger and blew out his breath. "How the fuck am I supposed to know what's important?"

"Ah, good point. What the hell. Go for it."

Logan stepped back, moving Katia behind him with his free arm, then he stretched out his hand, aimed at the yellow button, and fired. The roar was loud, sparks flew from the console, but there was no immediate change. He shot again, once, twice, three times and the console exploded. The shuttle lurched to the side, and he was thrown off his feet.

He landed on something soft, and it took him a moment to realize it was Katia. He blinked, trying to make sense of the chaos. The shuttle was obviously upside down—whatever that meant in space. But they were lying on the ceiling staring down at the floor and the chairs. He opened his mouth to ask if she was okay, just as the shuttle lurched again. Then they were spinning, and he grabbed hold of her and held on tight as they were tossed around. He landed on the bottom, and the air left him in a *whoosh*. They stopped for a moment, then they were spinning in the opposite direction.

He gritted his teeth. If he ever met Rico, he hoped he had a fucking bullet left.

Finally, they stopped moving. Katia lay still in his arms, and panic gripped him. He shook her gently. "Katia?"

She blinked her eyes open, and he went weak with relief. "I'm going to kill that bastard," she muttered.

"Get in line."

At least they were the right way up once more, lying on the floor at the back of the shuttle. "Are you okay?" he asked.

"I'd be better if you got off me and I could breathe again."

He pushed himself up and off her and sat leaning against the back wall, legs stretched out in front of him. He was still alive, though he could feel a trickle of blood down his cheek.

He raised his hand and rubbed his face. Beside him, Katia lay on her back. Logan concentrated on the rise and fall of her breasts to take his mind off the lost in space thing.

"Stop staring at my tits," she murmured, but she didn't sound particularly put out. She pushed herself onto her elbows. "Great, we're still alive. I wasn't sure there for a while." She looked at him. "You're bleeding." She sniffed her nostrils flaring. "You might want to clean that up. I find blood…distracting."

He frowned. "You don't seem the type to be scared of a little blood."

"I didn't say I was scared of it." She sat up and dragged herself over to sit, leaning against the wall beside him.

"What now?" he asked.

She didn't have a chance to answer. The shriek of an alarm rang out, red lights flashing on the smashed-up console in front of them.

Katia grabbed the pistol from where it lay on the floor, aimed it at the red flashing light, and shot. The alarm went silent. The red flashing lights stopped. Unfortunately, the main lights also went out, leaving them in darkness. The only light was the faint pinpricks of stars from the front screen.

He blew out his breath. "That was a bit stupid," he said.

"It was annoying me. And you really don't want to be in an enclosed space with me when I'm annoyed."

How much worse could it get?

The comm on her wrist lit up with a green light, and he could see her face in the faint glow. She raised her wrist. "Rico?"

"Hey, you're still with us," he said. "I thought I'd lost you there for a moment."

Logan closed his eyes and exhaled. They were not totally abandoned. He might not shoot Rico after all.

"And I'm sure you were very upset," Katia replied.

"I shed a tear."

"I'll bet. What's happening?"

"On the positive side, you've stopped moving. So good job there."

"And on the not-so-positive side?"

"Looks like you've knocked out the life support systems. I did tell you *not* to hit anything important."

And that sounded really bad. Beside him, Logan heard a low growl, almost animalistic.

"Don't lose it, kitten," Rico warned. "We're not done yet. I'm on my way."

"How long?" Katia asked.

"An hour, more or less."

"And how long have we got?"

"Long enough. I hope."

She was quiet for a moment. "Is there anything to eat on this pile of junk?"

"Nothing. They're not meant for extended trips."

"Crap."

"There is a flask of whiskey stashed under the pilot's seat."

"Thanks."

"I'll get you out of this, kitten, but there's one thing to consider," Rico said.

"And that is?"

"You're using twice as much air as you need to at the moment."

And what the hell did that mean? Logan wanted to ask, but something held him back. Maybe the fact that Katia still had the gun. It was rested casually across her thigh. In the dim green light, he could see her looking at him, her lips pursed. Was she actually considering it? She wouldn't. Would she? His muscles tensed, ready to leap into action if she made movement.

And what sort of fucking captain would suggest murder?

Maybe he'd totally misread the comment. Perhaps. Probably.

"Thanks for the advice," she said. "But I trust you'll get here in time. *We'll* be waiting."

"Well, don't do anything too energetic—you'll use up the air. I'm heading for you at full speed. Don't you fucking love space?"

And the comm unit went dead.

Chapter Ten

The scent of fresh blood filled her nostrils.

It was distracting as hell.

And she was hungry.

Hunger and fresh blood. Not a good combination.

The light from the comm unit had gone out when Rico signed off, leaving them in near blackness.

Katia took a few calming breaths. Beside her, Logan was rigid with tension, his breaths audible. She wasn't sure whether Rico's suggestion was serious or not. Probably knowing Rico, it was; he was nothing if not pragmatic. It had sure gotten Logan worked up.

He had nothing to worry about. She'd come to terms with what she was a long time ago. Even come to enjoy certain aspects. And she'd killed when she had to, and okay, once or twice, because she just hadn't liked the other person— some people deserved to die. There had been one guy she'd brought in for the murder of a prostitute. He'd gotten off on a technicality, and he'd grinned and given her the finger as he walked out of court a free man. He hadn't been grinning when she caught up with him in an alley later that night.

But that was just taking out the trash.

And while she'd only known Logan a short time, she perceived a...goodness to him. And he'd kissed her. And she'd enjoyed it. She couldn't kill him in cold blood just to give herself a few more breaths of air. No, they'd both live or they would both die.

Of course, there was always the chance that Logan would decide to move first and kill her. But she didn't think so.

Time to put his mind at rest.

She reached out in the darkness and found his leg. She patted it then moved up and found his hand resting on his thigh, curled into a fist. She opened his fingers and then placed the gun in his hand.

"Relax," she said. "You're breathing too fast. You'll use up the oxygen."

His fingers curled around the gun. Then she heard the clatter as he unloaded the bullets and they fell to the floor. Maybe he didn't want to be tempted. He blew out his breath.

"Your Captain Rico isn't what I'd call...typical."

She let out a laugh. "No. He's not typical." Not even a typical vampire. But then he was old, the oldest person she knew, and she suspected living a long time had a profound effect on who and what you were. You had to be ruthless and strong to survive. But at the same time, you had to want to survive. And be able to live with yourself. He'd taught her that a long time ago. Without him, she doubted she would have survived. So many shifters died through violence they brought on themselves. Suicide in a way.

"Will he get us out of this?"

"If anyone can." She shivered; the temperature was already dropping. Rico hadn't mentioned that, but she supposed it was inevitable. God knows what the temperature was outside the shuttle. She didn't want to die in the cold and dark. Though usually darkness didn't bother her; in fact, she relished the nighttime, and her eyesight was far better than most humans. But there was something about this darkness, the extent of it, seemingly spreading far out into infinity, that made her feel so small and insignificant. Pretty much what she was, she supposed. Which didn't mean she wanted it rammed down her throat during what might be the last hour or so of her life. "Christ, I wish we had a light."

"Let me go check in the cabinets," he said.

She heard him feel his way across the floor then the sound of a door opening, closing. Then another. "Here we go."

A torch flared to life, casting a beam of yellow light around the room. For a moment, it settled on her face, and she blinked. Then it moved on.

She blinked again, adjusting to the brightness. Logan was on his feet, holding the torch. He placed it upright on one of the chairs, so it cast a circle of light, reaching most of the room. Then he came back to her and held out his hand. She took it, and he pulled her to her feet. A shiver ran through her, and she rubbed her hands together. "I don't suppose there are any blankets anywhere."

"Didn't see blankets, but there might be something we can use." She watched as he wandered around the room, looking in the cabinets again. Finally, when he straightened, he was holding what looked like small silver packets. "Space blankets," he said. "We used them in survival training." He tossed her one, and she opened the packet. The blanket was made of thin silver foil. She shook it out and then wrapped it around herself. "Pretty nifty, huh?"

He glanced across. "You look like a superhero."

"I always wanted to be Wonder Woman."

Logan obviously wasn't feeling the cold yet. He tossed the rest of the blankets onto one of the chairs then sat down in the pilot's seat, reaching one hand underneath. He felt around. What the hell was he up to? He glanced at her and grinned. "Hurray," he said, dragging a flask out from under the chair. It was bigger than the last one. Must be a liter, and from the sound when he gave it a shake, it was full. "Typical or not, your Captain Rico does have his good points."

Katia sank down into the seat beside him and took the flask from his outstretched hand. She raised it to her mouth, swallowed, and handed it back, felt the warmth in her belly. "Yeah, he has his moments." And if he managed to pull this off, then she'd give him a great big hug.

They'd get out or they wouldn't.

She'd always expected a violent death. It was part of what she was. But she didn't think that running out of oxygen would actually hurt. She tried to remember what she'd read about it. Hopefully, they'd drift off into a peaceful sleep. All the same, she felt like she should be making the most of what might be her last hour. "It seems like we should be doing something…momentous. Just in case we…"

"Don't make it?" he finished for her then cast her a speculative look. "I suppose sex is out?"

The man had a one-track mind. He was holding out the flask again. This time she took two gulps while she actually considered his suggestion. "You suppose right," she said. "Way too energetic, and we need to conserve air."

"We could do it *really* slowly. I'm good at slow."

She'd bet he was. She'd bet he was good at fast as well. All the same, she shook her head, if not without a twinge of regret. "Do you ever think of anything else?"

He actually thought about the answer. "Yeah, sometimes. Deep meaningful stuff. Honest. When I can't help it. But sex is a good thing. People tend to over-complicate it. But it doesn't have to be complicated."

"I'll take your word for it."

"How are you feeling?"

She thought about it for a moment. "Lightheaded, but that's probably the whiskey. And cold. I hate being cold." At least that meant her cat would stay away—she hated the cold even more.

"Yeah." He rubbed his arms. "The temperature is dropping fast." He thought for a moment. "Why don't you come over here?"

She glanced at him suspiciously. "I thought we'd already agreed no sex."

He curved his lip in a sexy smile. "You know, I can be close to a woman and not actually turn into a raving sex monster. Come over here, and we'll share our body heat. In a purely platonic manner."

It did sound tempting. The chairs were big enough, and she'd bet Logan's body would give out some serious heat.

"I promise I won't do anything...sexy."

Hah, he was probably aware all he had to do was sit there and he exuded sexiness. But logically, it made sense. Why freeze to death when you had a soldier to keep you warm? A soldier who was ready, willing, and able. She got to her feet, hugging her silver foil around herself, and shuffled over, stood looking down at him. He really was stunning. Those eyes were mesmerizing, almost purple. He blinked, and she shook her head. "How do we do this?"

"Well, ideally, we should be naked."

"In your dreams."

"I thought you might say that, but all the same, as much body contact as we can." He rose to his feet, unbuttoning his uniform jacket as he stood. He stripped it off and handed it to her. "Put this on," he said.

She looked at it and then back at him. "What about you?"

"I'm a big tough soldier and you're obviously feeling the cold more than me." That was her fast metabolism again—she used up all the energy too quickly.

She placed the flask of whiskey—still clutched in her hand—carefully on the chair behind him, took the jacket, dropped her blanket, and pulled the jacket on over her shirt. The warmth of his body oozed through the layers of her clothing. It fitted easily on top, but then he was about twice as broad as she was. The sleeves came way past her hands, and she balled her fists. Logan reached down, picked up her blanket, and wrapped it around her shoulders.

Next, he reached behind him for the remaining blankets. He opened two and draped them around his shoulders. Then he sat down, tucking the whiskey inside his blankets. "For easy access," he said. "Now for the fun bit." He patted his lap. "Come sit on my lap, kitten."

She glared. "Don't call me kitten."

"Aw, your captain does. And it's cute and it suits you." He patted his lap again. "Come on, Detective Mendoza, do the sensible thing and get warm."

How could she resist? He opened his arms, spreading the blanket, and she shuffled the last step, twisted herself, and lowered herself gently onto his knee, sitting sideways, her legs across his, her hands awkwardly in front of her. He put his arms on either side of her and managed to open the last blanket. He shook it out and then wrapped it around their legs.

Already she was feeling warmer, the heat from his body seeping through to her, and she wriggled, getting comfortable and a little bit closer.

"Last bit." He wrapped one of his blankets around her and tugged the second higher so it covered the back of his head, then he pulled her closer and tucked her in. "How's that?" he asked.

Actually, it was lovely. "I can't move my arms," she said.

"You don't need to move your arms."

As if to prove it, he managed to unscrew the top from the

flask and held it to her mouth. "Open." She opened, and he tipped the flask, filling her mouth with whiskey. She swallowed quickly to avoid wasting any. He took a swig himself and then tucked his hands under the blanket.

She was drifting off. Probably a combination of Logan's hot body, the whiskey, and the lowering oxygen levels. But it was nice.

She wriggled a little, snuggling down.

"Stop wriggling," he murmured close to her ear.

"Why?"

"Because you're giving me a boner, and we've already agreed we can't do anything about it."

"Oh." She wriggled some more, and he flexed his hips beneath her so she could feel the length of a truly impressive erection pushing against her. Warmth flooded her system, her nipples tightening to hard little points. But was a shag worth dying for? She pressed down against him. Maybe. Sometimes. But not now. Besides, they'd have to somehow shed the blankets, and it was cold outside, and she was just getting warm. She lay still, her head resting against his chest so she could feel the steady thud of his heart. The rhythm was soothing, and for a moment she closed her eyes.

"Hey." He jiggled her in his arms, and her eyes flashed open.

"What?"

"Don't go to sleep."

She scowled. "You have an awful lot of rules."

"You go to sleep and you might not wake up. I'm not going to go to all this trouble to keep you warm only to have you die on me."

He was right. Was the air already thinning? It must have been half an hour since they'd shot out the systems. "Any whiskey left?"

"Do you have hollow legs?"

"It's that fast metabolism."

He gave her a drink, and they settled down again. For a while, she stared out of the screen in front of them, but it was lulling her to sleep, and she shook her head. "Talk to me."

"What about?"

"Anything?" She thought for a moment. "Why did you join the army?"

He was silent, and she'd decided he wasn't going to answer when he started talking. "I was seventeen, and I was offered the choice: the army or a young offender's institution. And I'd seen enough of institutions to last me a lifetime."

"Isn't the army just another institution?"

"Maybe that's why I felt at home."

"Oh? What had you done?"

"I killed a man." When she didn't say anything, his arms tightened around her. "Are you shocked, Ms. Homicide Detective?"

Maybe she should pretend to be. Would a "normal" person be shocked? But she'd killed people herself and knew plenty of killers. Some she had put away, others she hadn't. Rico, for instance, had probably killed more than any creature alive. Though not so much these days. Or rather the days before they left Earth. He'd claimed everything was changing, and they had to adapt or become extinct. "Did he deserve to die?"

"I obviously thought so at the time. And I was never charged with murder. Now, I've seen so many people who deserve to die and they get to live. And people who deserve to live and they end up dying. It almost seems a pointless distinction."

"Yeah." She thought of her own family. They certainly hadn't deserved to die. She shook her head. "Christ, this is too serious for what might be the last minutes of our lives."

"Should we check in with Rico?"

"No, he'll call if he has anything to say."

She was warm now. His hands were around her waist, holding her close. It was weird, but she actually felt safe. Totally weird. Because they were going to die, and soon. He was stroking little circles against her rib cage, sending tingles along her nerve endings. And he still had that erection. If they went *really* slow...

Then he prodded her in the ribs. "Don't go to sleep."

She smiled to herself. She could just imagine, great sex and then drifting off into post-coital sleep and never waking up. As good a way to go as any.

"So you won the lottery?" he asked

Well, no. But best not to tell him that. "I did. And it came as a total shocker."

"The odds weren't good."

In fact, what had happened was Rico had approached her. She'd known Rico for a long, long time. She wouldn't say he was a friend but probably as close as his and her side could get. She'd once done him a favor, and Rico always paid his debts. Anyway, Rico had decided that a lottery that didn't include certain sections of society—namely him—wasn't fair. He'd come up with a plan. He'd done research into the crews, found someone he thought might be susceptible, and bribed the captain of the *Trakis Two* into agreeing to ditch half of his Chosen Ones and replace them with people of Rico's choosing. He'd enlisted her to help spread the word among the supernatural communities, to make a list of potential people. The Unchosen Ones, he'd called them. Rico had made the final choice as to who got a place. There were plenty interested. All sorts. Werewolves, werecats, a few of the lesser shifters, demons, witches, warlocks, vampires, even some fae, who usually kept themselves totally aloof from the other races. Just under five thousand in all. She'd jumped at the opportunity.

"Do you have family with the fleet?" Logan asked.

"No. I have no family."

"Me neither."

"Aw, we're a couple of orphans."

"No one to mourn us if we die."

"We're not going to die." She snuggled closer. "So how old were you when you were orphaned?"

"I'm not actually sure I am an orphan. My mother left me at an orphanage in a small town in Colorado when I was three. I don't know why. There was nothing with me but my name pinned to my chest. Apparently, they looked for her, but she'd vanished."

"Do you remember her?"

"No. Except her eyes. They were the same color as mine, so I know she was probably my mother. But more a sensation than a memory. "

"Weren't you adopted?"

"When I was six and they finally gave up on my mother coming back, but it didn't work out."

"I bet you were a sweet little boy. What happened?"

"They sent me back."

"Why?"

She felt him shrug against her.

"I didn't fit in."

"And did you want to fit in?"

"It was all I ever wanted when I was a kid. So I learned to pretend, and I made a pretty good job of it. Then I joined the army, and I pretended some more, and I fit in just fine."

"And let me guess, you like women, but you stick to one-night stands because you can't let anyone close, because then they might see who you are and that you don't fit in and you never will."

"Something like that," he said, not sounding too put out by her assessment. "So what's your excuse?"

I'm a werecat and most men just don't understand me. "Being a cop makes things difficult. Long hours. You get distrustful. Lots of reasons. Besides, I like being alone. I like my own space."

She rubbed the dull ache pressing at her skull. Was the oxygen running out? Though she knew it wasn't lack of oxygen that would kill them but rather the buildup of carbon dioxide. "How's your head?" she asked.

"A little fuzzy. You?"

"The same." At least she was warm. She'd hate to die cold. And she wasn't alone. That was a comfort, which was strange considering she'd just said she was a loner. Her mind was probably wandering. How much longer? She rested her head on Logan's chest and tugged the blanket tighter around them. She didn't close her eyes, and she tried to keep her breathing slow and even, but everything was growing heavy.

A bright white light filled the screen in front of her, illuminating the cabin. She jumped. "What the hell?" At the same time, her comm unit buzzed, and she struggled to pull her arm free of the blankets, trying to get her brain working. Beneath her, Logan had tensed.

"You two look pretty cozy in there." Rico's voice came over the comm unit.

Relief flooded her system. At least there was a chance. She'd almost given up there. "Tell me you've got a plan."

"I have a sort of plan. It might not be a very good one, but it's the best I can come up with. I'm going to attach a tow rope and pull you in. That's what delayed me—I had to hunt one out from the tons of crap."

"How are you going to attach a tow rope?"

"I'm going to lasso you."

"Lasso?"

"You know, like a cowboy. And then I'm going to drag you back to the *Trakis Two*."

She thought about it for a moment. "How long will it take?"

"A couple of hours."

"I don't think we've got oxygen for a couple of hours."

"Why aren't you using the masks?"

"Masks?"

"Look above your head. You'll see a button. Press it."

She reached up and pressed. A flap opened and a gas mask dropped, dangling in front of her face. She stared at it blankly.

"Oxygen."

Katia glared at the comm unit. "Why the hell didn't you tell us before?"

"It never occurred to me that you didn't know." He sounded amused. "Now you do. That should be plenty to get us back."

She gritted her teeth. Then she pushed herself up. She swayed slightly, her head light, her vision blurred. A shiver ran through her. Already she missed the heat of Logan's body. She handed him the mask, and he tugged it and placed it over his face then gave her a thumbs up. She moved to the seat beside him, pressed the button above her, and tugged the mask over her own face. Immediately, her lungs filled with oxygen and the tightness eased from her chest. She looped the strap over her head and sat with her knees against her chest, arms wrapped around them, shivering in the frigid air.

The bright light went out, and through the forward screen she could see the other shuttle. It was so close it filled most of monitor. She hoped Rico was as good as he thought he was, because a collision would not be good right now.

"You might want to strap yourselves in or hold on," Rico said. "This will likely get a little bit bumpy."

No way could she fasten the harness without taking off her blankets, and that wasn't happening. She glanced at Logan. His hands came out and he gripped the arms of the seat, then he turned his head to stare straight out of the screen.

She didn't see Rico's lasso, but a minute later something sent a jolt through the shuttle. Her hands tightened, and she managed to keep her seat. Another jolt and then they were actually moving, jerking at first, lashing from side to side so she thought her neck might snap. But then they picked up speed and were moving more smoothly behind the other shuttle.

Maybe they were going to make it after all.

A hand reached out and rested over hers, squeezed.

She didn't pull free, but only because her fingers were freezing.

Best not to get too attached to Logan. She needed to spend the next couple of hours working out how to keep him alive once they got back to the *Trakis Two*.

It wasn't going to be easy.

Chapter Eleven

Logan's teeth were chattering loud enough to hear in the silence of the shuttle.

He was never going to be warm again.

On the plus side, against all the odds, they were actually still alive.

There had been a nasty moment right at the end when they'd landed in the docking bay on the *Trakis Two*. Though "crashed" was a better word. As they'd approached the bulk of the huge ship, Rico had shortened the tow rope until the two shuttles were almost touching. Logan had to give him that—the guy had balls of steel. And there was no doubt he was risking his life by doing this when he could have left them to float away in space.

Either the man was very fond of Katia or he was some sort of adrenaline junkie. Maybe a little of both.

The close proximity had given a little more control and also would allow both shuttles to enter the airlock together. But even with the short tow rope, as the speed decreased, they'd started a very unnerving side to side movement. It was only luck they hadn't hit the walls as they'd entered the airlock. And they'd banged into the shuttle in front as the doors closed behind them. He'd heard Rico swear through the comm unit.

Now the inner doors were opening, and they were inching into the docking bay, the shuttle in front barely above the floor. Logan glanced across at Katia, who was huddled inside her space blanket. She looked colder than him. As though she sensed his gaze, she turned to face him, pulling the oxygen mask free of her face. Beneath it, her lips were almost white. "Yay, we're alive."

He pulled his own mask off. "Yeah. For a while there, I thought…"

"Me, too. But here we are. Not where we planned to be, but it will do for the moment. At least until I've had something to eat. Jesus, I'm starving."

"Hell, and you say I have a one-track mind. Is food all you ever think about?" At that moment, his own stomach let out a growl.

"Pretty much. And being warm. I have never been so cold in my entire life."

In front of them, the other shuttle had come to a halt. They were still moving, and Logan tightened his hands on the arms of his chair in anticipation. Still he lurched forward as they hit, only just managing to stay seated. Next to him, Katia was thrown from her seat, and she swore loudly.

"You two okay in there?" Rico's voice came down the comm unit.

"Just peachy," Katia replied, and Logan heard the other man laugh.

"Okay, well, I've had enough of flying for the moment. So let's get out of these things."

The comm went silent. Katia struggled to her feet, clearly unwilling to release her hold on her silver blanket. Once standing, she looked down at him, as if considering what to say or maybe whether to say anything at all. "Look, just..." She trailed off then continued. "...be a little...careful around Rico."

What the hell did that mean? "Careful?"

"Try not to piss him off."

"Do you think I'm likely to piss him off? Does he piss off easily?"

"Oh yeah. He can be a little...unpredictable, and short-tempered, and basically pissy. Just be careful, and if I give you the look, then back off and shut up."

His curiosity was rising now. She sounded genuinely worried. "The look?"

She glared at him, eyes narrowed, brows drawn together. The "look," he gathered. It might have been scary if she hadn't been so tiny and wrapped in a silver blanket. "Got it," he said. He was definitely getting curious about the captain of the *Trakis Two*.

"Okay. And stick close to me. Don't wander off on your own." She thought for a moment. "Oh, and if I tell you to run, then run. Now, let's get off this pile of junk and find some food."

She shuffled off in the direction of the door. Logan pushed himself to his feet and tightened his blanket around himself. The air felt thin, and he was breathing faster than normal, but otherwise everything seemed to be working fine. Katia pressed her hand to the door panel, and absolutely nothing happened. She swore and kicked it, and it slid to the side. "Freaking load of crappy junk."

Logan followed her out the door and down into a space similar to the docking bay on the *Trakis One*. Large, cavernous—their footsteps echoing on the metal ramp—and packed with mostly unidentifiable stuff. A man stood beside the other space shuttle. He was no doubt inspecting the damage from where they smashed into it, but he turned as if he sensed them approaching. Rico?

The first thing Logan noticed was the man wasn't in uniform. He wore black pants, black boots, and a black shirt. He was tall, probably six-foot-four, the same as Logan, lean, with black hair and olive skin and dark eyes. There was a sense of...difference about him, something that made him stand out, and a feeling of leashed power.

As his gaze settled on the two of them, his dark eyes narrowed. A shudder ran through Logan. He'd thought he was cold before, but now his insides froze like he'd swallowed a ball of ice. He went still. This was the man who had suggested Katia kill him to conserve the air. At the memory, he had to fight the urge to take a step back. Instead, he stood his ground, returned the stare, and wished he had some bullets in his gun. Rico appeared unarmed, and Logan would have liked to have some sort of advantage. But his bullets were still strewn across the floor in the shuttle, and he wasn't going back for them. He thought about saluting but didn't want to let go of his blanket just yet, and besides, the man wasn't in uniform. Maybe he wasn't military. He didn't look military— might be the ponytail. He settled for a quick nod.

Finally, Rico turned his attention to Katia. Logan's tense muscles relaxed, and he could breathe again. Rico's gaze dropped over her small figure, and a smile curved his lips. "Hey, kitten, nice outfit. Silver is definitely your color. You look cold. You want something to warm you up?"

"Yes," she snapped. "I need food."

Rico laughed. "What a surprise." Then he nodded in Logan's direction. "Are you going to introduce us?"

"Yes, but only when I've had food. Oh, and by the way— your minor side effect sucked big time."

"I knew you would cope."

"No, you didn't." She glared. "Food, now."

Rico raised an eyebrow but nodded. "Let's go, then."

Katia shuffled forward, rustling as she moved, to walk

beside the other man, and Logan fell into place behind. They walked quickly, and Katia had to occasionally skip to keep up. Rico moved with an animal grace, seeming to flow, almost inhuman.

Yeah, he was being fanciful—probably suffering from shortage of oxygen to the brain.

He looked away, studying the ship instead. The first thing he noticed was that the *Trakis Two* appeared in much better condition than the *Trakis One*. The metal walls shone, and the lights remained on, not a flicker. Another difference— they never met any other crew members. He'd lost track of time on the shuttle. Maybe it was "night time" and everyone was asleep, but he didn't think that long had passed. It had been just after lunchtime when they left the *Trakis One*.

Finally, they came to a halt in front of a set of double doors. Rico placed his hand on the panel, and they slid open, revealing a galley similar in design to the one on the *Trakis One*. But again, it appeared in much better condition, everything sparkling. And it was warm...hot. The heat penetrated through his blanket.

Katia stood in the middle of the room and shed her silver blankets, dropping them to the floor in a heap. "Oh my God, that feels so good."

"I turned the heating up for you," Rico said.

"You're an angel," she said. "Don't let anyone tell you different."

Logan unwrapped himself, folded the blanket, and placed it on the end of the table.

Katia was already poking at the food dispenser. "How the hell does this work?"

Rico moved her aside and pressed a few buttons. Seconds later, a steaming bowl appeared. She picked it up, lifted it to her nose. "Beef stew?"

"Yes, but minus any real beef. I've been told it tastes the

same."

Was the guy a vegetarian?

Katia picked up her spoon and started shoveling the food in. Logan watched, and her gaze lifted, and she met his and grinned between mouthfuls. "It's *so* good."

He shook his head, but then his stomach growled.

Rico handed him a similar bowl, and he took it to the table, pulled out a chair, and sat down. It was sinking in. He was alive. His brain was starting to work again, to start turning the facts over in his mind.

There were way too many malfunctions going on around here. Or were there? The fact was he was out of his depth—he needed more information. Maybe he'd find this was normal and shuttles went off the rails regularly. After all, Security Officer Caldwell's shuttle had exploded. Perhaps they'd been lucky. At least they were in once piece, not blown into space dust. He took a mouthful of stew, chewed, swallowed. It was good. Considering it was over five hundred years old. But he supposed if they could keep live people in good condition for that amount of time, then food should be no problem. At least on the *Trakis Two*. He concentrated on the food; it was better than contemplating getting back on a shuttle and continuing with the investigation.

Rico placed a steaming mug next to him. Coffee. Then he took the seat opposite and sat back, watching the two of them. Katia was already on her second helping. Logan cleared his bowl, sat back, sipped his coffee, and watched her eat. He was warm at last and feeling sleepy. Probably reaction setting in. Coming down from the adrenaline high of imminent death.

Finally, she finished eating. She glanced up at him and grinned. "I feel better now."

"Good."

"Perhaps time for those introductions," Rico said.

She pursed her lips then nodded, albeit reluctantly.

"Logan, this is Captain Ricardo Sanchez."

Logan stood up and saluted. "Sir."

"Rico," he replied, "and please don't do that."

He sat down as Katia waved a hand in Logan's direction. "And this is Sergeant Logan Farrell of the New World Army."

"And what's he doing on my ship?"

"He's ex-military police, and when their security officer came to a sudden and unexpected end, the captain and first officer of the *Trakis One* decided to wake him up so he could carry on with the investigation. He was already awake when I arrived, and it was decided that the best interests of the fleet would be served by us working together."

"You've got a partner," Rico said. "That's nice, *querida*."

"Not really. But it is what it is. And we're making the best of it."

"So what happened to keeping the investigation away from here?"

Logan's ears pricked at that. Why didn't the captain of the *Trakis Two* want him, and more specifically anyone, investigating the deaths on the *Trakis Two*? What was he hiding? And a little worrying—why was he not concerned about talking about it in front of Logan? Would he meet an unfortunate accident on board the *Trakis Two*? Was that what Katia had been trying to warn him about?

Well, he was here now, so there wasn't a lot of point in worrying about it.

But if Rico had something to hide, why had he woken up Katia to investigate? Presumably, he wanted to know the answers. Which meant he didn't know them already. Unless she was merely a diversion and her job was to lead them away from the truth. He found he didn't want that to be the case. He felt they'd made a connection facing death together, and he didn't connect with many people.

He was watching Katia as she gave the other man

what looked like the "look." The one that meant: don't say anything else. Except it was aimed at Rico, not at him. What was Rico about to say that she didn't want Logan to hear? He remained still and quiet. The other two were entirely focused on each other now, and he didn't want to interrupt. This was getting interesting.

"You towed us here," she snapped. "That's why we're on board *your* freaking ship. Maybe you should have taken us back to the *Trakis One* or to the *Trakis Three*. Then there would be no problem."

"I don't do visiting, and you could have solved the *problem* before we arrived."

"Yeah, great idea. That might have taken a little explanation. And thanks for putting the idea into his head. He could have done the same to me."

"No, he couldn't," Rico said.

"But he didn't know that."

"And it's not too late to solve the problem."

She leaned forward. "Oh yes, it is. And anyway, there is no problem. Everything is under control."

"If you think so, kitten. But I'm not convinced."

Okay, Logan was totally lost. "Does someone want to tell me what the problem is?" Apart from lots of dead people and a lot of unexplainable malfunctions. And a really weird setup. And a captain who didn't behave like any captain he'd ever known. He studied the other man, trying to get a feel for who and what he was. Good or bad. But, like Katia, he was a complete blank.

Rico returned his stare. Outwardly, he appeared relaxed, leaning back in the chair, his eyes almost sleepy, but there was a coiled tension about him, a sense of power barely contained. Logan was being fanciful. Again. But there was plenty about this setup to get the alarm bells ringing.

"As I said, there is no problem," Katia replied.

She wasn't convincing anyone, but maybe he'd ask her when they were alone. If he got the chance and Rico didn't decide to get rid of the "problem" right now. He eyed up the other man again. Could he take him? He was unarmed, but then so was Rico. His muscles tensed.

Rico's lips curled into a small smile. As though he knew exactly what Logan was thinking. Logan allowed his own lips to curve into a smile, and he held Rico's gaze. It was like looking into a bottomless pit of darkness.

"Oh, for God's sake, you two," Katia snapped. "Cut the testosterone crap. There is no freaking problem." She glared at Rico. "You woke me up, took me out of my nice, cozy cryotube to solve this case. So let me solve it." She turned her focus to Logan. "And you? What do you think is going to happen here?" She got to her feet. "Christ, I can't do this on an empty stomach." She headed over to the food dispenser, came back to the table with another bowl of stew.

Unbelievable.

But it broke the tension. The tightness eased from his muscles, and Logan sat back, picked up his coffee, and drained the mug.

Across the table, Rico glanced between the two of them and then nodded. "Okay, kitten. We do it your way."

"Don't call me kitten. And yes, we'll do it my way."

There was a strange dynamic between the two of them, and Logan couldn't quite get a handle on it. He supposed Katia wasn't a crew member, she was a civilian, but all the same, Rico was captain. He would have expected a measure of respect. Also there was something quite...scary about Ricardo Sanchez. But Katia didn't seem in any way intimidated by him. The confrontation certainly wasn't affecting her appetite.

He looked back at Rico. The air of danger had drained from the situation. Rico pulled a silver flask from somewhere.

He leaned across and poured amber liquid into Logan's mug, then Katia's. "Okay, your way. For now." He raised the flask. "Welcome to the *Trakis Two*," he said with a grin. "I hope you enjoy your stay."

Logan lifted his mug and took a gulp, managed to keep his face expressionless. Strong stuff. He assumed he was safe for now, but he didn't want to outstay his welcome. Time to get to work. He looked at Katia. "You think someone didn't want us to get to the *Trakis Three*?" he asked.

"What? You mean you're not buying the malfunction crap?" She put down her spoon and sat back with a sigh. "Yeah. It had occurred to me."

"So you were right, and maybe the answers are over there."

"Of course I was right."

"Does someone want to bring me up to speed?" Rico asked.

"Not really," Katia said. "Because right now, we know sod all more than you do. We don't know who the victims are, we don't have a motive, and we've yet to visit a crime scene." She picked up her spoon again and ate for a minute. Then something obviously occurred to her. "Actually, now we're here, we might as well take a look at the scene of the crime. And you could get us the details on the victims."

"You didn't get that from the central database?" Rico asked.

"Nope. Would you believe there was a malfunction?"

"What are the chances of it being a real malfunction? Thirty out of ten thousand is not bad as far as losses go."

"Who knows?" Logan said. "Though the scientific officer on the *Trakis One* seems to believe it's a possibility." He thought for a moment. "I think if the news hadn't gotten out about the deaths, then they might have kept it under wraps. But it did get out, probably in the aftermath of Caldwell's mishap."

"So you think if Caldwell's shuttle hadn't exploded, then the investigation would have just gone away?"

Beside him, Katia let out a snort. Logan glanced at her and found her exchanging a look with Rico. A different look this time. But he'd given up trying to work out what was going on between these two. "Maybe. We'll never know. But now it's out in the open, and the people in charge have to look like they're doing everything they can to prove there's nothing shady going on here. Something like this isn't good for morale, and I get the impression that morale across the fleet is low already—but you'd probably know more about that than me."

"Morale is crap," Rico said. "We're five hundred years in. Things are running out, the fleet is falling apart, and there's no sign of our promised land in sight. All the ships are on their last crew rotation, and no one can decide what's the best move—wake up the decrepit and possibly senile old crews or train new people from the Chosen Ones."

"Which would be your choice?" Logan asked. Though Rico looked young, probably mid-thirties at the most. Like everything else on the *Trakis Two*, the captain seemed to be faring better than the rest of the fleet.

"Well, I'm not waking up the last captain," Rico said. "He was a total dickhead."

"I wondered what happened to Bastion," Katia said.

"He's asleep, and he's staying that way."

"Anyway, we should keep an open mind on the malfunctions," Logan finished. "Maybe we could have a talk with the chief engineer on board and get some more background."

Rico glanced at Katia then back at him. "Maybe."

"I'd planned to do it on the *Trakis Three*, but it might be good to get a few opinions."

"I'll see what I can set up. Sardi isn't the chatty type."

"Sardi?" Katia stopped eating momentarily. "Sardi is the engineer? You're kidding?"

"Nope," Rico said with a grin. "He's good."

"Well, it will be useful. But identifying the victims might also give us an insight on whether the deaths are random. So if you could dig out those back-up files, that would be great."

"I'll look into it. I take it there were no malfunctions on the *Trakis One*?"

"Not yet." Was that significant? "Could be the murderer is making sure he doesn't crap on his own doorstep." Again, Logan had no clue.

"Do the two of you still want to visit the *Trakis Three*?" Rico asked.

Right now, he didn't want to get on another shuttle as long as he lived. Which he was suspecting might not be very long. He glanced over at Katia as she placed her spoon in her scraped-clean bowl. She didn't look any more enthusiastic than he felt. But if he assumed that this was one malfunction too many, then clearly someone didn't want them to get to the *Trakis Three*. What secrets was the ship hiding?

"I think we have to," he said.

"Sadly," Katia said, "*I* think you're right. But before I get on another shuttle, I wouldn't mind a bit more information. That's if the *Trakis One* is responding yet. If so, can we get hold of that tech guy—Jake?"

He tapped a couple of times on his comm unit and held out his arm. She leaned closer as it cracked into life.

"Technical Support. *Trakis One*. Jake here. How can I help you?"

"Hey, Jake. Katia Mendoza here. Can you tell me who, if anyone, on the *Trakis One* could have changed our flight plan?"

"Your flight plan was changed?"

"Just a little."

"I should be able to." The man didn't sound convinced. "I'll get back to you."

"And one more thing. Can you tell me when the malfunction to the central database occurred?" He was silent for a moment. Hard question? "Jake?"

"I'm not sure. I can see when we last used the database and it functioned *properly*. That will give us a window."

"Then that will have to do." She sat back as Logan ended the comm. "Well, that gave us a whole load of nothing."

"Yeah." Rico rose to his feet. "I'll get Sardi to prep the shuttle once he's had a nose about. I, for one, would like to know why my perfectly maintained shuttle should suddenly decide to turn into a piece of crap. Hopefully, he'll be able to find out why you made your little detour. And make sure it doesn't happen next time."

"That would be nice. Is there a room I can use while we wait?" Katia asked. "Preferably with some sort of white board. I want to set up a timeline and get what little information I have down clearly. I work better when I can visualize things."

"You can use the conference room next door."

They followed him out and only a few feet down the corridor to another door. Inside was a room about the same size as the galley, with a circular table and chairs at one end. And a huge white board at the other.

"Perfect," Katia said.

"I'll go see if I can get that information on the victims," Rico said, "and then we'll visit your crime scene."

"Sounds like a plan."

Rico turned and walked away. He paused at the door and looked back at Logan. "Don't take this personally, but I look after my own. So if it ever comes down to you or Katia, I'm not going to choose you, sunshine."

And he was gone.

Chapter Twelve

Well, that could have gone worse.

Katia stared at the open door where Rico had disappeared. She didn't like that he had been so open about the "problem." It could mean nothing, but it could also mean that he was considering making the problem go away. And that parting comment hadn't put her mind at rest at all.

But hey, she was alive, her stomach was full, and she was warm at last. She was still wearing Logan's jacket, and she stood up, shrugged out of it, and handed it to him.

She knew he had questions. She could see it in his eyes and in the small line between his brows. And she had to decide how much to tell him. And more importantly, how much not to tell him. Probably he was better off not knowing most of it. It might increase his chances of getting off the ship alive. So she had to come up with something that would keep him happy. A little hard, though, when Rico had been such a dick.

"Do you want to tell me what that was all about?" Logan asked, walking farther into the room and tossing his jacket over the back of one of the chairs.

"No."

He ignored the comment. "Why did he tell you to keep the investigation away from here?"

Good question. She was silent for a moment. "It's nothing bad. Well, not *really* bad. Rico just likes to do things his own way. And maybe some of those ways are against standard fleet policies. So he doesn't want them nosing about the place, telling him how to run his ship. And you have to admit, this ship looks a hell of a lot better than the *Trakis One*."

She cast him a sideways glance. But he couldn't argue with that. It was staring them in the face, from the gleaming walls to the non-flickering lights. Whatever Rico was doing was working.

"Yeah," he said, though he didn't sound entirely convinced. "The place seems in perfect condition. Except for the malfunctioning shuttle, of course."

Which hadn't malfunctioned until it set down on the *Trakis One*. All the more reason to presume that someone had made the malfunction happen. Someone who didn't want them to get to the *Trakis Three*. But also someone who had access to the shuttle in the short period of time when it had been parked in the docking bay of the *Trakis One*. Unfortunately, she hadn't seen any real security, no guards anywhere on the ship, so likely the whole crew had access to the docking bay. And that wasn't including anyone who had remote access. She made a mental note to make a list of questions to ask Sardi—see if they could narrow down who could have sabotaged the shuttle. Right now, she wanted to get the facts organized in her mind, so she could pull something together.

• • •

Logan dragged out the chair so he could sit and watch her work. She went to the whiteboard and swiped a hand across the power button then picked up the stylus, tapped it against her thigh.

She wrote T1 to T12 down the side of the board. Then across the top, she headed columns for Date, Cryotube Number, and Victim. Along from the T2, she wrote the date the "malfunction" had occurred then, beneath that, the numbers of the cryotubes, leaving the victim column empty.

She repeated the process for the other ships where malfunctions had occurred. Ten in all, including two on the *Trakis Six*. Then she swiped her hand across the board, sorting the list into chronological order. T3 first, T7 last, and T2 somewhere in the middle. Then she stood back and looked at her work. "There's an awful lot we don't know."

"Three victims in every case," Logan said. "Could the number mean something to our killer?"

"Like his lucky number? Maybe, but right now, who knows? Not me."

She opened up a new page, wrote *Things We Need to Know* across the top.

"Maybe we should look at it from a different angle," she murmured, almost to herself. "For the moment we forget about who actually did the crime—because right now we have no clue, or even if there was a crime at all—and just list out who could potentially do it?" She wrote the question on the blank sheet. "Can it be done remotely?" She added that question. "Or does our murderer need to be there in person?"

She looked so goddamn cute when she worked, nibbling on her lip and wrinkling her nose as she stared at the board.

"If that was the case, then it would be easy," Logan pointed out. "We look at the shuttle logs and see who went where and when. There can't be that much travel between ships."

"Easy would be nice." She sucked in the end of the stylus. "Except we know no one has visited the *Trakis Two* in the time frame, so it must be possible to control the cryotubes remotely."

"How do we know that?"

"Rico told me."

"Unless the murderer is based on the *Trakis Two*," Logan suggested. Why *had* Rico wanted the investigation kept away from here? Logan wasn't buying Katia's explanation. Not entirely at least.

She turned to look at him, eyes narrowed, as she considered it. "Unlikely. But we'll keep an open mind. We can check the outgoing logs."

She stared some more. He could almost see her brain working. "That covers who could do it physically, but what about who has the capability to do it? How hard is it technically? Who can access the cryotube systems?" She added the questions to the list. "And if it was done remotely, who can do that and from where? Hopefully, Rico and Sardi can answer most of this stuff between them."

She swiped the board again to bring up another page. "And now for the difficult one." She wrote *Motive* across the top then stared at it. "What possible reason could there be to murder someone who's been asleep for five hundred years? And why three at a time?"

"Could be someone our murderer knew from back on Earth. An old grudge? Settling scores?"

She wrote *grudge* and *revenge* on the board, but her brows were drawn together. "Honestly, I just can't see it." She shook her head. "Maybe once we have the victims' details, we might see if there's any pattern or if they're purely random."

She paced the room a couple of times then came back to stand in front of him. "You know, there are about thirty crew members per ship and ten ships surviving. That's only around three hundred potential suspects. Maybe we could do a process of elimination. Who *couldn't* be our killer?"

"Unless it's not a crew member."

She glared at him, hands on her hips. "Who else could it be? Everyone else is asleep."

"Maybe someone woke up from Cryo. And got…bored."

With a sigh, she went to the board and scribbled—*anyone else awake?*

She scratched her head then came over and plonked herself down on the chair next to him, a scowl on her face. "We need more information."

"Then it's your lucky day," Rico said from the open doorway. "I have your victims." He crossed the room and handed her a piece of paper. "I've also been in contact with the *Trakis One* to let them know the good news that you're here and not halfway back to Earth."

Logan was guessing there was someone, somewhere, not too happy about that. He just wished he knew who.

Katia glanced at the paper and smiled. Then she got up and walked to the white board, swiped it to bring up the first page.

Against the first number on the T2, she wrote: *Peter Stewart, 13 years old*, the next: *James Stewart, 15 years old*, and finally: *Jacob Stewart, 17 years old.* She turned back to Rico. "There's a CF next to each name. What does that stand for?"

"Crew family."

And there it was. Their first breakthrough. Each crew member was allocated three places for family members on the ships. Though, apparently, they were always allocated tubes on a different ship than the crew member was serving on. No doubt there was some psychological bullshit reason for that. Maybe they would be a distraction or there would be an overwhelming urge to wake them up, have a chat…

"That's why there are always three victims," Logan said. "I'm betting if you got the rest of the victims, they'd all be crew family."

"Clever boy," Katia said. "Do we know who the crew member was?"

"The captain of the *Trakis Eight*, third rotation," Rico replied. "But the *Trakis Eight* hit an asteroid field about two hundred years ago and was destroyed, so Captain Stewart is no more."

"Great. So now all we need to do is find someone with a grudge against a dead captain. Any ideas? No?" She sighed. "Then let's go see some empty cryotubes."

Chapter Thirteen

They made their way through the cryotube storage area, or the "fridge" as Rico called it. The air was cool, and Katia shivered, pulling her shirt close around her. Rico was right, this place was creepy. Thousands of tubes, all with their little green lights glowing—well, obviously not all. They were on their way to examine the cryotubes that had "malfunctioned."

"Did Caldwell visit the cryotubes?" Logan asked.

"He did," Rico answered. "Not that there's a lot to see."

She caught sight of faces through the clear lids as they passed. So peaceful. Maybe it wasn't a bad way to go, to fall asleep and never wake up. Maybe they could put Logan back into cryo if it looked like he was going to be a problem. And maybe she'd request it as well. She gave herself a little shake. First, they had a case to solve. A murderer to expose.

Finally, they arrived at their destination. She could tell that, not only by the absence of green lights, but the lids were open.

Three of them in a row.

She came to stand beside the closest. It was empty. She

didn't know what she'd been expecting. A corpse maybe. There was no evidence of a dead body, no sign of a struggle. A little plaque with a number on the base was all the identification there was. C2341. She glanced at the paper in her hand. The number corresponded to Peter Stewart, who was thirteen years old at the time he had come into the hold of the *Trakis Two* and gone to sleep. At least he had lasted longer than half the Chosen Ones on the *Trakis Two* who hadn't even reached their tubes. How had Rico organized it? She'd never thought about the details before. Now she felt maybe just a little bit of guilt. She was guessing they'd never made it on board but had been re-routed from the holding facility where the Chosen Ones had spent the last few weeks before takeoff. Had they known what was happening? That their dream of survival had turned into a nightmare?

"Where are the bodies?" Logan asked, pulling her from her thoughts.

"We tossed them out the airlock. We don't have a morgue on board, just the medical center, and no space for three bodies. And they were a mess. They'd been dead for over two years."

"Had they struggled?"

"Oh yeah. That much was clear. Fingernails gone, they'd torn off the monitors—not that it made a difference. The alarms were all 'malfunctioning' anyway. Not even a flicker. Looked like they'd died of asphyxiation. Or maybe they died of shock or fright. Not a good death, either way."

Maybe she wasn't going back in a cryotube after all.

They looked at the other two tubes, but there was nothing new to see. Katia smothered a yawn with her hand. "It's been a long day."

"Sardi will be a while with the shuttle, " Rico said. "Why not go get some beauty sleep? You both look a little peaky. I allocated you a cabin, D101, on the other side of the docking bay, and there's an empty one next to it for your sergeant."

"Sounds like a plan." She yawned again then turned to Logan. "Let's go, soldier."

They didn't talk as they made their way along another corridor. As they got closer, she cast Logan a quick look. What to do with him? Did she trust Rico? In this particular instance—hell, no.

They were coming up on the cabin Rico had allocated to her. And the one next door that he'd said Logan could use. She came to a halt in front of D101 and considered how to word her idea.

"Don't take this the wrong way," she said. "But I think you should share my cabin."

He looked down at her, eyebrow raised. "What's the wrong way?"

"I'm not suggesting we have sex or anything. But I'll sleep sounder knowing you're close by."

"You don't trust Rico?"

"Actually, I trust him with *my* life." And it was true; once Rico accepted you into the circle, then he would protect you with everything he had. Unless you betrayed him, then all bets were off.

"You just don't trust him with mine?"

"You're probably all right." She wrinkled her nose as she considered what to say next. "If he was going to do anything, likely he would have done it by now. All the same, as I said— I'll sleep sounder knowing you're close by."

"Balls," he said with a grin. "Admit it. You're just trying to get into my pants."

To be honest, she was too tired to think about it. But she didn't want him dead. Maybe facing death together had forged some sort of bond between them. She would worry about it when she'd had some sleep and her mind was functioning a little better. Pressing her palm to the door panel, she stood to the side and gestured for him to enter. He gave her a sideways look and a wink but walked into the cabin.

She hadn't realized how small it would be. Logan filled the space. It had curved silver walls, a bed, a chair, and a small table. There were built-in cupboards, and a chute that she guessed was for laundry. The bed had a dark pink cover and was maybe big enough for two, but it was going to be pretty cozy. She couldn't get worked up about that right now, and she was guessing Logan was the same. There were shadows under his eyes, and his skin was drawn. Besides, snuggling up to a warm body was exactly what was needed to banish the memory of how freaking cold it had been on that shuttle. A shiver ran through her.

Rico had left her bag on the bed, and she went across and rifled through it, pulling out the contents, looking for something suitable for sleeping in. She found a long T-shirt in soft, black material. It would do. She bundled the rest up and shoved it, and the bag, on the single chair by the bed.

"I'll only be a moment," she said and left him standing in the middle of the room while she went into the bathroom. She tied her hair in a ponytail and then stood under the steaming water for an age. It felt so good. Then she switched the shower to air and let the heat dry her skin. Afterward, she felt almost human, which was a bit of a joke. She hadn't been human for a long time.

She slipped the T-shirt over her head and smoothed it down—it came to mid-thigh, perfectly adequate. Then she released her hair from its ponytail and ran her fingers through the curls. And she was ready. She felt a little reluctant to go back to the bedroom, and she didn't know why.

Logan had removed his boots and his jacket and was seated on the bed, back against the wall, legs stretched out. He had been pressing buttons on his comm unit, but he looked up as she came in, a slow smile curving his lips. "Nice,

Detective Mendoza."

She shook her head then waved a hand at the bathroom. "It's all yours."

He got up and stretched, all long, lean muscle, and disappeared into the bathroom. She stood unmoving as the door closed behind him, and a few seconds later, she heard the water running. She sat on the bed and took off her comm unit from her wrist and placed it on the shelf by the table. Then she crawled under the covers and rested her head on the pillow. It felt so, so good.

She fought to keep her eyes open, not wanting to be asleep when he returned. Finally, the door opened, and there he was.

Holy freaking moly.

He came out wearing nothing but a pair of black boxers and looking pretty good. She tried not to stare, but there was a lot of him on display, all perfectly toned muscle and golden skin. Obviously, you didn't lose your tan in cryo. Broad shoulders and narrow hips, long legs. She sighed then held up the sheet and patted the spot in front of her, scooting over to the far side of the bed.

He slipped under the sheet and lay down, turning on his side and backing up against her. She wrapped her arm around his waist, trying to ignore how good his skin felt, satin soft over the firm resilience of hard muscle. And he was so freaking hot. She pressed herself against him, trying to get in contact with as much of that bare, hot skin as she could.

"Oh my God," she murmured, "you feel so…warm."

A chuckle shook his body. "Glad to be of some use. I am also so wrecked."

"Me, too."

"Then go to sleep."

She reached out and flicked the switch to turn out the light. It wasn't totally dark, just a dim glow. Probably you could reprogram, but it was good enough for now. She closed her eyes and breathed in the scent of warm, clean man. It had been way too long, but her body was too tired to respond.

She waited for sleep to take her. And waited. Beside her, Logan's breathing was slow and deep. She'd thought she would drop straight off, but now she was here, her mind couldn't switch off; it kept going over and over the case. The shuttle. The rescue. How close they had come to dying. How long they had left. Whether Rico would try to kill Logan. Whether she would let him.

"Relax," he murmured.

"I'm trying, but I can't shut down my brain."

"Turn over," he said.

"Why?"

"Don't sound so suspicious. Just turn over."

She did. He pushed up behind her, so she could feel his hard stomach and his chest against her back, his legs tangling with hers. It felt sort of right. He came up on one elbow behind her, then his fingers burrowed into the hair at the back of her neck. "You have beautiful hair," he whispered. He stroked through the long strands then massaged her scalp, sending tingles down her nerve endings. His fingers felt so good, wiping the churning thoughts from her mind. She couldn't hold onto consciousness, and finally, she drifted into sleep.

She woke to the almost forgotten sensation of an erection pushing against her ass. Instinctively, she pressed back against it, because it was huge and hot and felt amazing…and totally unexpected.

She went still.

Where the hell was she? And who did that erection belong to?

Her mind was all fuzzy, and she concentrated to bring it back. She was in a cabin on the *Trakis Two*, five hundred years away from Earth, and the erection belonged to Sergeant Logan Farrell.

It probably wasn't the best idea to get any closer to Logan, either physically or emotionally. But she never did her best thinking first thing in the morning. She wriggled her ass against him, and a shudder of tension rippled through his body.

He was awake.

He nuzzled his face against the back of her neck, kissing her, and a shiver of pleasure prickled across her skin.

"Good morning, kitten," he whispered in her ear, and his warm breath tickled her skin. "If it is morning."

"Near enough." They'd slept around twelve hours.

His teeth nipped at her neck, then his tongue licked the spot, and a sudden warm wetness flooded between her thighs. Oh, she was in trouble. This felt too good. But did it need to be trouble? Logan struck her as the "love them and leave them" type. Just like her. So why shouldn't they get a little fun while they could? After all, the end of the human race was close at hand. And she didn't have to worry about pregnancy or STDs. She'd had an implant to cover the former, and everyone on the ship had undergone a comprehensive medical exam to ensure there were no nasty diseases heading for the new world.

Logan was kissing down the side of her neck now. He had such a clever mouth; what would it feel like if he—? But then he nipped the soft place where her shoulder met her throat, and rational thoughts fled. For a moment, she closed her eyes and enjoyed the sensations, the little tingles shooting down her nerves, coalescing at her nipples, the junction of her thighs. It wasn't enough, and she wriggled around so she was facing him, really close, but there weren't any other options;

the bed was narrow.

God, he was gorgeous, with his messy hair and a shadow of stubble on his chin, and his eyes were so pretty, almost purple in the dim light.

"I didn't think you would ever wake up," he murmured. "I've been lying here thinking about all the reasons why this"—he flexed his hips so she felt the scalding heat of his erection up against her stomach—"would be a bad idea. But you know what? We nearly died yesterday, and there's no certainty that we won't die today or at least some point in the not-too-distant future. So I thought—why not?"

His views so reflected her own that a smile tugged at her lips.

"You're smiling, kitten. I'll take it that's a good sign."

"Don't call me kitten. And I was thinking something similar myself." She pressed herself up against him. "It would be a shame to waste this."

"A total shame. Almost a crime against humanity. Now, at this point in the proceedings, I usually give out my standard expectation clause—along the lines of…this is just a little fun and don't expect a happily ever after, because I'm not that sort of guy. But I'm guessing we don't need that between the two of us?"

She didn't bother to answer the question. "Get on with it, soldier, or I might change my mind and tip your ass out of *my* bed."

He grinned, then he moved quickly, and somehow, she was on her back and Logan loomed over her. For a moment, she tensed up. She didn't like being on her back; the position made her feel vulnerable. Then she forced her muscles to relax, because he was lowering his head, and if she remembered rightly, Logan was a hell of a kisser.

She parted her lips, but instead he kissed her cheek, then her eyes, so she fluttered her lashes closed, finally, her mouth.

His lips were warm and firm, and his tongue was hot and wet, pushing inside, sliding along her inner mouth, her teeth, her tongue, filling her. He tasted of heat and spice and something uniquely him, and her head swooned.

"Naked. I need you naked." He threw off the cover and straightened so he was straddling her hips, then he grabbed the hem of her T-shirt and dragged it up her body and over her head, tossing it on the floor behind him. Then he sat back on his heels and stared.

"Damn, but you are gorgeous."

His gaze was almost a caress in itself, trailing down from her face to her breasts, so her nipples tightened, then lower, and a pulse throbbed between her thighs. He shifted down the bed, so he could lower his head, and he licked one taut nipple then suckled it, and she squirmed at the sensations coursing through her. He bit down gently, and she pushed against him, a purr rumbling in her throat. Need was building inside her, an ache at her core.

She tried to wriggle closer to the erection she could see poking at his black boxers, but he held her steady with a hand on her hips as his mouth moved lower, trailing wet kisses down over her stomach, dipping into her belly button, and she went still, realizing where he was heading and wanting to do absolutely nothing to change his mind. He lifted his head slightly and blew gently on the curls at the base of her belly, his breath cool against her wetness. Her thighs parted of their own accord, and he lowered his head, and then his mouth was on her, his lips and his tongue nuzzling her. She parted her thighs further to give him access, another purr rumbling from her throat as he used his thumbs to separate her sex. He glanced up the line of her body, caught her gaze.

"You are so wet. I like that. I like that you want me as much as I want you. And you can't hide it and I—"

"Logan, you talk too much."

He smirked and shut up. She held herself still as she waited for his touch. Then he was French kissing her sex, his mouth open, long wet kisses that never quite reached where she needed him most. His tongue was circling her, and her hips were pushing against him. She was so close, and a moan escaped her. She didn't like to beg, but she was getting pretty close to where she would do anything, say anything...

At last, he kissed the little bundle of nerves, drawing it into his mouth, sucking, and her back arched as she exploded into a thousand pieces, pleasure throbbing through her. He bit down, and she came again, screaming, pushing against his mouth, giving herself up to pleasure, totally mindless.

Finally, her body quieted, and she lay still. She felt so, so good, languorous and sated. Why had she denied herself for so long? She'd been right, Sergeant Logan Farrell had a clever mouth. Now to see how good he was with the rest of his body. A twinge in her sex showed she was ready and willing to find out.

"Well, that was easy," he said, and she blinked her eyes open. Her gaze lowered and snagged on his cock.

Logan straightened, wiping his mouth with the back of his hand. "My turn now."

His hand went to his shorts, and he pushed them down and fisted his cock. It was thick and long, the head purple and swollen. Her inner muscles clenched as her mouth went dry, and she licked her lips.

He rested his weight on one elbow and lowered himself slowly toward her—

And Rico's voice crackled over some sort of comm system all around them. "Wakey, wakey, rise and shine, children. And get to the docking bay now. We have a problem."

Logan went completely still, cock in hand, and was looking around wildly. She held a finger to her lips, and he gave a small nod. He didn't look happy.

"Jesus, Rico, you nearly gave me a heart attack."

She shook her head, trying to get her brain to function. Then she thought over his words. He obviously knew Logan was with her. How? Had he made a visit to Logan's room and found him absent?

"Sorry, kitten. But needs must."

The voice wasn't coming from her comm unit by the bed—there must be one built into the room. She gritted her teeth and glanced at Logan, more specifically at his penis. She wanted that penis.

"We'll be there in ten minutes," she said.

"You'll be there in ten seconds or I'm coming to get you."

And the transmission went dead.

Chapter Fourteen

His dick ached.

He considered begging, promising he didn't need ten minutes; ten seconds would be perfectly adequate. But the mood had been broken. He swore viciously but pulled up his shorts at the same time.

Katia cast him an amused glance.

"You can smile," he muttered. She'd already come and come hard.

She patted his arm and slipped out from under him. "We'd better get down there. Best not to piss him off if we can help it."

He lay for a moment, watching her move around the room, picking up her clothes from the chair beside the bed. She was small but perfectly formed, her breasts full and round, her nipples dark and prominent. His dick twitched, and he looked away.

Heaving a resigned sigh, he rolled onto his feet, stretched, found her gaze on him. She wanted him. And she was going to get him. As soon as they'd found out what this new problem was.

She finished dressing—jeans and another flannel shirt, in one piece this time—pulled her hair into a ponytail, and sat on the bed, chewing on a protein bar. Logan yanked his pants on, wincing a little as he fastened them, then sat beside her to put on his boots. She handed him a bar, and he bit into to it— quite nice, sweet and fruity. She got up again, tossed him his shirt. He put it on as she opened the door, and she headed out as he fastened it. They didn't talk on the way to the docking bay. Again, they saw no other crew members. Where the hell was everyone?

They found Rico pacing the docking bay floor. He whirled around and stared at them as they crossed the space toward him. He was dressed the same as before, with the addition of a weapons belt, a pistol at his hip, and a long black leather coat over the top. He looked more like a goddamned pirate than a spaceship captain. He waited for them, hands on hips as they came to a halt in front of him.

He looked at Katia, and his nostrils flared. "You smell of sex and look like you just got laid." Then he turned his attention to Logan, and one eyebrow rose. "You don't." He smiled. "Don't tell me I interrupted something."

"Fuck off," he growled.

Rico snorted then rubbed his chin. "This is getting out of hand."

"What's going on?" Katia asked.

"*Dios,* five hundred years and not a single visitor. Now three in nearly as many days. Did I mention I don't like visitors?"

"Yeah, you did. So who's coming?"

"The Scientific Officer from the *Trakis One.* Her shuttle will be arriving any moment now."

Layla?

"What the hell does she want?" Katia asked.

"How would I know? Just said she had information for your boyfriend"—he nodded toward Logan—"and clearance from the Captain of the *Trakis One* to board us. What the fuck right does *she* have to give permission to board *my* fucking ship?"

"She is in charge of the fleet," Logan pointed out. The other man's focus turned to him, and he almost wished he'd kept his mouth shut. But he had an idea that he wouldn't earn any points with the captain of the *Trakis Two* if he backed down every time the other man looked in his direction. So he stared back. And continued staring until something jabbed him in the side. Katia. He turned to her with a frown. "What?"

"Don't wind him up."

"Good advice," Rico said, but the tension seemed to have drained from him. "So what are we going to do with this woman? How do we get rid of her?"

Get rid of her? He didn't like the sound of that. "Why don't we get whatever information she has for me, and then she'll no doubt go back where she came from?"

"Maybe." Rico didn't sound convinced. "But if that were the case, why come at all? Why risk a shuttle trip? They haven't come across as a particularly safe means of transport recently. So why not just comm us with your information?"

"She probably wants to see Logan in person," Katia suggested. "Check him over. Make sure he's okay."

"Why?"

"I think she likes him."

"So problem number one is responsible for problem number two?"

Katia scowled. "I told you there are no problems."

"Hmm. Well, get rid of this woman." He turned to Logan. "Bang her, do whatever you need to. But get her off my ship."

He was starting to believe that Rico must have something

big to hide. But what? He was also thinking it wasn't anything to do with their case, something unrelated. So it wasn't his job to find out. And maybe it was just as Katia had told him—Rico liked to do things his own way and didn't want anyone interfering.

But what the hell did Layla hope to achieve by coming here? Perhaps she had some information she didn't want to send via the comms. Maybe she'd found something implicating someone and didn't want to be overheard.

"You think she's found something she doesn't want to share with the Captain or Pryce?" Katia asked.

"Maybe, but she must have gotten permission from one of them to come here. So unlikely. No doubt we'll find out soon enough."

"Perhaps she just wants to get laid."

"She's not the only one," he grumbled.

"Well, it sounds like she's docked," Rico said. "So we're understood here? Find out what she wants and get her off my ship. No finishing anything. Information, and good-bye."

Logan shrugged. Until he knew what she wanted, he wasn't promising anything.

The inner docking bay door slid open, and the shuttle flew through, the door closing behind it. The vessel touched down lightly just inside the doors. Watching it, he realized that the horror of their near-death experience the previous day was fading. And he was ready to go again, a tingle of excitement in his gut.

The door opened, and Layla stood framed in the doorway, hand on one hip, looking around the docking bay. She went still as she caught sight of their little group. Then she focused on Logan, and a smile flashed across her face as she hurried down the ramp toward them. She ignored Rico and Katia and headed straight toward him. He braced his legs for the onslaught. Her arms came out and then she was on him, arms wrapped around him, her long blond hair tickling his nose. His arms hovered at his side. What the hell was he supposed to do? He patted her back with a tentative hand.

He caught Katia's gaze above the other woman's head, and she raised an eyebrow. She didn't seem too bothered, though. Was she forgetting only minutes ago he'd had his head between her legs and she'd been screaming in pleasure?

Layla's head was on his chest. Christ, they'd only met yesterday, and she was acting like he was the love of her life. He put his hands on her arms and gently pushed her away.

"I thought you were dead," she said. "We got the news that your shuttle had gone off course, and we couldn't get in touch. Travis said you were finished. I didn't believe it, but they wouldn't let me come after you. They said it wasn't worth risking the other shuttle. I was so scared."

"Aw, sweet," Katia said.

Logan bit back a smile—maybe she was a little bit jealous—as Layla went still in his arms. He dropped them to his side and she turned slowly. "Detective Mendoza. I'm so glad you're okay, as well."

"I'm sure you are."

Someone coughed from behind him. Rico. He turned and found the other man watching them, a small smile on his face.

"Layla," he said, "this is Captain Ricardo Sanchez of the *Trakis Two*."

Layla looked past him, snapping to attention. She saluted Rico, then a frown crossed her face, and her eyes widened a little.

Rico stepped forward and held out his hand, and she shook it. "Welcome on board the *Trakis Two*, Scientific Officer..."

"Langdon," she said.

"Perhaps I could call you Layla," he murmured. "We

don't go much for formality on the *Trakis Two*."

She cleared her throat. "Of course."

"And you must call me Rico." They were still holding hands.

"Jesus," Katia muttered. "Excuse me while I go throw up."

A laugh escaped him, and she glanced over. He looked down at her, then lower, his gaze wandering over her body, letting her know that as far as he was concerned, Rico was welcome to the other woman. All the same, he was eager to find out what had brought her here.

Finally, Layla got her hand back. She looked around, appearing a little lost.

"So," Katia said, "what's this information you have for us?"

"Why don't we take this somewhere more comfortable?" Rico said.

What the hell had happened to getting her off the ship as soon as possible? He exchanged a look with Katia, but she gave a sigh of resignation. "Lead the way," she said.

Rico put his hand to Layla's waist and led her through the docking bay. Logan let them get a little ahead and then followed with Katia. "What's going on?" he asked quietly. "I thought we had a plan."

"Looks like it's changed." She nudged him in the side. "I think you might have a little competition," she whispered.

"Good." He rested a hand on her arm, lowered his head, and kissed her. She tasted sharp and sweet, and his dick twitched. "Come on, let's go find out what she's got for us." And then maybe they could go back to bed before heading out to the *Trakis Three*. If he was going to risk getting into a shuttle again, then he really wanted sex with Katia before he ventured into the unknown. But maybe whatever Layla had to tell them would change their plans to visit the other ship.

They arrived at a small meeting room with a circular table and six chairs. Rico sat down, reached beneath the table, and pulled out a flask and four glasses. Did he have the stuff stashed *everywhere*? He poured the amber liquid while they took seats around the table, Layla next to Rico, him and Katia opposite. He wanted to be able to see Layla's face while she spoke to them. She took a sip of the liquid, and her eyes widened. She swallowed and put the glass down.

"So, talk," Katia said.

Layla seemed a little put out at her abruptness, her eyes narrowing, then she took another sip and started talking. "We have uncovered a possibility that the malfunctions might be the result of a terrorist attack."

Well, that wasn't what he'd been expecting. Though he wasn't sure why. In the last years before they had left Earth, there had been a plethora of terrorist organizations sprouting up all over the place. Lots of disgruntled lottery losers who weren't too happy about the idea of being left on a dying planet. It had been fueled by thousands of conspiracy theories as to what was happening, why the ruling body—the federation—wasn't telling the people exactly how the planet was going to come to an untimely end.

Some were affiliated to one of the many religions, but there were also plenty with no obvious beliefs at all. Many had vowed to prevent the ships from ever leaving Earth. That they were an abomination. That Earth was the home of mankind... Others had tried to take over the ships and escape themselves. Most had been tin-pot organizations without the resources to be any real threat. It was the ones who had no real agenda other than wanting to cause total chaos—*if we're going to die then so are you* sort of mentality—that were the real danger. It was easy to create havoc if you didn't care whether you lived or died.

"Go on," he said.

"There's an indication that one of the cryotubes on the *Trakis Three* might have contained a sleeper."

He grinned. "A sleeper? A little ironic, don't you think?"

Obviously, Layla didn't do irony. She frowned then continued, "We believe this person was secreted on the *Trakis Three* by one of the terrorist groups, in place of one of the genuine Chosen Ones. He was pre-programmed to wake at a certain time."

Logan wasn't convinced, on a few levels. Mainly because if it was the action of terrorists then they could cause way more terror than what was going on right now. A few dead Chosen Ones who wouldn't have even been uncovered if it hadn't been for a random audit? And why arrange for the sleeper to be awoken now, nearly five hundred years into the trip, when, if everything had gone according to plan, they would have already found their new home and been awake anyhow?

But he kept his opinion to himself. For now. He wanted to hear what else she had to say first.

"So how did you come across this new information?" Katia asked. She sounded as skeptical as he felt. They were definitely on the same wavelength.

"It was Travis. He was going through the logs, concentrating on the time around the original…incident. He found a malfunction recorded in one of the cryotubes on the *Trakis Three*, shortly before the first deaths. The tube went offline. It was apparently a temporary glitch, and the tube came back online almost immediately. At the time, no one thought to check out the actual tube." She paused, and he got the distinct impression that she was building up the tension. Actually, she was just pissing them off.

"And?" Rico prompted.

"And we requested they go have a look. They did. And the tube is empty."

Now that did make a difference. It still didn't make sense, but it made a difference. He cast Katia a sideways glance, and she gave a small shrug.

"Any sign of foul play?" he asked.

"Apparently not. No damage at all. Just an empty tube, still functioning."

She sounded pleased with herself.

"Do they know who was supposed to be in the tube?" he asked.

"Jack Burton. He was a nine-year-old son of one of the lottery winners."

"So we're looking for a little terrorist," Katia said, her face totally serious. His lips twitched.

Layla wasn't amused. Her mouth tightened into a thin line. "The terrorists must have killed the boy and taken over the tube before we left Earth. He woke up and murdered the first people. Then he got access to the remote systems and started killing people on the other ships."

"Why?" Logan asked.

She glared at him. "Why?" Her tone translated as: are you stupid? "Because he's a terrorist. That's what they do. Kill people."

"No, they don't just 'kill people.' Their primary function is to create terror. Killing a few people in their cryotubes—and not telling anyone about it—is hardly terrifying."

Katia leaned across the table, grabbed the flask, and filled her glass. The woman was hollow and seemed to show no effect from the amount of alcohol she was consuming. "Maybe little Jack woke up and decided to go for a walk and have a play with a few cryotubes and switched them off by mistake, and…" Except maybe an increase in sarcasm.

Layla sat up very straight. "Captain Stevens believes that this is a valuable lead and would like you to follow it through."

"And of course they will," Rico said smoothly. He topped

off her glass then turned his attention to Logan and Katia. "Won't you?"

"Why not?" There was obviously something going on. Cryotubes didn't suddenly empty themselves. But he wasn't buying the terrorist sleeper theory. Too many holes.

"You're the captain," Katia said. "You order, and I obey." Rico snorted. She ignored him and continued, "We'd already decided to go there anyway, so no biggie. We can take a look at the empty cryotube, have a talk with the crew. If this guy is wandering around the ship, then someone might have noticed him. Or at least noticed any unauthorized entries into the systems."

"Good. That's sorted. And will you wait here for them to return?" Rico asked Layla. "I'm sure we can keep you... entertained for a few hours."

Layla twisted in her seat, gave him her full attention and a pout. "That would have been wonderful."

Beside him, Katia made a gagging noise.

Layla sighed dramatically. "Unfortunately, I have orders to accompany them to the *Trakis Three*. The captain decided this was far too important to leave to—" She broke off, looked at Logan with an apologetic lift of her shoulders. "He thought a senior member of the crew should be present."

"Surely that's not needed," Katia said. She sounded a little desperate. "And it might not be safe. Who knows what will go wrong next time? Do they really want to risk their scientific officer when they've already lost one crew member this week?"

"I'll have to take the risk," Layla said. "Orders are orders." She turned back to Rico. "Maybe there will be time to show me around your ship when we get back. I must say you've kept it in very good condition. Though from the look of you, you can't have been captain for very long."

"A few years. I just take care of myself. Don't

overindulge," Rico said, and beside him, Katia nearly choked on her whiskey.

There was definitely something between her and Rico, but Logan had no clue what. There didn't seem to be any sexual tension, so it wasn't that. But they clearly knew each other well.

Logan swallowed the last of his whiskey and looked pointedly at the flask. Rico filled up his glass and Katia's, which was empty. Again.

He sat back and sipped it. He'd been almost looking forward to the next shuttle trip. Alone in space with Katia, time to finish what they started. The added adrenaline rush of possible death to add a little edge to the encounter. Now, that wasn't going to happen. Maybe they'd get a chance to slip back to the cabin for a quickie before they set off. Rico could entertain Layla.

"So when do we go?" Katia asked.

Rico pushed himself to his feet. "Now is as good a time as any."

Balls.

There goes my quickie.

Chapter Fifteen

They were on their way to the docking bay after a detour via the galley. Katia had insisted. She didn't want to die hungry. She'd wolfed down two bowls of porridge and then stuffed her pockets with protein bars. This time she was going to be prepared. Okay, maybe not prepared for a nine-hundred-year trip back to Earth, but really, could lightning strike twice? No, this trip was going to go smoothly.

Katia hung back a little with Rico and allowed Logan and Layla to lead the way. She wanted to talk to Rico in private. He'd been on the ship a long time, part of the fleet. He must have a good idea of how things worked, what was possible, what was impossible or just unlikely.

In front of them, Logan did not seem happy with their visitor. He strode along, shoulders hunched, hands thrust in his pants pockets.

Layla walked beside him. Every so often, she would reach across, touch his arm, say something. He usually replied with a twitch. His body language said, "Keep away." But Layla obviously wasn't a good reader of body language. She stepped a little closer.

"I'm surprised she's not holding his hand," Katia muttered.

"Hmm, I don't think you need to worry," Rico said. "He's definitely not interested."

"Who said I was worried?" She gave what she hoped was a disdainful sniff. "So what do you think?"

"I like her."

Of course he did. Rico liked anyone with tits. "That wasn't actually what I was asking. Besides, you just want to shag her."

"Maybe not *just* shag her. I'm hungry."

That wasn't good. How had he been feeding, anyway? There didn't seem to be a lot of crew awake. Maybe they didn't need to be awake. *Ugh.* "We'll try and bring her back alive for you."

"Do that. We might have gotten away with offing their security officer, but if their scientific officer comes to a bad end after a visit here as well, there's a good chance they might get a little suspicious."

"You think? Anyway, on the slightly more important issue of the case—what do you make of the sleeper/terrorist idea?"

"Load of bollocks."

Yeah, that was pretty much in line with what she'd come up with. "So what's going on?"

"Damned if I know. That's why I've got my little detective team heading over there to find out. I'm sure you'll come up with something. Talk to the crew. They'll know what's going on. If someone who's not supposed to be there is wandering around, then someone else will have picked them up. They've got to eat."

"We plan to."

"And be careful with your new boyfriend. If you reveal

anything to him, be aware that you might have to kill him afterward."

It wouldn't come to that. "You don't like him?"

"Actually, against all probability, I do like him. But there's more than just you at stake here. And he's career military. I've dealt with them a lot—scratch the surface and you'll usually find a dickhead. In the end, they follow orders and cover their own asses. That's what they're trained to do."

"I won't reveal anything."

"Hmph. I've never seen you like this with a man."

She scowled. "Like what?"

"Your eyes go all soft when you look at him."

"Do not." *Did they?*

"And your reaction to the beautiful Layla would have given you away."

"Would not."

He ignored her. "I won't make you kill him yourself. If necessary, I'll do it for you."

"Sweet. Thanks for the offer, but it won't be needed. After the *Trakis Three*, we'll collect Layla's shuttle and head back to the *Trakis One,* and I'll keep everyone away from here. Hopefully, we can close the case and you'll be left alone again with your secrets."

"Yours as well," he reminded her.

Hers as well. She glanced at Logan and briefly wondered what his reaction would be if he knew the truth. Better not to think about it. "So did Sardi find any evidence of sabotage on the shuttle?"

"Nothing. If your little detour was planned, then whoever made it happen knew what they were doing. You didn't have a chance with the autopilot locked in and no way to change back to manual. They thought of everything."

"Clever." Not a happy thought. A shiver ran through her, and she wrapped her arms around herself. "Did I actually say thank you?"

He grinned. "Take it as said. Most fun I've had in centuries."

They were walking through the docking bay now, approaching the shuttle, and her steps slowed. "So what are the chances of us making it to the *Trakis Three* this time?"

"Sardi reckons pretty good. You'll be using the other shuttle. You well and truly fucked up yours."

"You told us to shoot it."

Rico ignored the comment. "Sardi checked it over, and he's been keeping an eye on it since. No one's been near in that time."

That sounded good. "Where is Sardi?"

"Keeping a low profile. He's not exactly inconspicuous. But he's gone over your shuttle in fine detail. Left nothing to chance. You'll be okay."

"Fingers crossed."

They came to a halt in front of the shuttle, where Layla and Logan were waiting. Another shiver ran through her. God, she'd been cold. She glanced at Rico. "Give me your coat."

"This coat? I love this coat."

"And I promise to bring it back. But I'm sure Logan would like to keep his clothes this trip. So the coat. Hand it over."

"For you, kitten, anything."

Hah. As if. He shrugged out of it and handed it to her. She pulled it on. It smelled vaguely of the vampire, cold and musky, but mildly reassuring. It reached the ground, and she had to roll up the sleeves. She glanced up and caught Logan watching her, a smile on his face.

She glared. The smile broadened.

"Right, trip to the *Trakis Three*, take two. Let's go."

. . .

She looked so goddamn cute in that huge coat.

He'd never considered that cute did it for him, but he was battling an almost overwhelming urge to pick her up and kiss her.

Maybe it was just that she was such a contrast. She looked young. If he had to guess—and didn't know better—he'd put her at around twenty. And sweet. But in reality, she was tough as nails—it was one of the things he liked best about her. And she'd said she'd been a homicide detective for nine years, which must put her in her middle thirties at least. About the same age as him.

She shoved up the sleeves and glared at him as she passed, slamming her palm on the panel. The doors slid open, and she disappeared inside.

Rico still stood at the bottom of the ramp. "Don't let anything happen to her," he said then turned and walked away without waiting for an answer.

How the hell was he supposed to do that? He'd certainly do his best, but hell, if anything else went wrong, he wasn't sure what he was supposed to do.

Layla tugged at his arm. "Let's go. I'm eager to get this over with, then we can return to the *Trakis One*."

He found he wasn't so enamored of the idea. The *Trakis Two* had coffee and whiskey. And Katia. Though, unless they managed to solve this case on the *Trakis Three*, she would likely be coming back with them.

He turned and followed Katia into the shuttle, with Layla close behind him.

Katia had already seated herself in the pilot's chair. Damn. He wanted to be pilot. She grinned at him as if guessing his thoughts. He took the co-pilot's seat beside her and fastened his harness. He glanced up to find Layla hovering beside him, looking from him to Katia as though she wanted to say something. Had she expected him to sit next to her? Christ, it was like being back in high school.

"Can you sit down and fasten your harness?" Katia said. "We're getting ready for take-off."

Layla shot him another look but then moved to the seat behind his. A moment later, the throb on the engines vibrated through his feet as the shuttle came to life around him. A shudder ran through him. But nothing was going to go wrong this time. Absolutely nothing.

"You nervous?" Katia asked.

"Hell yeah."

"Me, too."

They lifted into the air, and the forward screen came to life, showing the docking bay. They floated gently toward the doors. So far so good. The doors slid open to the airlock, and they were in. And there was space in front of them. A thrill of excitement tightened in his gut. He was glad his previous experience hadn't completely put him off.

He gripped the arms of his seat as they shot forward.

His heart was thudding, but as nothing bad happened, he slowly relaxed. He turned to Katia. "So are we going where we're supposed to be going this time?"

She pointed at the console in front of her. *Trakis Three.* Forty-two minutes to destination.

He blew out his breath. Katia handed him a protein bar, and he ate it while staring into space and thinking about the case. Sleepers and dead Chosen Ones. "What do you want to do first?" he asked.

"I think stick with the original plan and visit the cryotubes of the dead Chosen Ones."

Behind him, he heard a *humph* from Layla. She clearly didn't think they were taking her terrorist theory seriously enough. Katia ignored her. "Then we'll talk to the tech guys, see if we can pull out any more information from the ship's backup files, get confirmation the victims were crew family. And then we'll go see if we can't find any evidence of our sleeper."

"Sounds like a plan."

Thirty-nine minutes. He tried not to think of what he could have been doing if Layla wasn't along for the ride. Why was she here? He peered sideways at Katia; she was nibbling on another bar. He liked the look of her strapped in like that. He could imagine her... She caught his gaze and blew him a kiss, her expression amused, as if she knew exactly what he was thinking. And he shook his head to banish the image.

"Logan, come and talk to me," Layla said. "I'm a little nervous."

Katia snorted, and he cast her a baleful glance but unfastened his harness and got to his feet.

Layla was a little pale. He came around and sat in the seat behind Katia. He couldn't resist banging on the back of her chair with his booted foot. He turned to see Layla watching him, her brows drawn together. "So," he said, "tell me what it's like living on a spaceship."

"Pretty boring. Not a lot happens."

"How many crew exactly?"

"Thirty-four—well, thirty-three now that Caldwell is dead. I have a team of six. They're good people but considerably older than me. Did I mention I was the youngest on the ship?"

"You did. It must be hard for you."

"Well, it's nice to have some younger company now. I hope we can be friends." She reached across the space between them and rested her hand on his thigh. "More than friends." She squeezed, and he glanced up and found Katia peering over the back of the pilot's chair, a grin on her face.

He picked up Layla's hand and placed it on her own leg.

"I'm sure we can be friends. Let's solve the case first, though. After that, I don't know what will happen."

"I'm sure the captain will offer you Caldwell's old position. Especially if I put a good word in for you."

Did he want that? If the alternative was going back in his cryotube, then probably yes. Did he want to get more than friendly with Layla? He found the answer was a resounding no. So he hoped the position wasn't reliant on Layla's good word. He had an idea that she was a woman who wouldn't take rejection well. And she was making her intentions perfectly clear.

"Thank you," was all he said.

Maybe he could put in for a transfer to the *Trakis Two*.

The thought brought him up short.

What had happened to "love them and leave them?" *Coffee and whiskey*, he reminded himself. He just wanted the coffee and whiskey.

Katia was in her seat, making notes on a tablet. Maybe he should go and talk about the case some more. So they were prepared. He made to get up, but Layla's hand was on his thigh again. "Talk to me some more. I can't stop thinking about what happened to you yesterday. You almost died."

"We're going to be fine," he said soothingly. "The shuttle was checked over. We'll be there soon. In fact, why don't I go check how long we have to go?"

He picked her hand up again and placed it on her lap then got up before she could say anything else. He went back and sank into the chair next to Katia, closed his eyes for a moment, then glanced at the console. "Twenty minutes to go," he said. He got up and walked around the room a couple of times, peered into the cupboards. Pretty much the same setup as their shuttle yesterday. Which gave him a thought. He went back to where Katia sat in the pilot's chair, crouched down beside her, and reached underneath.

"Ha ha," he said, pulling out the flask, unscrewing the top, and taking a gulp.

"You're going to turn into a lush," Katia said, grabbing the flask from him and raising it to her mouth. He offered it to Layla next, and she sipped delicately before handing it back.

"Hey," Katia said. "Come look at this."

He came around to stand beside her and studied the screen. Off to the right, he could make out an object. Small, it was about an inch across, but growing bigger.

"That must be the *Trakis Three*," Katia said. "Looks the same as the *One* and *Two*. You would have thought someone would have had the imagination to paint them different colors."

He doubted any paint job would have lasted five hundred years. The ship was a drab, khaki-gray color. He could make out the details now. Of course he'd seen pictures before they left Earth. They were huge, probably a quarter of a mile across, and shaped like a bullet. The exterior was mostly smooth, no windows or anything that could slow them down. Ugly, really. But he supposed they had done the job. While they might be falling apart, they had lasted five hundred years. That was an amazing achievement. Mankind pulling together.

The ship filled half the screen now. He could make out the name, *Trakis Three*, in black along the side. Only ten minutes to landing. It did actually look like they were going to make it this time.

And what would they discover?

The truth was he had no clue. And he was intrigued to find out. He guessed it would turn out to be nothing more than a series of system malfunctions.

Something flickered at the edge of the screen.

"What the fuck is—"

The whole screen erupted in a ball of orange flame. There was no sound, and for a second, he stared, trying to make sense of what he was seeing. Then the shuttle was hurled backward as though by an invisible fist, and Logan flew through the air. He hit the back wall with a bang, and everything went black.

Chapter Sixteen

Katia was pushed back against her seat by the force of the explosion then rolled upside down then right way up and upside down again. The harness held her in place, biting viciously into her shoulders and breasts. Her eyes squeezed tightly shut as the shuttle leveled out. She took a quick peek. The screen in front of her was filled with fire, and she shut her eyes again before her they burned. The temperature inside the shuttle shot up until sweat broke out all over her body. She preferred freaking freezing to death than roasting like a pig on a barbecue. Looked like she wasn't going to get a choice.

Someone was screaming, a continuous, high-pitched, shrill screech that drilled into her head. Super loud, right behind her. Layla?

They were slowing down, and she forced her eyes open. The main lights were out, but the room was lit by the flames from the front screen. She shook her head; her ears were ringing, probably from all that screaming. She stared, trying to make sense of what she was seeing.

The whole of the *Trakis Three* was a burning mass, with occasional flashes of brighter light as explosions shook the dying vessel.

Jesus.

The strength of the explosion had saved them, blown them outward and away from the burning ship. Otherwise, they would have been engulfed. As it was, they were being slow-cooked instead of fast. She fumbled with the harness.

Where the hell was Logan? He'd been standing beside her when the ship had exploded. Finally, she managed to free herself, and she twisted around. He was lying on the floor at the back of the shuttle, lazy bastard, but already he was stirring. He'd be fine. She shifted her gaze to where Layla sat, still held in by her harness. Still screaming.

"Shut up," Katia snapped.

The other woman went instantly quiet. Thank God. Then she sat staring straight ahead, eyes vacant, sweat gleaming on her face. Obviously, she was in shock. Katia hoped she didn't have to slap her. Actually, that was a lie.

Layla shook her head then caught Katia's gaze and looked at her accusingly. "You said we'd be fine."

Had she?

"Hey, it wasn't us. We were just caught in the blast. We're alive, aren't we?" What more did the woman want? Some people were impossible to please.

"Logan?"

"Having a nap behind you. But he's fine."

Well, until his brains, along with the rest of him, fried. Time to get the hell out of there. Right now, they were floating aimlessly in space. They needed to get away from the burning ship. Preferably a good deal faster than they were floating. She stared at the console in front of her and wished she knew how the hell to fly the stupid thing.

She tried pressing her comm unit, but it was dead. Maybe

the blast wave was interfering. Or it had been damaged while she was being flung around. She glanced at the reading on the autopilot. *Destination: the Trakis Three, two minutes to arrival.*

Jesus, two more minutes and they would have been entering the docking bay when the explosion went off. They'd be well and truly burned to a crisp. Dead. Gone.

Her stomach churned, and for a moment she was pretty sure she was going to lose her breakfast. But she managed to swallow it down again. Sweat dripped from her forehead, and she stripped off the coat, but that only exposed her to the hot air.

She studied the console, trying to remember what Rico had said yesterday. The yellow button would turn off the autopilot and give them manual control. Without giving herself time to think it was a bad idea, she leaned forward and slammed her hand on the yellow button. The display went dead.

Now what? She turned to Layla. "Do you know how to fly this thing?"

Layla sniffed. "Of course."

Well duh? "Then do you think you could get the hell up and get us away from here. Preferably before we all roast?"

Layla unfastened her harness and stood up. She swayed a little, resting her hand on the seat in front. But she appeared okay. "What just happened?" she asked, coming around to stand in front of the console.

Katia waved a hand at the screen, where the burning hulk of the dying ship could still be seen. "At a guess, the *Trakis Three* exploded."

Could there be any survivors? It didn't seem possible. All those Chosen Ones dead. Burned in their cryotubes. At least they'd have been asleep, unlike the crew. Poor bastards.

"What?" Layla didn't seem quite with it. Maybe she'd

banged her head. "How?"

"Maybe it was your sleeper. Perhaps he decided to up the terror factor." Well, he'd certainly done that. She'd been well and truly terrified. Layla cast her a look of dislike then a pointed glance. It took her a moment to realize she was in the pilot's chair. She got up and stepped out of the way so Layla could sit. She flicked a few switches. "Where are we going?"

"Right now, I don't care. As long as it's away from here and somewhere cold."

Jesus, freezing yesterday. Cooking today. What would be next? At least Layla seemed to know what she was doing.

"Is it working?" she asked. They hadn't taken a direct hit, but the force of the blast had been strong enough to roll them. They could have sustained damage. And then there was always the possibility of another malfunction. Those were pretty common around here.

"It's working," Layla said.

If she concentrated, she could feel the difference. Where before the shuttle had been floating aimlessly, now there seemed a purpose. They were turning, the burning remains of the *Trakis Three* sliding from the screen, replaced by the vastness of deep space.

"Can you get us back to the *Trakis Two*?"

"Of course."

"Then let's go."

She blew out her breath. Time to get Logan checked out. He was still lying on the floor, where he'd landed. As she approached, she saw his eyes were open and he was staring up at the ceiling.

He rubbed his head. "Balls," he muttered. "Lots and lots of balls."

She came to a halt beside him and stood staring down, hands on her hips. She couldn't see any damage, and there was no blood. Maybe he was comfortable down there. Maybe she should join him.

"Guess we aren't going to make it to the *Trakis Three* after all," he said.

"Guess we're not."

He pushed himself up and leaned against the wall behind him, ran a hand around the back of his neck. "Christ, it's hot. Tell me I'm not dead and gone straight to hell."

"You're not dead. But honestly, I'm not sure how long that will last. You do seem to attract trouble."

"Hey, it's not my fault. At least I don't think it is. Did I touch something I shouldn't?"

"I don't think there's anything you can touch that would cause the *Trakis Three* to explode. Come on, up you get."

She held out a hand to him, and he slipped his palm in hers. As she gave a tug, the shuttle lurched to the side, and he was thrown back to the floor. Katia, still holding his hand, landed on top of him with a *whoosh* of air. "What the…?"

She pushed herself up as the shuttle lurched again. They must be dodging debris from the ship. Deciding she was better off where she was, she collapsed on top of Logan. His arms came around her, and she buried her face in his neck. If she was going to die, this was as good a place to go as any she could think of. She couldn't even drum up any fear—her system had obviously been overloaded with emotion.

Logan's hands slid down over her until he reached her ass. Then he gripped her tight and held her to him. She was plastered against the length of his body, her breasts crushed against his hard chest, her thighs tangled with his. His hands tightened, and he held her closer so she could feel him hardening against her. Actually, there were definitely worse ways to go.

He thrust his hips against hers, and she pushed herself up a little so she could look down into his face. "I like a man who can get it up in times of stress."

A bead of sweat rolled down her forehead and off the end of her nose then landed on his chin. "You are so fucking hot," he murmured.

"So are you." She lowered her head and licked the sweat from his face, bit at his lower lip, slanted her mouth over his, pushed her tongue inside. She was alive and so was Logan. He kissed her back, one hand sliding into her hair to hold her steady.

"What are you two doing?" At the sound of a voice, they both went still. Katia glanced over her shoulder.

Layla was peering over the back of her seat, glaring at them with accusing eyes. Katia had forgotten the other woman was even there.

"Nothing, Miss," Logan said. "Honest."

Katia looked back at him, and his lips twitched, and suddenly she was giggling. Beneath her, Logan's body shook with laughter. They were both slightly hysterical, because it wasn't every day you survived a life threatening incident. Just two days in a row. She giggled some more.

Finally, they both sobered. He put his hands to her waist and shifted her so she sat on the floor, legs sprawled in front of her, back against the wall, Logan beside her. Layla was obviously still waiting for an answer. "I was checking Logan's vital signs," she said. "You'll be pleased to know he's functioning as normal."

Logan snorted, and Layla's eyes narrowed, but she turned back to the console.

Katia rested her head back against the wall and stared straight ahead. The adrenaline was draining from her body, leaving her shaky. A few feet away lay the silver flask, and she crawled toward it then brought it back to her place next to Logan. She thought about getting up, sitting in a chair, strapping herself in, just in case. But she couldn't be bothered. She unscrewed the top, took a gulp, and handed it to Logan.

He seemed as dazed as she was. Reaction setting in, that was all. They passed the flask back and forth, not speaking, until she felt the buzz in her head. It was nice.

"Christ," Logan said. "All those people. Dead. Just like that."

"It would have been quick."

"Yeah. Probably no warning at all." He was quiet for a moment. "So are you thinking now this is more like a terrorist attack? Or that someone *really* doesn't want us to get to the *Trakis Three*?"

"Truthfully?" She raised the flask to her lips and took a swallow, felt it warm in her stomach. The temperature was dropping inside the shuttle, and her body temperature was returning to normal, the sweat cooling inside her clothes.

"Yeah," he said, "I think we should have nothing but truth between us."

Hah. That was never going to happen. Logan couldn't deal with the truth. Some things were better kept secret. "Well, truthfully…right now, I don't give a toss." She giggled again. She was a little drunk. That wasn't maybe the best of ideas, she had to keep her wits about her, but somehow, she couldn't give a toss about that, either.

He drained the flask and slid it across the floor. She reckoned he was a little inebriated as well.

Leaning back, she closed her eyes, and the world spun. She didn't open them again until she felt a jolt as the shuttle landed back on the *Trakis Two*.

Rico was going to be pissed, and not the nice, drunk, giggly sort of pissed, either.

Chapter Seventeen

Logan contemplated getting up. But he couldn't seem to move. Beside him, Katia wasn't moving, either.

She was a little drunk.

So was he.

A lot of that was reaction. Way too much going on.

He was going to have to consider the implications at some point. Was the destruction of the *Trakis Three* a logical progression for a terrorist who, up until this point, had seemed pretty unterrifying? And had the terrorist died on the *Trakis Three* or had they abandoned ship before the explosion?

Or was the whole terrorist thing just smoke to get them away from the real truth?

He turned his head to look at Katia; her eyes were open, and she gave him a lazy smile—definitely drunk.

His attention shifted to Layla as she rose from the pilot's seat and came to stand over them. She'd gotten them back safely.

"Thanks," he said. "We would have been in trouble if you hadn't been with us."

She opened her mouth to answer, but at that moment, the outer door slid open, and Rico stood there. He stepped through the open doorway, hands resting on the holster at his hips. His lips were tight, his eyes narrowed. "I'm not happy," he said.

Beside him, Katia snorted. "If you're not happy, then very soon we're not going to be happy, either."

He strode into the shuttle, came to stand over them. "You know me so well."

She heaved a sigh. "And I was feeling all sort of mellow and...alive."

Rico cast her a look of disbelief.

"They're drunk," Layla muttered.

"Am not," Katia said. Logan decided to keep quiet on the subject. His head felt distinctly woozy, though he supposed he might have landed on it after the initial explosion. Now he came to think about it, his head did hurt. He reached behind it and ran a hand through his hair, felt a huge lump. *Ouch.*

"What I want to know is," Rico said, "what is the chance of my ship exploding in a fireball anytime soon?"

Katia shrugged. "Your guess is as good as mine." She held out her hand, and Rico grasped it and pulled her up. She brushed her hands down her sides then pressed a finger to the spot between her eyes.

Logan pushed himself to his feet and swayed. He balanced himself with a hand against the wall and closed his eyes for a moment. When he opened them, everyone was watching him. "I'm not drunk," he said. "Well, not very. I must have banged my head. It's okay, just a little lump."

"Oh, you poor thing," Layla said. "That's probably why you're acting so strange. We must get you to the medical center."

"Not necessary," he muttered.

"Of course it's necessary," Rico said. "You can't be too

careful with a concussion. Layla can go mop your fevered brow, and I'll take Katia to the galley—get her some food. She's a mean drunk when she's hungry."

He was guessing that Rico wanted to talk to Katia alone. What about?

Problems and how to eliminate them?

He glanced at Katia, and she shrugged but seemed to be trying to convey something with her expression. Trouble was he had no clue what. No help there. But he suspected that Katia was starting to like him a little. He didn't think she'd agree to any sort of elimination going on. Or was that merely wishful thinking?

He gave her a nod. "We'll see you in the galley, then."

He followed Layla out of the shuttle. He had no clue where the medical center was, but the layout was the same on this ship as on the *Trakis One*, and Layla certainly seemed to know where she was going. They didn't talk on the way; she appeared a little preoccupied. He supposed a near-death experience would do that. He'd had two now in two days, and he was a little preoccupied as well.

Again, they met nobody. It was like a ghost ship.

The medical center looked pristine, as though it had never been used. Maybe the crew were all really healthy as well as invisible. And there was no medic in sight. Layla frowned. "Where is everyone?"

Damned if he knew.

She shook her head. "Never mind. I can deal with a sore head. Actually, I just wanted to talk to you away from the others."

She did? What about? Obviously she'd noticed the lack of crew, and maybe the seriously weird captain, and come to the same conclusion he had—that everything was not quite right on the *Trakis Two*.

He sat on the gurney in the center while Layla moved

around the room, getting supplies. She seemed to know what she was doing, and that put him at ease a bit. She came back to where he sat and placed a bowl next to him. "Bend forward," she instructed.

He leaned forward, and she probed the back of his head for a moment, then he felt the cold touch of some sort of liquid, and the sharp scent of antiseptic filled his nostrils. "The skin's not broken," she said. "You'll be fine." He straightened, and she handed him a couple of painkillers.

He swallowed them dry.

"So what did you want to talk about?" he asked warily. Maybe she just wanted to spend alone time with him. But he didn't think so.

"Don't you think there's something...not quite right about this ship?" Layla asked.

Hell yes. While he still hadn't seen anyone but Rico, the place appeared to function perfectly. But he wasn't sure how far he wanted to go with this. There was more than a hint of danger surrounding the captain of the *Trakis Two*. While he seemed to be playing nice at the moment, the man had an air of almost tangible danger. As if he could lose his civilized face at any moment and descend into...what? Logan didn't want to know.

Maybe if they had any sense at all, they would get themselves off this ship and back to the *Trakis One* before Rico decided they'd overstayed their welcome.

But he wasn't quite ready to go yet. There was a mystery here, and he was a nosy bastard. Plus there was the possibility that whatever was going on here was tied to the deaths. Besides, heading back to the *Trakis One* would involve another trip in a shuttle, and he wasn't quite ready for that, either. He thought a limit of one trip and near-death experience per day was quite reasonable.

"Logan?"

Layla was still waiting for an answer. "What are you thinking?" he said. "You have more experience than me. I've no idea what's normal and what's not."

"Well, apart from the missing crew, Captain Sanchez isn't like any of the other captains I've ever met. And this place looks as good as new."

"They still have coffee," he offered. Maybe Rico had made a pact with the devil.

"How? You know..." She took a step closer and lowered her voice as though they might be overheard. "As far as I'm aware, no one has ever visited the *Trakis Two* before. Except for Stuart Caldwell, and it didn't end well for him. Not since I've been awake, which is unprecedented. I mean, there isn't a lot of traffic, but occasionally we get requests for help, or we have socials...not often, but sometimes. Never on this ship, though, and as far as I'm aware, no one from here has visited the other ships."

Rico didn't actually seem much of a party guy. "And that means...?"

"I have no clue. And believe me, I've given it a lot of thought since I got here. I think we should try to get a look at the ship's logs."

No, that was a very bad idea. He remembered Rico and Katia's conversation about keeping the investigation away from the *Trakis Two*. And the other bits about eliminating problems. If they were found snooping around, then they would rapidly move up to problem status and be prime subjects for elimination. And he didn't want to be eliminated. He was owed an orgasm, and he didn't want to put his life in danger—again—until he'd gotten what he was due. He could hardly say that to Layla, though. She was watching him earnestly.

"Maybe we should wait until we're back on the *Trakis One*," he suggested. "And instigate a formal report and investigation."

"Perhaps. But right now, all we have is a feeling. We need some proof that something is wrong."

"What could be wrong? What do you think could be going on here?"

"Maybe the crew are all dead. I mean—they've still got *coffee*."

"Then how is the ship running itself?" he countered. "You said it yourself—it's in better condition than all the others."

"Hmm." She wrinkled her brow. "What about the Chosen Ones? Maybe they're all dead?"

"But why? How would that benefit anyone?" And that would be quite easy to verify. He didn't think it was the case, from what he'd seen in the cryotube storage area everything seemed to be functioning fine, but he added it to his mental check list.

"Okay, I admit it," she said. "I don't know. I just know that something is not right. And it's our duty to find out what."

No, it wasn't.

He blew out his breath, scrubbed a hand through his hair, winced when he touched the tender spot.

Right now, all he wanted was some food, a hot shower, and to crawl into bed with Katia and finish what they'd started that morning. "I think we need to complete the investigation first. One thing at a time. And we need the captain's and Detective Mendoza's help to do that."

"Do we?" She stopped her pacing and turned to face him, eyes narrowing. "And what is it with you and the detective? You're all over her. Tell me you're just using her to get the investigation moving?"

Why would she think that? The idea pissed him off. But he wasn't about to explain his feelings for Katia to another woman. Hell, he couldn't even if he wanted to; he had no clue how he felt. "Yeah, I'm just using her. I want to make a good impression with this investigation, and she's a good detective. Working with her is my best chance of solving the case." He jumped off the gurney. "Let's go find them." She didn't move. "Look, I know you think there's something weird about the setup here. But we've got bigger issues. The *Trakis Three* was blown up."

"You don't think it was the terrorist? Or maybe a malfunction?"

His lips twitched. "A hell of a fucking big malfunction." He had two theories right now, but he'd wait to share them until he was with Katia. The first was that Layla's terrorist had indeed decided to up his act and done so spectacularly well. Or the second, that someone *really* didn't want them to get on board the *Trakis Three* and find the answers.

He was keen to get back to Katia, find out her take on the matter. He was leaning toward one of those, and he was interested to know if Katia was leaning the same way.

Balls. He just wanted to get back to Katia.

It was weird, he'd only known her a couple of days, and yet he liked her. He wasn't used to liking people.

And strangely, he trusted her. She was hiding something, but at the same time he had faith that she would do her damnedest to keep him safe. Hadn't she shared her cabin with him last night, so she could protect him? He'd never had anyone want to protect him before. It made him feel strangely warm and fuzzy.

"You're smiling," Layla said. "What are you smiling about?"

"Nothing." He shook it off. "Come on. Let's get back to work—and be vigilant. Keep your eyes open. There's probably a simple explanation for the differences you're seeing. The captain's a maverick, that's all."

"If you say so."

"I got the impression you liked him."

"He's…charming," she admitted. "When he's there, you can't see past that, but then when he's not there, it's…" She shook her head. "I'm just being fanciful."

Well, that made two of them.

Chapter Eighteen

"*Dios*, I don't like this." Rico paced the galley, running his hands through his long hair, which had come loose from its ponytail. "A few dead Chosen Ones, a malfunctioning shuttle—those I can get my head around. But an exploding ship. Nope. Not one bit. Makes me feel a little...vulnerable. And I don't do vulnerable."

No, she could see that. She hadn't often seen Rico rattled. In fact, she might never have seen it. "And you weren't even there."

She wasn't sure what she was feeling. The buzz from the alcohol had gone. Unfortunately. If someone could destroy the *Trakis Three* just like that, then the same could happen to the rest of them. Not a comforting thought. Maybe it had been a malfunction. A *really* big one. But she wasn't buying that. No, she was definitely moving toward the someone didn't want them to get to the *Trakis Three* scenario. What would they have found? They'd never know now—all the evidence had disappeared with a bang.

So they had to think around the issue. What could they

be hiding? If they assumed the malfunction to the central database was the killer covering their tracks, then that took them back to her original theory—that the first victims would have given them a direct link to the killer. They were somehow connected.

Were they crew family? And if so, why would someone want them dead?

She needed the details of the victims from the other ships—they'd already been requested, but she would chase them up. And a visit to one of the other ships would be good, if they got the chance.

And a list of all those who had access to the central database would also be useful. Surely the list couldn't be that long. Something else for Jake to look into. Though he hadn't got back to her with the other stuff yet.

Her stomach rumbled. At least she was getting the hang of the food dispenser in the galley. She flicked through the screens. So many choices. She finally settled on a vegetable curry and rice. Then added bhajis and naan bread—double portions of each. The hot, spicy scent filled her nostrils, and her stomach rumbled some more.

She took the piled-up plates to the table and sat down, trying to ignore Rico's pacing at least for the first few mouthfuls.

Trouble was Rico didn't like to be ignored. "Describe what you saw," he said, dragging out the chair opposite and plonking himself down.

She shoveled in another mouthful then sat back and thought while she chewed. "It exploded. What more can I say?"

"All in one go? Or a small explosion followed by a bigger one? Think."

She closed her eyes and tried to envisage the explosion. She'd been staring straight at the screen when it happened.

Though she'd been a little distracted by Logan, who'd been hovering by her shoulder at the time. "I think a smaller one somewhere near the back of the ship, followed by a super big one almost immediately after."

"Sounds like the engine room went first. Probably caused a chain reaction."

"And boom."

"*Si*. And I'd like to not go boom in a similar manner if I can possibly help it. So we need to know why, and we need to know who, and then we need to kill them."

He was right. This upped the stakes. No longer just a few dead Chosen Ones. Ten thousand of them dead. Plus the crew. No one was safe. "Have you heard from the fleet?" she asked.

"Yes. We're on red alert. But they're going through the motions. Captain Stevens believes that the threat is over, that the *Trakis Three* was blown up by the terrorist, and he—or she—conveniently died in the blast. And now we're all safe and sound. Apparently, it's a tragedy, but we must have faith in God. I don't like it." He shot Katia a sharp glance. "Do you like it? What's your take on the terrorist angle?"

"Well, it would wrap everything up all nice and neat." She scraped her plate, popped the last bit of bread into her mouth. What next? Puddings. Nice stodgy puddings like her mom used to make. Apple pie. And coffee. At least all this food was keeping her cat at bay—she hadn't had a twinge since before they'd left the *Trakis One* yesterday.

She got up, dumped her plates into the cleaner chute, and went back to the dispenser. She found the apple pie, got a coffee, and came back. Rico was glaring at her.

"But?" he snarled.

She took a mouthful...yum...closed her eyes to savor it. He was still glaring, and she grinned. "But I don't believe a word of it. Too neat. I don't like neat." She turned her attention back to her food.

"Kitten, if you don't stop eating for one minute and give me your full attention, I'm likely to get a little antsy. So...?"

She heaved a huge sigh but put her spoon down. "I think someone didn't want us to get to the *Trakis Three*. They tried to stop us by sabotaging the shuttle yesterday. That didn't work—and obviously you didn't give them a chance to repeat the process today. So they did the next best thing and made sure we would never step on board the ship. Or more likely they intended to blow us up as well. Whatever answers were there are now up in smoke." She thought for a moment. She didn't want to say this—it went totally against the detective in her—but it had to be said. "You know, maybe it would be better if we went along with the terrorist story. Let this all go quiet. Perhaps if whoever did this believes they've gotten away with it, then it will finish."

"How likely do you think that is?"

"I think it won't stop the deaths. Our killer has gotten a taste for it now, and I'm guessing they have convinced themselves they have a just cause. But it might stop them blowing up any more ships."

"It's the 'might' that's making me twitchy," Rico said. "I don't like the thought that there's someone out there with the ability to blow up my ship and the total lack of conscience to enable them to kill ten thousand people when it's expedient."

"Yeah, and if we don't know the who and the why, we have no clue what else might trigger them. How about we pretend that we're going along with the terrorist theory but continue to investigate under the radar. See if we can't uncover our killer and then decide what to do."

"We?" His eyes narrowed. "You want to keep soldier-boy on the case with you? You don't think the sensible thing would be to keep this between us? Perhaps put a little distance between you and Sergeant Farrell. He doesn't strike me as stupid."

No, he wasn't stupid, but she didn't think he would stumble on the truth. And yes, she did want to keep him around. She had a flashback to the feel of his mouth on her that morning. Holy moly, it had felt good. And she owed him an orgasm. She always paid her debts.

"He won't be a problem. And he can help—we can tell the *Trakis One* we're compiling a report so we can shut the case and they can publish it, so people can sleep easy in their beds."

"Or their cryotubes," Rico said. "Okay, your decision. But I won't risk anyone uncovering what's happening on my ship. So you make sure he doesn't find out. If he does, he dies. That simple." He sat back and stretched. "Anyway, we're stuck with both him and the lovely Layla for the moment. All movement between ships has been prohibited until further notice. Probably until the red alert has been downgraded." He sat back and regarded her out of half-closed eyes. "So what do you make of the beautiful Scientific Officer Langdon?"

"She's actually very competent. I thought she was going to go all hysterical on us after the explosion, nearly burst my eardrums with her screaming, but then she pulled herself together and flew us back here. I'd say she's brighter than she lets on."

"Maybe I'll keep her out of trouble while you continue the investigation with your soldier. Do my part. It's only fair."

"You're such a hero," she said.

"Yeah." He grinned. "And maybe we'll both get laid. Watching you eat has given me an appetite."

"Jesus," she muttered. "And you talk to me about being sensible?"

"The difference is I can make sure she remembers nothing about our little fling. Though I suppose I could do the same for your friend. He's not my type, but for a favor, I could lower my standards."

"Gee, thanks." Rico was capable of wiping the memory of anyone he had taken blood from. A very useful trait. If worst came to worst, he could do the same with Logan. He'd have to drink from him first, and somehow, she doubted that would happen voluntarily, but Logan could be made to forget the coercion as well as anything else that was likely to put them at risk. She'd worry about it later. If everything went to shit.

Voices drifted in from the corridor. Looked like they had company. "So we're agreed?" she asked. "We go along with the terrorist is dead theory and everything is okey-dokey and we're just closing up the case."

"We do."

"But we could really do with an excuse to visit one of the other ships if you can come up with something believable."

"I'll give it some thought."

Logan and Layla appeared in the doorway. They made a striking couple. Both tall and good-looking. Prime material for building a new human race. They entered the room, and Logan took the seat opposite her, and she avoided meeting his eyes. Layla sank down onto the chair beside him as if staking her territory. A growl rumbled in her throat—her cat was awake, after all—and Rico cast her a sharp look of speculation. She forced a smile. She was good. Logan wasn't hers. The growl echoed deep inside her. Someone was grumpy and didn't agree.

Layla smiled at Rico. "Logan says you have coffee. Could I have a cup? I haven't had coffee in...five hundred years."

"Of course." Rico rose to his feet. "Let me get it for you. Sugar? Cream?"

Her eyes widened. "Wow? I'm impressed. And yes to both."

"We aim to please."

Katia rolled her eyes, but luckily, no one saw her as they were all focused on the beautiful, charming Layla. She gritted her teeth. What the hell was wrong with her?

Rico got a mug from the dispenser and placed it in front of Layla then placed a bowl in front of Katia. "Ice cream," he said. "I think you could do with a little cooling down."

She lifted the corner of her upper lip in a snarl then turned it into a sweet smile. "Thank you *so* much. I'm super impressed as well. You're *so* impressive, captain."

He snorted a laugh and then took the seat next to Layla.

"Hey, don't I get anything?" Logan said. Rico reached into his pocket and tossed him a flask. "Thanks."

Katia placed a spoonful of ice cream on her tongue and closed her eyes as it melted. Chocolate. She licked her lips, opened her eyes, and found Logan staring at her mouth. She held his gaze and stroked the spoon with her tongue, and heat flared in his eyes. That was better; she almost purred. Rico cleared his throat, and she broke the contact.

"So how are you?" she asked. He looked okay, not cross-eyed or anything. She sniffed. No blood, just a whiff of antiseptic.

"Good." He rubbed the back of his head. "Just a lump. So what's happening?"

"Well, the fleet is on red alert, but they believe the explosion on the *Trakis Three* was a suicide mission, and the terrorist died, and the threat is over."

"Balls. You don't actually agree, do you? It's a load of bullshit."

She glanced at Layla and decided she didn't want to say any more in front of her. Presumably her loyalties lay with the crew on the *Trakis One,* and she would report back to their captain. Which was exactly what Katia didn't want. She'd already decided she would wait to brief Logan on the ongoing investigation when they were alone. She tried to convey a message with her eyes. *Shut up.* But he obviously wasn't paying attention.

"No way was that a terrorist attack. It was an obvious action to keep us away from finding whatever answers were on the *Trakis Three*."

"You really believe that?" Layla said. She sounded almost bewildered. "But what about the empty cryotube?"

"You have to admit, there's an awful lot of evidence supporting the terrorist theory," Katia said.

He snorted. "A lot of awful evidence you mean."

She ignored the comment. "It makes sense if you think about it." He opened his mouth, and she continued before he could get any words out. "Why don't you sleep on it and we can talk about it later? Maybe you'll have joined up the dots by then."

His eyes narrowed on her. She flicked a glance at Layla, who had leaned in close to Rico, listening to something he was saying. She finally saw the understanding dawn in Logan's eyes. Took him long enough. "You're right," he said. "I'm probably not thinking straight at the moment."

"Don't worry, we make allowances for you."

"I did just get banged on the head."

Her bowl was empty. She sat back and smothered a huge yawn with her hand. It had been a long day. Well, actually, not that long, it was probably only late afternoon, but she'd had enough. She looked at Logan. "I think I'm ready for a shower and a sleep."

"Me, too." He winked and pushed himself to his feet.

Layla looked up. "Is there somewhere I can clean up?"

"Of course," Rico said. "Katia will show you where." He turned to look at her. "The cabin on the other side of you is empty. I need to check up a few things with the…crew." He turned to Layla. "Then after you've had a cleanup and a rest, and you're feeling a little better, I can give you a tour of the ship, show you a few things."

"That would be lovely. I appreciate you taking the time. And I'd love to talk to your Scientific Officer here. I met her in training."

"I'll see what I can do."

Hah. How likely was that?

Layla frowned as something occurred to her. "If there's a ban on moving between ships, then what's happening about the party?"

"The party?" *What freaking party?*

"On the *Trakis Seven.* There's always an anniversary party on one of the ships. Who goes along is rotated as the shuttles can only carry four. This year, it's on the *Trakis Seven*, and I was going. It's a special one—five hundred years in space. I was looking forward to it. I met Callum in training. He was a nice guy."

"Callum Meridian?" Katia asked. "He's the captain of the *Trakis Seven*?"

"Yes. He's been awake about the same time as me. You know him?" She sounded skeptical and well she might.

"Only by reputation," she said. Callum Meridian had been a goddamn hero fighter pilot in the years leading up to the exodus from Earth. He'd also been engaged to the daughter of the President of the Federation of Nations. The planet's most famous couple, though they'd broken that off before they'd left Earth. She sighed. Callum Meridian was gorgeous, and he was free. He'd just about replaced Han Solo in her fantasies. Because that was what he was, an out-of-reach fantasy—the way she liked her men.

She glanced at Logan. He was watching her out of narrowed eyes. Was she looking a little dreamy? Probably. She smirked. They needed an invite to that party—the perfect excuse to visit another ship. There had been some deaths on the *Trakis Seven*, the most recent ones chronologically.

Definitely worth a visit. Yay, she was going to meet Callum Meridian.

Logan leaned in close. "Get that look off your face. He's likely a total asshole."

"Only thinking about the investigation," she said smugly. "But he was a hero." She sighed dramatically. "Come on. Let's go."

Chapter Nineteen

Logan strode down the corridor, flanked by the two women. It was making him a little twitchy. He could almost feel their gazes locked on his ass.

He considered pointing out that they shouldn't objectify him. But he didn't mind Katia objectifying him as long as she was on the same wavelength as he was, which was, basically, burrowing himself deep inside her as soon as possible.

He recognized the corridor. It was where the room they had slept in was situated, and he slowed his footsteps, glanced back at Katia for directions. They would need to get rid of Layla first.

She came to a halt in front of one of the identical doors, and he and Layla came to a stop beside her. "This is your cabin," Katia said to Layla.

Layla looked between the two of them then rested a hand on his arm. "I was hoping we could talk some more," she said.

Not on his agenda. He gave her what he hoped was a rueful smile. "Later, huh? Right now, I need a shower and a rest. My head is killing me."

"I could take another look."

"I think I need to lie down somewhere quiet. But thanks."

Katia placed her hand on the panel, and the door opened. Layla went in, reluctantly, casting him an almost hurt glance. But then the door shut on her, and he released a sigh of relief.

"A headache?" Katia said, turning to him.

"I didn't want to hurt her feelings. But I have places I need to be right now."

She studied him, her head cocked to one side. "You're a nice guy, Logan Farrell."

No, he wasn't. "Bed. Now."

She waved him down the corridor, but something occurred to him. "Is Layla safe on her own? You said last night we were sharing because you thought I might be in some sort of danger."

She flashed him a grin. "I lied. I just wanted to get into your pants."

Did he believe her? Maybe fifty-fifty. He had no doubt she wanted in his pants, but at the same time, she had been protecting him. As Layla had said, there was something not quite right about the setup here on the *Trakis Two*. Rico didn't want anyone looking too closely, and he was likely to stop any information coming to light. But how far would he go? Logan couldn't help but wonder if Caldwell had stumbled upon something Rico didn't want to get back to the *Trakis One*.

He pushed the thoughts aside. For now, at least. He reasoned he was pretty safe for the next few hours. He walked beside Katia the few feet that took them to the next door. He would have liked a little more distance between them and Layla, but he'd take what he could get. Katia pressed her hand to the panel, and the door opened. Logan hustled her inside, and she was in his arms and plastered against him before the door even closed.

He had to lower his head to kiss her—she was so much shorter than he was—but it was worth the effort. His mouth slanted over hers, and she tasted hot and sweet, and he parted her lips with his and pushed inside, his tongue filling her. His cock had jerked to life as soon as they'd touched, and he pressed against her, walking her backward to the bed. He kissed her until they ran out of air and he had to fill his lungs.

Her skin was flushed, her lips swollen, her eyes darkened with desire. Sliding his hands to her waist, he picked her up, tossed her on the bed, and came down quickly on top of her, his hands framing her shoulders to hold his weight above her. He was rock hard now, his dick pressing against his fly almost painfully. He pushed one leg between her thighs and lowered his hips so she could feel how much he wanted her.

She stared up into his face and licked her lips. "I need a shower."

"I need a fuck, and you smell pretty good to me. Sort of hot and sweaty…" He punctuated his words with biting kisses down her throat, along her collarbone, burying his nose in her cleavage and breathing in deeply. "…and sexy as hell. But you are wearing way too many clothes. They have to come off. Right now."

He sat up on his heels, straddling her hips, and came up with a plan of action. It was pretty simple. He clasped his hands on the front of her shirt and ripped it open. No bra, and he stared at her breasts, small but full and perfect, tipped with dark red nipples that pointed up at him. She made no move to cover herself, just allowed him to stare.

"Hey," she said. "We have limited resources, you know. I can't pop down to the shops and replace that."

"Darling, you're mistaking me for someone who gives a fuck. We'll turn up the heating—you won't need clothes." His hands covered her breasts, and she closed her mouth. He massaged them gently, watching the pleasure flash across her face, her cheeks flush with color. A low purr rumbled from her throat. Shuffling down, he lowered his head and sucked one tight nipple into his mouth, and her back arched beneath him. He could do this forever, except just not right now. Because right now, he was working on the presumption that if anything could go wrong, then it would. Like the ship might explode around them at any moment. And the only thing he wanted exploding right now was his dick while it was buried deep inside Katia.

He gave one last suck, nipped it with his teeth, then sat up, his hands going to her waist. She came up on her elbows and watched him as he unfastened her pants, raising her hips to help him as he tugged them down. She kicked off her shoes—looked like she was as eager as him. Thank God. He finally managed to tug them all the way off, and he threw them on the floor. Apart from the torn shirt, she was naked in front of him. And so beautiful he ached. Tiny and perfectly formed. She had such a big presence that he sort of forgot how small she was. He wanted to take her in his arms and protect her. But later. Right now, he wanted inside her so bad, his dick ached. His hand went to his waist, and he unfastened his pants, shoved them down over his engorged shaft, groaning in relief as it sprang free.

He glanced up to find her staring, and he twitched under the hot desire in her eyes. She was sprawled open before him, and he cupped a hand between her thighs. Her eyes drifted closed, and that purr came again. He curled his fingers so they slipped between the folds of her sex, and she was so wet and warm. She pushed against him, and he swiped his thumb over her clit. She jumped. She was so ready.

He removed his hand, gripped his cock, lubricating it with her juices, then he lowered himself on top of her and positioned himself at the entrance to her body. Her eyes were open, she was watching him, and he couldn't resist a quick kiss on her full lips, then he thrust inside in one smooth move. She was so tight, but she welcomed him inside easily, wrapping her muscles around him, pulling him in.

Fully inside, he went still for a moment, savoring the sensations, then he slowly pulled out. Her legs wrapped around his hips as though she was trying to keep him inside. Any second now, things were going to get hard and fast, and he wanted nothing in his way when that happened. Placing his hands on her knees, he pushed her legs up against her sides, opening her to him, still deep inside. "Trust me, kitten."

Her eyes flashed at the nickname. "Give it your best, soldier." But her voice was breathy with desire. This time as he pulled out, she stayed still, watching him out of half-closed eyes. He shoved back in slowly, and she...*growled*. Pleasure shot from his balls up his spine, through his body. He'd never felt anything so good. He ground his hips against the sensitive spot between her thighs, and she moaned and pushed up against him. Her arms came around him, her fingernails digging into his skin, raking down his back.

The sharp pain loosened the tight hold he had on his control, and he let the power flow through him. He pulled out and shoved back in again, harder this time, and she took him easily, rising up to meet him, growling again when he withdrew. There was something so primal, almost animalistic in her responses.

Then he sped up, and rational thought left him completely. His every cell concentrated on the sensation of pushing into her, pulling out, faster and faster. He was vaguely aware of her frantic movements beneath him. She was with him all the way, and a moment later, she went completely still then threw back her head and screamed.

Fucking awesome.

He released the last little bit of his control and felt the pleasure swell through his dick, his balls, filling his body as he pulsed inside her. She bucked against him, tightening her inner muscles, so he kept right on coming.

Finally, he was spent, weak, lost. Where the hell was he? Cupping her face, he lowered his head and kissed her. He felt the sting on his back where she'd clawed him and grinned.

"You're an animal," he murmured then collapsed onto her, rolled and pulled her so she sprawled on top of him.

She licked his neck. "More than you will ever know."

What did that mean?

But he was too sated to worry. Closing his eyes, he let the sense of well-being wash over him. And for the first time, he accepted that, yeah, he was glad they had woken him up. Just for this one fucking awesome moment. Sleep was pulling him under, but he didn't want to go to sleep yet, maybe never again. He wanted to savor the feeling. He wanted to know if Katia had found it as good. From that scream, he was guessing she'd enjoyed herself as much as he had. He hadn't screamed, though. Maybe he should have, to show his appreciation. She felt good in his arms, all soft and small. Her breathing was even—had she fallen asleep?

He opened his eyes and found her sprawled across his chest, chin in her hand, gazing up at his face.

"I thought you were asleep," he said.

"Time enough to sleep when you're dead," she said with a grin. "Or so Rico tells me." She sighed. "That was amazing. You are one good fuck, Sergeant Farrell."

He grinned. "Ditto, Detective Mendoza."

She wriggled against him. "So what do we do now?"

He couldn't do it again right now. No way. Then her hand slipped between them, wrapping around his dick, squeezing soft then hard. He came to attention under her touch, and he decided that maybe, with the right incentive, he could manage once more.

• • •

Her third—or was it her fourth—orgasm of the day ripped through her. For the second time that day, she was covered in sweat, but the effort had been worth it.

She twitched her hips, and a ripple of residual pleasure shot through her. They'd come together that time, they were getting in sync, and now he was sprawled beneath her, looking totally spent. She'd worn him out. She liked that idea.

She needed a shower before she fell asleep. Really, she did.

Beneath her, Logan's eyes flicked open, and a slow smile spread across his face. "You are the best."

"I need that shower."

His hands tightened on her hips. "Not yet. Lie with me for a while. I like you dirty."

"Okay." That worked for her; she couldn't actually be bothered to get up yet.

He was still lodged deep inside her, and she raised herself up so he slipped free. A sense of loss washed over her. She ignored it; she hadn't lost him...yet. That was no doubt somewhere in the future, but one of the things she had learned in her long life was to enjoy the moment. She snuggled herself at Logan's side, breathing in the scents of sex and sweat and something spicy, unique to Logan. "So talk to me," she said, "or I'll fall asleep, and I do want to shower first."

"Talk to you about what?" He sounded wary, but she realized she wanted to know about him. Where he came from, who he was, what he wanted out of life. He came across as a mixture of cynicism and naivety. He'd told her he didn't believe in dreams, but he believed in the hope of a brave new world for mankind. "You told me you didn't believe in dreams," she said. "Why? What happened?"

He was silent for a long time. Either he'd fallen asleep or

he was avoiding the question. She poked a finger in his ribs.

"Ow."

"Talk or I get up and shower."

He heaved a huge sigh then dragged himself up a little so he was leaning against the wall, pulling her closer against him.

"When I was young, very young I mean, my mom abandoned me on the steps of an orphanage. I was three, I think."

Aw. How sad. She remembered now that he'd mentioned it that first shuttle ride but then closed up. Was he willing to tell her more now? She hoped so. "I bet you were such a cute little boy. Those pretty eyes."

"Well, they were all I got from my mom. I have one memory of her looking down at me, out of eyes like mine. She was telling me that I had to be a good boy. And that she was sorry. I never saw her again."

"And were you a good boy?"

"For a little while. I lived in the orphanage for the first couple of years. They couldn't put me up for adoption straight away, in case my mom came back for me. Of course, she never did. The orphanage was run by the Catholic Church, and let's just say there were certain facets of my…personality that they believed needed to be beaten out of me."

"I hate the church," she said.

"I'm not too fond of them, either. But they had a point with me."

She twisted a little so she could see his face. "What point?"

"I was different from other children. I felt things too much. I saw things in people that they usually didn't want me to see. I would know if someone was good or bad, and I hadn't yet realized that people usually didn't want to know that sort of stuff."

"But how? How did you know?"

He shifted, looked a little uncomfortable. "I found out later, a lot later, that I was an...empath." He sounded almost embarrassed by the word. And she tried to remember what she knew about empaths. Not a lot. He was continuing, and she concentrated on his words. This was far more than she had ever thought she would get out of him.

"I went through a lot of therapy as a teenager," he said. "They were trying their best to find out why I couldn't fit in. One particular therapist had worked with empaths before. She recognized me right away, from the information in my files, but also from my eyes. Apparently, a high proportion of people with empathic abilities have pale purple eyes. But we're getting ahead of ourselves. I was telling you about when I gave up on dreaming."

She snuggled closer, resting her palm on the hard muscles of his belly. "Go on."

"When I was six, I was adopted by a couple. They had a daughter about the same age as me. Apparently, they'd been trying for another child but had finally accepted that it wasn't going to happen. So they would do their godly duty and adopt a little unwanted child of God. Me. They were nice enough people, took me in, tried to show no difference between me and Dora, their daughter. They were 'good,' and I had no problem with them. I thought maybe it was going to work. That I had a chance to be part of a real family. I relaxed."

This wasn't going to have a happy ending. She kept quiet, though, because she was guessing he'd never spoken of it before and that he needed to get this out.

"Mrs. Dobson had a brother. He turned up after I'd been there maybe six months. And he was not a good man. I learned later he'd been in prison, though I didn't know then. I just got these waves of badness that rolled off him. I couldn't be in the same room. I tried to tell my new mother. She said 'someone like me,' who'd spent years in an institution, should be more charitable. As though it was my fault my fucking mother had abandoned me. And the Catholic Church was no better than a prison—though she wasn't far wrong there. Anyhow, she doted on her brother."

He went quiet. "Go on," she said.

"You really want to hear this crap? You wouldn't like to see if you can get it up again instead?"

"Later. I want to know what happened."

"Not a lot else. I started having dreams of fires. I knew they were something to do with the brother—my 'Uncle Theo,' as I was supposed to call him. I didn't want to tell her. I knew it would make her mad. But I was so scared, sure something bad was going to happen. Wasn't it my duty to try and stop that? So I told her that I thought Uncle Theo was a bad man and was going to burn the house down."

"I gather she didn't believe you?"

He grinned. "Hell no. She sent me to school with no breakfast and a stern admonishment not to make up stories about my elders and betters." He stared into space for a minute then ran a hand around the back of his neck. He winced. "I remember the school bus dropping me off that afternoon. The sound of fire engines and the stench of smoke in the air. The fear. And I ran, still thinking I could do something to help. That someone would listen to me. When I got there, the house was engulfed in flames. Theo was sitting on the grass with a blanket around him. My new mother and father were sobbing on the lawn."

He blew out his breath. "Dora was inside. They couldn't get to her. Her mother blamed me. Somehow, I'd willed it to happen. I was the evil one. She couldn't actually accuse me of setting the fire, I'd been at school and had plenty of witnesses, but I saw she would have liked to. She screamed at me. Called me a spawn of Satan, if I remember right. Theo was some sort of hero—he'd tried to get into the house to save her. I remember him looking at me, a smile on his face. It goes without saying that they sent me back to the orphanage. That was when I stopped dreaming about a family, fitting in, anything, really."

Her eyes pricked, and she blinked. "So did you stay in the orphanage after that?"

"No. They decided they didn't want me, either. Might be something to do with the fact that I told the priest that the head of the orphanage was buggering the little kids."

"Jesus."

"He never touched me. I think he was a little bit scared of me. As usual, with the Church, it was hushed up—anything to avoid a scandal. And I was shunted off to social services, ended up in and out of foster homes. They never worked for long. I was a fucked-up mess. One thing I learned later, though, by a strange twist, when they finally put out the fire at the Dobsons', they found little Dora's body was hardly damaged. She'd been raped and strangled. Theo had set the house on fire to hide what he'd done. Ended up back in prison where his sister dutifully visited him every week. Denial is a wonderful thing."

"That's a horrible story," she said.

"All the real ones are."

There was that cynicism again. He ran his hands through her hair, massaging the back of her neck. It felt so good, blurring her brain, but there was something else she wanted to know. "The empathy thing? Do you still get the feelings? Do you know if people are bad or good?" What would he see in her? Hell, what about Rico? Scary stuff.

He shook his head. "Not so much, unless I actively try, and I don't. The therapist I met, she said she could help me control it. I didn't want to know whether people were bad or good. I wanted to find out for myself—besides, it doesn't mean a lot. Good people can do bad things and vice versa. She taught me how to build a wall around it, shut it inside the walls, build a big door with a big lock, and then throw away the key."

"So it's still there inside you?"

"I guess. But mostly it stays behind the wall."

"So now you're all nice and normal. No doubt you fit right in with all your nice, normal army buddies."

He looked down at her, lips pressed together. "Truth?"

"Why not?"

"No. I've never felt like I fit in anywhere. I feel like there's this great lump of difference inside me that will never belong anywhere that normal people are. And if anyone looks too closely, then they'll recognize right away that I'm an impostor."

"So you don't let them look too closely."

"No. And I've learned to pretend. It doesn't bother me anymore."

Liar.

He went silent for a moment. "What about you?"

"What about me?"

"No sad stories to tell?"

"Plenty." If he thought he had problems fitting in, he should try her life. "But we'll leave mine for another time. Right now, I'm going to go have that shower and get some sleep." She sat up, swung her legs out the bed, stood up, and stretched. She felt good. There wasn't room in the bathroom for two, which was a pity. But there was something he could do while she was showering. "Why don't you nip back to the galley and get me some more of that ice cream?"

He shook his head. "You are unbelievable," he said, but he was already out of bed and pulling on his pants. "What flavor?"

Chapter Twenty

Logan couldn't believe he had told her all that stuff about his childhood.

He'd never told anyone before.

But the sex had been out of this world. Hey, literally. He'd never had sex in space before. Maybe it was always that good—though somehow he doubted it would be anywhere near as good with anyone else.

He felt great and curiously optimistic. Katia was right. He'd never allowed himself to get close to anyone, because he knew they would see him as the fraud he was, a weird misfit. But Katia had appeared unfazed by his revelations.

He was eager to get back, and it wasn't only because the ice cream was melting. Normally, at this point, he'd be working out ways he could extract himself without upsetting the woman he was with. But right now, all he wanted was to get back to Katia, crawl into bed, and watch her eat. Then curl himself around her and go to sleep. Then wake up and make love.

Maybe he could talk to Rico about getting that transfer

to the *Trakis Two*.

Would Katia want him to, though? She didn't seem any more into relationships than he was. That was a good thing, wasn't it?

He wasn't thinking permanent. Not marriage and kids or anything like that—although Katia would have cute kids. But after all, there was a seriously good chance that they weren't going to last much longer anyway. How long until something on the *Trakis One* went really wrong? And while this ship seemed in better condition, could it survive alone without the back-up of the fleet?

Things to worry about tomorrow. Or the next day... Right now, he had a warm woman waiting for him.

He arrived at the door and juggled the two bowls of ice cream—he hadn't been able to choose between cherry and chocolate—and pressed his hand to the panel. Nothing happened.

Balls. Had she locked him out?

Or was this yet another malfunction?

Some premonition of disaster churned in his gut. He did his best to ignore it. After placing the ice cream on the floor, he banged on the door. "Katia." He couldn't hear anything from inside. Were the rooms soundproofed? He didn't know. He banged again. Nothing.

What the hell?

His heart was beating fast. He looked around as if he might find answers in the empty corridor.

Maybe she'd fallen asleep. But that bad feeling in his stomach was spreading. Swelling and growing and...

He punched a finger on his comm unit. He didn't have a direct link to Rico but flicked through the possibilities. He pressed the bridge but got no answer. Then he tried the docking bay, and finally someone answered.

"What?"

Not Rico. "Is the captain there?"

"Yes."

"Can I speak with him?"

Silence. Then a second later, Rico's voice came over the comm. "What do you want? I'm busy."

"I can't get in the room. And Katia isn't answering the door."

"Maybe she's had enough of you."

"She sent me for ice cream."

Rico was silent for a moment. "I'll be there in a minute."

He paced in front of the door then came back, banged on it again. Glared.

Down the corridor, a door opened, and Layla appeared. Didn't look like she had gotten around to that shower yet. She peered at Logan, her eyes widening. "What's happening? What's wrong?"

"Katia. She's not answering. I brought her some ice cream." How pathetic was that?

"Maybe she's asleep."

God, he hoped so.

Rico appeared at that moment. He glanced between the two of them then shoved Logan out of the way and stepped in the ice cream. "*Mierda*," he muttered, slamming his hand on the door panel. Nothing happened.

He took a step back and drew the pistol at his waist, shot at the door panel, sparks flying, but the door slid open.

Logan pushed past him. The bed was empty, so she wasn't asleep. There was a strange smell in the air, and he coughed and choked and pulled his T-shirt up to cover his nose and mouth. Crossing to the bathroom, he pushed open the door, and she was lying naked, crumpled on the floor. For a second, fear held him immobile. He shook it off, crouched down, ran a trembling finger down her throat. Her pulse was racing. His own ratcheted up.

"Get her out of here," Rico snapped from behind him.

Logan scooped her up in his arms, cradled her against his chest, mind blank. He spun around, almost running across the small space. Once outside the door, he laid her on the floor.

He swallowed, his throat constricted, his lungs tight. "Katia, wake up."

"Let me see." Rico pushed him out of the way and hunkered down, lifting her eyelids. "She's out cold. What the hell? I'll take her to the sick bay." He picked her up, turned to Layla. "Go back to your room but stay awake and keep the door open." He glanced at Logan.

"I'm coming," he said before the other man could suggest anything different.

Rico snarled but didn't waste any more time arguing, just turned and hurried down the corridor. Logan had to run to keep up.

Once in the medical center, Rico laid her on the gurney where Logan had sat only hours earlier. Katia appeared totally lifeless, but as he stared, he could make out the slight rise and fall of her chest. She was still alive, and there was always hope where there was life. He wasn't a praying man, but he'd give it ago. He'd been so optimistic only minutes ago. Why hadn't he remembered how quickly life could turn to shit? He searched his mind for anything he could do, but they had no clue what had happened. Some sort of poisoning, but how? Why?

"Come on," Rico muttered. "Wake up, kitten." There was no response, and Rico swore. "*Dios*, she's too far under. I need her awake." He crossed the room, opened a drawer, and came back with a syringe. Without any warning, he pulled the top and stabbed Katia in the chest. Logan took a step forward, but Rico glanced up and growled. "Stay back. I know what I'm dealing with. You don't."

What the hell did that mean? But he didn't have time to think about it, because Katia took a huge breath, her spine bowed, and she rose up from the gurney then collapsed back. She was gasping for breath, wheezing. She needed oxygen, something… Christ, he felt so helpless.

Rico took hold of her shoulders and gave her a shake. "You need to shift."

Shift? Shift what? Why wasn't Rico doing something more productive? He took a step forward, and Rico turned to him and growled again. Like an animal. Logan stopped. There was something going on here he didn't understand. But she was dying. He could see that. He wouldn't let her die.

"Shift, goddamn it," Rico said. "You're dying."

Her head lolled to the side, and she looked at Logan, standing stiff by the side of the gurney. Totally fucking useless. No clue what was going on.

"You said you'd kill him if he found out." Her voice was breathy, and Logan had to lean in to hear her words. She swallowed, forcing the words out. "Promise you won't kill him."

Kill who?

Me?

"Shift!"

She gritted her teeth, and he could see the physical effort it took her to get the word out. "Promise."

Rico took a deep breath, his hands fisted at his side. Logan could almost hear the grinding of his teeth. His fear turned to bewilderment. This whole thing was surreal.

"I promise. Now fucking shift."

She looked past Rico for a moment, and her gaze caught Logan's. She gave a tiny shrug. "Normal is overrated anyway," she whispered. Then she closed her eyes. Was she dying?

He stood locked in place, unable to move, his mind screaming to do something, to save her, but his body unwilling to comply. If he didn't move then this might all go away.

"You might want to step back," Rico said, and he shook his head.

"What's happening?"

"Why don't you wait and see?"

He forced his feet backward as Katia's body arched up off the gurney. Something shivered in the air, and his skin prickled. A change was flowing over her, black fur sprouting from her skin. Her bones snapped—the noise loud in the silence—and then realigned, her face changing shape. Then her eyes flashed open, and they were no longer human, glowing bright green flecked with yellow, as they stared at him. He wanted to look away, as though that might change the reality. Maybe it wasn't real. Maybe he'd fallen asleep and was dreaming this. Because yeah, this was the stuff of dreams...or nightmares.

It seemed to last forever but in fact took only seconds. Where Katia had lain, a huge black cat—a jaguar, he was guessing, but bigger than any he'd ever seen in a zoo— sprawled, legs hanging over the edge. Huge paws. Claws. It opened its eyes and peered at him then rolled onto its front and rose to its feet. All fucking four of them. It shook itself, the huge body rippling with muscle, then leaped down off the gurney. It gave Logan a narrow-eyed stare then cast Rico a dirty look before padding across to the corner of the room and collapsing onto its side, eyes closed.

Logan released the breath he hadn't been aware he was holding. He blinked. The cat was still there. He cleared his throat, opened his mouth. Closed it again. "That's Katia?" Stupid question. But his brain wasn't functioning too well right now.

"Yeah. Cute, isn't she? Sort of furry and..." Rico shrugged.

"Will she be all right?"

"Now she's shifted, she'll be fine. She'll stay like that for a few hours, and when she shifts back, she'll have cleared the poison from her system."

"She's a…?"

"Werecat. Jaguar, actually. Quite rare." He turned away and spoke into his comm unit. "Sardi, get to the sick bay. Now." He glanced at Logan, lips pursed. "We have a… problem."

It occurred to Logan that Rico had promised he wouldn't kill him—at least he was presuming he was the person Katia didn't want killed—but maybe he would get someone else to do the job. He considered making a run for it and must have glanced at the door.

"Don't," Rico said.

Something else occurred to him. "Are you…?" He waved a hand toward where Katia lay sleeping.

"Hell, no."

"But you're not human, are you? If you're not like her, then what are you?" Maybe he shouldn't have asked. Maybe he really didn't want to know.

Rico didn't answer, just curled the corner of his upper lip in a snarl, bearing the tip of one white fang. "Guess."

Logan's heart stopped beating. When it started again, it was racing. "Christ," he muttered.

Rico grinned. "Not even related."

Someone cleared their throat in the doorway, and Logan nearly leaped out of his skin. Hell, he was jumpy. He turned slowly. A man leaned in the open doorway. Sardi, he guessed. At least at first sight he appeared to be a man. Albeit, probably the tallest man Logan had ever seen. That wasn't what made Logan's mouth go dry, though. He swallowed. The "man" had horns. Real, honest-to-fucking-God horns. Sticking out the top of his head. And that would make him… Logan's mind seized up.

Rico let out a short laugh. "You know, this was almost worth it to see the expression on your face."

Logan shook his head, trying to make his brain function again. "Yeah, right, and people usually just take you in their stride, do they?"

He gave a slow smile. "They usually don't last long enough."

"Balls," he muttered.

"Sardi, this is Sergeant Logan Farrell, Katia's new boyfriend."

"Isn't that nice."

He had a low, gravelly voice that grated on Logan's ears. Was he supposed to shake hands? He decided not. "So what happens now?"

"Well, I'm not going to kill you. I made a promise. But I don't want you wandering around the place, either. So until Katia wakes up and can take charge of you, I'm afraid you're off to the brig. And I need your comm unit."

He unfastened it from his wrist and handed it over, though comming anyone had actually not occurred to him. Hell, no one would believe him anyway. "Why are you not killing me?" he asked.

Rico considered him for a few seconds then shrugged. "You saved her life. If she'd been in there any longer, she would never have come around."

"Yeah, but the question is: why did her life need saving? What the hell happened? And if you say a malfunction, I might very well..." What? What could he do?

"I don't have malfunctions on my ship. And I'm off to see if I can find the answer to that question right now. But one thing you might consider—if this was a murder attempt, then there's a good chance you were also a target." Cheerful thought. "Sardi, can you lock him up in the brig and meet me at Katia's cabin?"

Sardi tossed him a salute. "Aye, aye, Captain."

Did he detect more than a hint of sarcasm?

Logan followed him out of the room. He wasn't used to people towering over him, but Sardi had a good six inches on him. Plus the horns. "So what are you?" he asked.

"Demon."

Of course he was. "Is anyone on this ship human?"

"There are a few." He cast Logan a sideways glance. "So you're with Katia? You're a brave man."

He wasn't sure how "with" Katia he was. Or even how "with" Katia he wanted to be. The whole changing into a cat thing was hard to take in and a lot to get his head around. Though she obviously liked him well enough not to let Rico kill him off. "I wasn't actually aware she was a…" He couldn't make himself say the word "werecat."

"Ha. Like that, she's a pussy cat. It's her human form that's a complete bitch."

The day was taking its toll. Exhaustion rolling over him in waves. The brig actually sounded like a good idea right now. Maybe not so much locking him in but locking the monsters out.

Sardi opened the door and waved him inside. The cell wasn't that much different than the cabin he'd shared with Katia. A little smaller, but it had a bed, and that was all he was interested in right now.

"How long?" he asked.

"Until Katia wakes up? Could be a few hours." He gestured to a panel on the wall. "You can get drinks from there. And here…" He dug into his pocket and pulled out a flask. "Something to keep you company."

Logan took it and sank down onto the bed as the door slid shut behind the…demon.

He kicked off his shoes, rested his back against the wall, stretched out his legs, unscrewed the top from the flask, and took a long swallow.

His back stung where she had clawed him. It seemed like a lifetime ago.

"I had sex with a werecat."

Hey, he could say it. He wasn't in denial. Not at all.

And he'd just been thinking about asking for a transfer to the *Trakis Two*. He'd actually considered that here was someplace he could fit in. At the thought he snorted and nearly choked on a mouthful of whiskey. Yeah, it seemed he was a misfit wherever he went.

He took one last mouthful then stretched out on the bed.

He was asleep in seconds.

No dreams.

Chapter Twenty-One

Katia had slept for nearly twenty-four hours then woken up in her cat form, curled up on the floor in the sick bay. A combination of exhaustion and needing to heal.

According to Rico, she'd nearly died. If she'd been human, she *would* have died. She couldn't remember what had happened. She'd been about to shower and then... nothing. Rico was having a full analysis done on the air in the cabin, but he didn't think it would reveal much. Whatever had been used had obviously broken down by the time they'd got into the cabin, as it'd had little effect on Logan.

Could it have been Logan?

But why? That didn't make sense.

Plus, he'd alerted Rico. Although, at that point, he'd believed she was human and should have been already dead. And by alerting Rico, he would have shifted any suspicion from himself. *Unless you were a really suspicious person like Rico.* "You need to think with your head and not your—"

"Shut up," she'd snapped. She was thinking with her head. And her head didn't think it was Logan.

Which left Layla and Rico and whoever else was awake on the *Trakis Two* right now. Layla, like Logan, made zero sense. What possible motive could she have? Unless she was jealous that Logan was with her. A woman scorned? She couldn't see her going that far.

Rico was in the clear. He'd saved her life. The adrenaline shot had woken her up. Without that, she would never have shifted, and she would be dead.

The rest of the crew? Rico was organizing a get-together so she could interview them. Maybe there was someone awake who didn't like her. It wasn't beyond the realms of possibility. She tended to piss people off. But Rico didn't think there was anyone on the crew who would kill like that. Try and rip her throat out, maybe, but not poison. It wasn't their way.

What if there actually was a terrorist and they had somehow got on board the *Trakis Two*? Could they have left the *Trakis Three* before it blew? Taken a shuttle? No, someone would have noticed a shuttle landing. Wouldn't they? Maybe they'd come earlier and remote detonated whatever had blown up the *Trakis Three*. But according to Rico, the only shuttle that had landed on the *Trakis Two* in the last few decades, apart from hers and Layla's yesterday, was the one that brought the security officer from the *Trakis One*.

Maybe unknown to them, they'd had a stowaway.

Unlikely.

Which left her…nowhere.

She came to a halt in front of the brig. Logan had been locked in here for over twenty-four hours. He was probably going to be pissed as hell.

And now, he knew what she was.

How was he dealing with that? She was about to find out.

She tapped the monitor screen outside the cell, and it lit up. Logan was stretched out on the bed, hands behind his head, gazing at the ceiling. For a moment, she stared. He was still dressed in the clothes he had pulled on to get ice cream for her. His uniform pants and a white T-shirt. He was stunning, and she had a flashback to how he had felt on her, in her, and heat pooled in her belly. She might as well enjoy the memories. She probably wouldn't be getting her hands on him again anytime soon. Likely the whole cat thing might be a bit of a turn off. She tried not to analyze how that made her feel. What good would it do? She was what she was. There was no changing that, and she didn't want to. Not really. Just for a while there, she'd felt close to Logan. Closer than to anyone since her family had been slaughtered by the werecat who had turned her.

There was no point in putting this off. She placed her palm on the panel, and the cell door slid open.

Logan turned his head, his eyes narrowing on her as she stood in the open doorway. He glanced past her as if to check if she was alone then swung his legs off the bed and sat up, running a hand through his short hair. He studied her, his eyes wandering over her body, finally returning to her face.

"You can turn into a cat," he said.

She nodded, though it hadn't been a question. "A jaguar."

He pressed a finger to the spot between his eyes. "And your friend Rico is a vampire."

"I'm afraid so."

He shook his head then rose to his feet. "I'm starving."

"No one brought you any food?"

"No. I thought you were dead and they were going to leave me here until the problem went away."

She bit back a smile. "Sorry. I only just woke up. I came straight here."

He raised an eyebrow in obvious disbelief. "Balls."

"Okay, I had a slight detour via the galley. I was *really* hungry—a side effect of...shifting." She shook her head.

"Anyway, come on, we'll go get you something to eat and we can talk."

"Yeah, talking would be good."

Screwing would be better. She had an overwhelming urge to shut the door behind them and drag him to the bed and lose herself in him. Forget everything for a while. But she couldn't bring herself to take the step and close the space between them. And risk rejection. He was giving nothing away, his expression blank. And he certainly wasn't giving off any sexy vibes. That was a first, and she could only suppose it was because of his new knowledge of her. She gave a mental shrug.

"Let's go."

He pulled on his shoes and followed her out of the cell. She led the way down the corridor to the galley. The room was empty, which was just as well; she didn't think Logan was ready to meet any more of Rico's crew yet. Best to ease him in slowly.

Her stomach churned. She never got nervous, but for some reason, she was not looking forward to this conversation. She couldn't even face any food, which was unheard of. Instead, she sat at the table, gnawing on her fingernails while Logan helped himself to the food dispenser. He came over, hesitated, and then took the seat opposite her, placing his plate on the table. He started eating without saying a word and didn't stop until his plate was empty. Then he got up, got two mugs of coffee, placed one in front of her, sat down again, and leaned back in his chair.

"So how safe am I?" he finally asked.

The question took her by surprise. "From me?"

"Well, not from you personally. I was thinking more of your friend with the big teeth."

A smile curved her lips. Except she didn't really feel like smiling. "Rico won't harm you. Not on purpose, anyway. He promised, and while I'm not going to try and convince you he's a nice guy, or anything even approaching a nice guy, he sticks to his word."

"He's not a guy at all. He's a goddamn blood-sucking monster."

And there it was. "So what am I?" she asked.

Shock flared on his face, eyes widening. He clearly hadn't thought about that. Which was odd.

"Come on, Logan. You can say it. Am I a monster, too?"

He looked into her eyes. "I don't know. Are you?"

She shrugged. "It's not the monsters you should be worried about. While you might be safe from Rico, there is obviously someone else around who wants you gone. If you'd have been in that room with me, you'd be dead."

"So would you."

She nodded. "Good point. Thank you. You saved my life. I hope you're not sorry about that."

The shock flared again. "Hell, no. I don't want you dead." He put his untouched coffee down and raked a hand through his hair. "Come on, Katia, you can't expect me to not be a little shocked by all of this. You can change into a big fucking cat and probably eat me. For all I know, you eat people regularly. It's a lot for a guy to take in, so cut me some slack if I'm not coming across all diplomatic right now."

"Okay. But my point was there is someone out to kill us both. They've tried three times now. And I'm betting there's a good chance they'll try again."

"You think it's the terrorist?"

"Who knows? It's as good a theory as any right now. Rico went over every inch of the cabin but found nothing. We have no clue how the poison got in. And no clue even what it is. In fact, we have no clues at all." She took a sip of coffee. "But I don't think there's a terrorist. I think someone wants us and the investigation to go away."

"I think you're right. I always found the terrorist theory a little too pat. Which means we've got to find the murderer. Before they try and kill us again and this time, no doubt, succeed."

"Sardi is going to explain some of the mechanics to us—what can be done remotely. What needs to be done from on the ship. If the malfunctions have to be done on the ships, then our murderer has been visiting. And there must be logs that cover the shuttle trips. We can try and match them up. We'll work that out when we know more. We'll go get that information next. Then tomorrow we go to a party and we can somehow wrangle a visit to the crime scene, get the names and details of the victims."

"Yeah, I'm really in the mood for a party," he said flatly. "And getting on another shuttle. You might have to drug me."

"Me as well. Layla can wake us up when we get there."

"Where is Layla, anyway?"

She looked away. She wasn't sure how he would take the next bit of information. "She's with Rico."

"*With* Rico?"

She waggled her eyebrows. "You know."

"Is that safe?"

She shrugged. "Probably. As long as she doesn't piss him off."

"So she knows what you are?"

"No. Rico can do this mind control thing. If he drinks from a person, he can make them forget."

"Balls. Could he do that to me?" His hand moved in what she was sure was an involuntary reaction, touching his neck as if to check for bite marks.

"He could, but he won't."

"Well, I probably should be a bit offended, but I'll take that as a good thing." He drained his mug. "I've been doing some thinking."

"Is that wise? Why change the habits of a lifetime?"

"Ha ha. I'm guessing the reason Rico wanted you to keep away from the *Trakis Two* is because if anyone looks too closely, then there's a good chance that they'll realize you're not who you're supposed to be. I'm also guessing you didn't actually win a place in the lottery?"

"No," she admitted.

"And Rico isn't really captain of this ship."

"He is now."

"And how did that happen?"

"Does it matter? You really think most of the Chosen Ones are here because they legitimately won a freaking lottery? Of course they're not. They're here because they knew someone or paid someone."

"I'm not interested in most of the Chosen Ones. I'm interested in you."

He knew so much already. Why not this? If he decided to turn on them, then Rico would wipe his memory. That was the deal they'd made. Before they left this room, she had to find out whether Logan would work with her or whether he intended to reveal the truth about them to his buddies on the *Trakis One*. If the latter was the case, then Rico would do his thing, and while she wasn't entirely happy about that, it was the only option.

"Rico bribed the first captain of the *Trakis Two* to swap half his Chosen Ones for Rico's people."

"The first captain?" She nodded, and he said, "Sebastian Falk?"

"I think that was the guy. Rico always referred to him as Bastion. Bastion the Bastard most of the time. I don't think he likes him very much."

"And what did he bribe him with?"

"What's one thing Rico could offer?"

He shook his head. "No clue."

"Eternal life."

For a moment, his expression remained blank. Then she caught a glimmer of understanding in his eyes. "He turned the captain of the *Trakis Two* into a goddamn vampire?"

"Yeah."

He peered around the room as if expecting a second blood-sucking monster to leap out at him. "So if he's now immortal, then where is he?"

"Rico locked him in a cryotube and put him to sleep— said he was pissing him off."

"A lot of people seem to do that."

And thinking about people who had pissed off Rico, she wondered how long it would take Logan to put the pieces together and question what had happened to the security officer from the *Trakis One*.

"So what happened to the five thousand Chosen Ones who didn't get their places?" he asked.

"I have no idea." Actually, she did have an idea. She suspected they were dead. Well, they'd be dead anyway after five hundred years. But they couldn't have been left alive or they would have informed someone. And the fleet had been in contact with Earth for the first few years.

"Look, I'm not going to go into the morals of whether he was right or wrong. Morals aren't Rico's strong point anyway. But most of his people on this ship never even got entered into the stupid lottery, so how fair was that? They deserved as much a chance as anyone else."

"They probably didn't get entered because no one knew they actually existed."

"Beside the point." She waved it off. "The more important question is are you going to finish this investigation with me?"

Katia held her breath as she waited for his answer.

He didn't hesitate. "Hell, yes. I want answers as much as you do."

And she released her breath. "Good. Then let's go investigate."

· · ·

Logan glanced around. They'd all met up in the conference room to discuss the investigation and were sitting around a circular table. Him: the human, Katia: the werecat, Rico: the vampire, and Sardi: the demon.

Maybe he'd gone insane.

He was trying to concentrate on the case and not think too much about the whole werecat/vampire/demon and God knew what else situation. He'd had enough time to think about that stuck in his cell for twenty-four hours. He'd relived the moment when she'd turned into a big black cat over and over again.

Perhaps his brain had fried in the explosion and he was now hallucinating after all. But he didn't think so, because it all made a sort of sense. He'd always recognized that there was something weird happening on the *Trakis Two*. Though without the big reveal, he was equally certain that he would have never stumbled across the correct explanation.

It was a lot to take in.

He'd never believed in God, pretty much turned his back on religion after his early experiences, so he never thought much about the good versus evil debate.

If demons existed, did that mean God existed as well?

But whatever Katia was, or could turn into, he didn't believe she was evil. He had a flashback to the feel of her beneath him, on top of him, and his dick twitched. She hadn't made any indication as to whether she wanted a repeat performance. In fact, he had no clue how she felt. Except she had risked her own life to make Rico promise not to harm him. And that made him feel a little bit warm and fuzzy.

But he had to accept he'd been living a delusion. He would never fit into her world—she wasn't even human. And he still had to decide whether he had an obligation to report them—of course, that was assuming he ever got the chance. He didn't think Rico would allow him the opportunity. So he either had to escape the *Trakis Two*—maybe when they went across to the *Trakis Seven*, he could somehow make contact with someone… Or he had to persuade Rico that he wasn't a threat and he wouldn't blab about what was going on here.

They'd been responsible for the probable deaths of approximately five thousand Chosen Ones. He'd seen Katia's shifty expression when he'd asked what had happened to them. She might not know for sure, but she suspected they'd been disposed of somehow as well. But maybe she was also right—didn't people like her—and that covered a multitude of sins—deserve the chance to survive as much as anyone else? A place in the brave new world. Or was that only for humanity? Hell. It was giving him a headache.

What if he couldn't persuade Rico that he wasn't a threat? Would he just be kept here until Katia decided that she didn't care if they got rid of him? She didn't seem to care that much now. She hadn't looked at him since they'd sat down. Was she already regretting making Rico promise not to kill him? Maybe she'd had her wicked way with him and now she wanted him out of the picture. After all, she had said she didn't do relationships.

Back to the case…it didn't hurt his head half so much as his love life or lack of it. If they were right, and there was a murderer on the loose, then they had killed over ten thousand Chosen Ones. So get them first and then worry about the rest.

Around him, the table had gone quiet. Were they waiting for him to say something? There was actually one thing he really needed to know.

"So the three dead on this ship were human? Real crew

family, not…"

"More interesting supernatural beings?" Rico finished for him. "Yes, they were humans."

The crew family link was the only concrete clue they had right now. "Have we got confirmation from the other ships that the victims are crew family?" he asked.

"No, we haven't received anything," Katia said, still not looking directly at him. "Now they're saying the investigation is closed, so we don't need the information, and why waste resources? And I don't want to push it. If we want to appear as if we're not pursuing the investigation further, then perhaps it's best not to ask too much."

"You can find out about the victims on the *Trakis Seven* when you get over there tomorrow," Rico said. "Do you think it's significant?"

Logan scratched the back of his neck. His scalp was itching where he'd banged his head. "No clue. But right now, we have to treat everything as significant. Hopefully, knowing more about the victims will enable us to pinpoint why they were selected, which might give us an idea who wants them dead."

Sardi had taken them through the ship's systems, trying to isolate what could be done remotely. Quite a lot, it seemed. Most of it had gone over Logan's head, and he suspected Katia's, too. A great big thick report lay on the table between them. Katia leaned across the table and picked the folder up. "I'm wrecked," she said. "I'm going to take this and read it in bed then get my beauty sleep." She still didn't look at him while she spoke. In fact, she looked anywhere but at him, so he was guessing he wasn't invited to join her.

"Where?" Rico asked.

She grimaced as if she hadn't considered that. "I don't fancy going back to my cabin. I think I'll go crash out in the brig. Unlikely a murderer will look for me there."

"Okay. Sleep well, kitten."

She opened her mouth but then snapped it closed again, whirled around, and stalked out of the room.

Logan watched her go. Would she turn around at the last minute? Ask him to go with her? But no, she disappeared out the door without a backward glance.

But why should she want him? She'd told him she wasn't into relationships, and anyway, he was a mere human. She probably looked down on him as an inferior species. He'd bet male werecats had bigger dicks than humans.

Though she'd seemed to enjoy herself plenty when they'd been in bed together. Unless she'd been faking it.

"Not going with her?" Rico asked, dragging him from his not-so-happy thoughts.

"Maybe he doesn't like the idea of sleeping with someone who's not completely human," Sardi said.

Christ, now they were accusing him of some sort of racism against werecats. Was that even a thing? And it hadn't occurred to him. Yeah, he had to admit if she turned all furry on him while they were in the act, then he might be a little freaked out. But she wouldn't do that. Would she? So he just glared at the two "men" opposite. "Did you hear her inviting me?"

"You didn't strike me as the type who waits to be invited," Rico said.

He gave a small shrug. "Katia's...different." She knew her own mind for one thing. If she'd wanted him, she would have said so. But she hadn't.

"*Dios*, save me from the mating rituals of others," Rico muttered. "I, for one, need a drink. And you look like you need a drink, as well. It's not every day you discover that the monsters really do exist."

"Hey, who are you calling a monster?" Sardi complained. He reached beneath the table and dug out three glasses and a bottle of amber liquid, poured generous amounts into the glasses, and pushed one toward him.

"Well, at least it's not boring around here right now," Rico said, raising his glass. "To fun times ahead." He downed the whiskey in one go and looked at Logan, one eyebrow raised, a challenge in his dark eyes.

Logan picked up his glass. Getting drunk in the company of a vampire and a demon was not the most sensible of ideas, but what the hell? He raised his own glass and swallowed it down, just managing not to choke. He slammed the glass on the table, and Sardi filled it again. He blew out his breath then glanced at Rico.

"How long have you known Katia?" he asked.

The vampire's lips twitched. "If this is leading up to you asking me the best way to get into her pants, then I have to admit I've never been there."

And *he* had to admit he had wondered. And he couldn't deny that he was more than pleased that they'd never had a thing. He glanced at Sardi.

"Me neither," the demon said. "I'm not that brave."

"I just wondered. She seems to know you pretty well."

Rico shrugged. "To answer your question, I've known Katia for around seventy years."

Logan had been about to take a mouthful of whiskey, but he went still with the glass halfway to his mouth. "Seventy years? She's seventy years old?" No way. She didn't look seventy. He remembered her saying about Rico being immortal. Would she live forever?

"At a guess, she's around a hundred. When I met her, she'd been changed for ten years, and she was nineteen when she was bitten…so yeah, about a hundred now. A baby."

So she'd been nineteen; that accounted for why she appeared so young. Maybe they didn't age. She'd stay looking nineteen, and he'd grow older and eventually die. He'd be a lecherous old creep, like Major Pryce. What must that be like, watching the people around you die while you lived on? It maybe explained some of her reasons for avoiding relationships. But then again, he didn't think there was much of a chance of him surviving to old age, with all this murdering going on around them. So why not enjoy the time they had?

"Is she immortal?" he asked.

"In theory, all weres are immortal, but they usually come to a bad end. They're a violent, undisciplined bunch. Really more animal than human."

Now who was being racist? "Katia's not an animal," he said.

Rico snickered then filled up his glass. "I think our boy's in love."

"No, I'm not." He wasn't *that* stupid. But he liked her, and he didn't like many people. "So how did you meet her?" he asked. Was there some sort of club where people who weren't human could go to meet other people who weren't human?

Rico sat back and regarded him for a moment then shrugged. "I think that's a story for her to tell you. If she wants you to know." He reached into his pocket and placed something on the table in front of them. A pack of playing cards. "Let's play poker."

He didn't want to play poker. He wanted to…

Except Katia didn't want him. He might as well play cards. There was nothing else he could investigate until tomorrow, and he was good at poker. Plus, he wanted to understand a bit more about what made these people tick, just in case Katia decided to look at him again.

Rico spoke into his comm unit for a moment then settled back to study Logan. "So do you have family with the fleet?" he asked.

"No."

"Family anywhere?"

"Obviously not." Stupid question. Even if he'd had family back on Earth, they'd be long dead by now. But he hadn't, so it was a moot point.

"You've been in the army how long?"

"Eighteen years. Christ, what is this, Twenty Questions?" Logan emptied his glass and held it out for more. He felt like getting seriously shit-faced; he'd worry about his liver tomorrow. If only to stop himself from running to Katia. Begging to share her bed.

"Just trying to decide how much of a liability you are and what we're going to do with you long term. You're a career soldier. I'm guessing you were an orphan and the army is the only home you've ever known."

"So?" he growled.

"So it gives me some idea of where your loyalties lie."

Did it? Logan wasn't so sure. For a long time, he'd been going through the motions. He'd stayed with the army because it was a life that suited him and maybe because it was all he'd known. But did he feel loyal? Probably not. The army was run by a load of assholes. And he hadn't really felt like he belonged. Any more than he'd belonged anywhere else in his life. He was saved from answering by the door directly opposite him sliding open. Two men stood there. So there were other people awake on board, after all.

Both were tall; one had short dark brown hair and amber eyes. He was smartly dressed in black pants and what looked like a white silk shirt. The other had long red hair, pale skin, and blue eyes and wore jeans and a T-shirt. Despite the differences, they had a similarity about them, and they both moved with the easy athleticism of trained fighters as they crossed the room to where they all sat.

"You called, oh Lord and Master?" the dark-haired man said. And Logan detected more than a hint of sarcasm in the voice.

Rico grinned up at them. "We're playing cards. Poker. We needed more players."

The man rolled his eyes then looked at Logan, a frown forming on his face. "Who's this?"

"Sergeant Logan Farrell of the New World Armed Forces," Rico said.

"No way. Is that even a real thing?"

"Apparently, yes. They have tanks and everything. Obviously, the president is not going to tolerate any insurrection when we get to our brave new world." He turned to Logan. "And this is Dylan"—he nodded to the dark-haired man—"and Adam." The redhead. "Adam is ex-military, so you should be real buddies. Except he's also Scottish, which probably means you won't."

Neither looked like they wanted to be buddies. Both had closed expressions. And despite the "lord and master" comment, they behaved more as equals to Rico than subservients. Maybe that was how things were on the *Trakis Two*.

"What's he doing here?" Adam asked, taking the seat on the other side of Logan, while Dylan sat down in the chair Katia had vacated, crossed one leg over his knee. Sardi grabbed two more glasses and pulled another full bottle from somewhere.

"He's investigating the…malfunctions. With Katia."

Adam leaned forward. "Katia's awake?" He sounded eager, and Logan twisted in his seat so he could look at the other man.

"What's it to you?"

"Och, the wee lassie likes me."

"No, she doesn't," Rico said. "She thinks you're a tosser. Just like I do. Anyway, you might be interested to know that Katia has given Logan here her protection."

"A human?"

He might as well have said a slug. Logan could hear the

complete disbelief in the other man's voice. Though Logan was starting to believe that "man" might not be a totally accurate description.

"Why would she have done that?"

"Probably his pretty eyes, but you'll have to ask her. In the meantime, you two are on guard duty. There have been three attempts on our investigators' lives. I want you to make sure that nothing happens to them until they finish the investigation."

"You're serious? You want us to babysit?"

"Do I look serious?" Rico asked, dealing out the cards. "In case you were undecided, the answer to that is yes—deadly serious. But it does mean that you both get to go to the party."

"In which case," Adam said, rubbing his hands together, "no problem."

Logan shifted his chair a little closer to Sardi. He could feel the alcohol like a buzz in his head, numbing out the chaotic thoughts. He liked it and took another gulp. "What are they?" he asked in what he hoped was a quiet voice. Obviously not quiet enough, as everyone at the table turned to stare at him. "What?" he asked. "You can't expect me not to be curious."

"What do you think they are?" Rico asked.

He didn't think they were vampires. There was something cold about Rico, and these guys came across as definitely hot-blooded. No horns, so he didn't think they were demons, either. What did that leave? How the hell was he supposed to know? They had a slight flavor of Katia about them. Something he hadn't even recognized, but now he knew what she was, he could sense the air of difference about her. But not quite the same.

"Werewolves," he said. It was as good a guess as any.

Rico raised his glass. "The man got it in one. Very

impressive."

"Really? They're actually werewolves." Fucking hell, but that was cool. He wondered if they'd give him a demonstration if he asked nicely. He decided they might, but they might also eat him afterward, so another time perhaps.

An hour later, he had all the chips in front of him, and he was receiving some very dirty looks from everyone around the table. He guessed none of them were used to losing. Too many top dogs around here...ha ha, he liked that, werewolves—top dogs. He chuckled to himself. He was definitely drunk. He needed to lie down. He swallowed the last of his whiskey and slammed the glass onto the table.

Tomorrow was party day. Getting-in-a-shuttle-again day. How likely was it to all go to shit three times in a row?

Time to find somewhere to lay his fucking head for the night. He certainly wasn't going to the room he'd been allocated; it was too close to where Katia had been poisoned.

Katia had said she was sleeping in the brig.

Likely she would be in bed by now. That small bed, all warm and cozy and maybe naked. Yeah, she'd definitely be naked. Maybe he'd go and offer to share some body warmth. Purely platonic. He didn't think he could get it up right now anyway.

He pushed himself to his feet, swayed, and balanced himself with a hand on the back of his chair.

"Where are you going?" Rico asked.

"I have to go see Katia. Tell her I don't think she's an animal."

Rico shook his head. "God help us all."

He was aware of their eyes on him as he wended his way out of the room; there seemed to be an awful lot of obstacles to maneuver. He was on autopilot on his way back to the brig. Bouncing off the walls, but he made it eventually.

There were two cells. One was open and empty. The

other—the one where he'd been locked up—was closed. He tried to focus, but everything was blurred. Finally, he managed to get his hand on the door panel. Nothing happened. He banged on it and still nothing happened.

"Balls." She'd locked him out. Then his heart rate spiked. Or had someone gotten to her?

Suddenly, the door in front of him slid open. And there she was. Sitting in bed. He peered closer. Everything was slowly rotating. "You locked me out," he said, swaying slightly as though in a breeze.

"No, actually, I locked out anyone who might be trying to murder me."

"I'm not trying to murder you. You left me with a vampire."

"I told you, he won't touch you now."

"My protector."

He lurched inside the room, and the door slid closed behind him. He took that as a positive sign. He didn't say anything else—he had an idea nothing of any sense would come out of his mouth right now. She sat watching as he stripped off his clothes.

"What are you doing, Logan?"

Wasn't it obvious? He finished taking off his pants... slowly. Otherwise, he was likely to trip and brain himself. She was still watching him through narrowed eyes, tapping her fingers on her sheet-covered thigh. What was the question?

"I just had to come and tell you—" He hesitated. What could he say? "That I like cats," he mumbled.

She shook her head, but a small smile flickered across her lips. She held up the sheet, and he crawled underneath. He wrapped his arms around her, and the world stopped spinning.

He felt...safe.

And within seconds, he was asleep.

• • •

Katia lay with her eyes closed. He was sprawled half across her, heavy, but she didn't move him. Instead, she shifted on the bed so she could wrap her arms around him, burrow her nose against his skin. He was warm and smelled of clean sweat and hot man, mixed with the sweetness of whiskey. His chest rose and fell beneath her, and the steady thud of his heart soothed her agitated thoughts.

Since she'd left him, she'd been desperately fighting the urge to go back and…she wasn't sure what. She was scared by how much she needed his…again, no clue. Acceptance maybe. That's what had held her in place. Fear. What if he *couldn't* accept what she was?

But—aw—he liked cats.

It was enough for now.

Chapter Twenty-Two

She woke and lay with her eyes closed. She was warm and cozy and vaguely…happy.

Was she crazy? How could she possibly contemplate happiness considering the total mess they were in? Someone with the ability to blow up spaceships was wandering around on the loose, blowing up spaceships and killing thousands. Whoever it was, they clearly had no conscience.

A sociopath.

But she'd lived to fight another day. No one had killed her in the night.

Unless she was dead and this was…heaven or hell?

Logan spooned her from behind, one hand around her, clasping her breast through the material of the T-shirt she'd slept in. From the sound of his breathing, he was deep asleep. Or passed out cold. He'd been pretty far gone when he came to her.

She slipped out of bed, stopping midway as he rolled onto his back. But he didn't wake, and she was glad. She felt good right now, and she didn't want that to change just yet. She'd learned a long time ago to accept and enjoy the good times when they occurred. And she had no clue how he would feel when he woke up. Would he even remember what he had said last night?

He liked cats.

The memory made her smile.

God, he'd been drunk.

She stood by the side of the bed, staring down at him. He was lying on his back, snoring softly. In sleep, the lines on his face smoothed out and he appeared younger. And without the purple eyes to distract, he looked more masculine, pure male, all harsh lines, a big beaky nose, nice lips. And he knew how to use them.

He showed no sign of waking up as she dressed quietly and let herself out of the cell. Time to earn her keep and solve this case—too much time had been wasted over people trying to kill her. She had a few notes she wanted to make. So after a quick visit to the galley, she was heading to the conference room to update her whiteboard.

She pressed the panel to open the door and almost jumped when Adam Murray straightened up from where he'd been leaning against the wall opposite. Adam was one of Rico's wolves, though not too high up in the pack. Rico kept a few of them for protection. She'd been part of that for a while, after she'd first met the vampire. He'd offered her a safe place, which she hadn't had for a long time. All he'd asked in return was the occasional blood donation and her absolute obedience. It had been a little enough price to pay. Without that time, she doubted she would have survived. She'd been such a baby, had no clue about anything—her old master, the werejaguar who had changed her, had kept her a virtual prisoner.

Until she'd killed him.

"What the hell are you doing lurking out here?" she

asked.

"Och, aye, you're pleased to see me, really." He grinned. "I'm here because I'm your new babysitter."

"You're kidding me?" She didn't need a babysitter. So she might have nearly died three times in little more than three days, but she could look after herself. Okay, maybe the third time had come a little close. But the last thing she needed was a goddamn horny werewolf dogging her footsteps.

She glanced back at the closed door. "Maybe you'd better stay here and guard Logan."

"Your boyfriend?"

She frowned. "You've met him?"

"Aye. Last night. Plays a mean hand of poker but can't hold his liquor."

She didn't know whether it was good or bad that Rico was letting Logan meet the others. It could mean he'd decided Logan could be trusted. Or it could mean that he'd decided to resolve the problem once the investigation was over and neither she nor Logan were of any further use. She sort of trusted him not to go back on his word, but there were other ways to render a problem not a problem without actually killing him. He might put him back into cryo, and she was beginning to think that was as good as a death sentence. If they went back to sleep now, then they would never wake up. The systems would eventually shut down and everyone would die—the ships would be huge graveyards carrying the last dead remains of humanity.

"He's safe in the brig," Adam said. "We're monitoring the surveillance cameras. All the cells have them."

Her eyes narrowed. "You watched us sleep?"

"Yeah, pretty boring. I headed over as soon as you woke. Left Dylan watching sleeping beauty in there. Nice underwear, by the way."

She snarled, and he grinned and stepped back, held out

a paper bag he'd been hiding at his side. "Here," he said, holding it out at arm's length as if she might bite. "Peace offering."

She took the bag and peered inside. It contained two chocolate muffins, and the warm sweet smell filled her nostrils. Her stomach rumbled.

"And coffee," he said, holding out the cardboard mug in his other hand.

She bit into a chocolate muffin, closed her eyes as she chewed, swallowed. "Okay," she said grudgingly. "You can stick around."

Adam sat at the table and watched her as she stared at the board, trying to think of something useful to add. She checked her comm unit, just in case someone had decided to send some of the information she'd asked for, despite the investigation being officially closed. But nothing.

Hopefully, she could fill in more information for the *Trakis Seven* after they visited the ship today. Something occurred to her, then, and she turned to Adam.

"Are you coming to the party?" she asked.

"Wouldn't miss it for the world. Dylan's been brushing off his tux."

She grinned. Dylan was the pack alpha, a total badass, but he'd been a rich city stockbroker before he was changed.

"We'd been banned," Adam continued. "Rico doesn't believe that we can behave in a sufficiently civilized manner, but obviously, keeping darling Katia and her new boyfriend safe overrides any social gaffs we might make."

"You want to go?"

"Och aye. Things can get a bit samey around here."

"How long have you been awake?" she asked.

"Fifty years, give or take a few. I trained as tech support when the last guy decided he'd had enough and wanted to go back to sleep. Fae—absolute pussy. No disrespect."

She snorted. "None taken." She wasn't too keen on the fae herself.

"By the way, Rico said he'd sorted you out a dress for the party. Your boyfriend is to go in uniform—look the part, give us an official appearance."

She didn't want to think where Rico had gotten a party dress—was he raiding the cryotubes? The man had no morals.

She took a step back and examined her board. Considering she'd been awake for four days, she'd managed to gather very little information. All they really had was the crew connection, and that was tentative. But then, she had been expending an awful lot of energy just staying alive.

With that thought, she swiped the board to a new page. Down one side she wrote, "autopilot malfunction," "*Trakis Three* exploding," and finally, "poison gas." Next to them she wrote down the possibility of remote activity resulting in the occurrence. She'd gone through Sardi's notes last night in bed. It had been interesting reading—at least for someone trying to work out who had tried to kill her, three times. The answers as far as she could tell—and she'd check with Sardi—were "no," "yes," and "no clue."

The autopilot could only have been tampered with from on the shuttle. That reminded her—they'd asked that question of Jake, the tech guy on the *Trakis One*. And as far as she was aware, he'd never gotten back to them. She made a note to chase him up and find out why. That also reminded her of something else—hadn't his supervisor told them that Jake had family on the *Trakis Three*? Poor man. Maybe he was in mourning.

From her understanding, while someone could have redirected the shuttle remotely, no way should they have been able to stop the people on board from switching to manual control. It just didn't have that functionality. So they must have actually been on board. But that didn't narrow things down much. Pryce had programmed the shuttle. Layla had been on board, waiting to talk to Logan, if she remembered rightly. Neither seemed a likely suspect. But the docking bay on the *Trakis One* was not a restricted area—anyone could have entered the shuttle. She made a note in her file to ask Pryce for any surveillance footage for the time she'd been on the *Trakis One*. If she could work out a good reason why she wanted the information when the case was supposedly closed.

Apparently, the explosion on the *Trakis Three* could have been remote detonated. By a number of means. The easiest would be if there was some sort of explosive device strategically placed on the ship, say in the main engine rooms.

But even more worrying, apparently no explosive device would have been necessary if the person knew what they were doing and had access to the *Trakis One*'s systems. The *Trakis One* had the ability to monitor and also change the running modes of all the ships. If they overrode the *Trakis Three*'s own systems, they could input code to make the engines overwork and eventually implode, leading to a chain reaction that could blow up the whole ship. Which reflected what they had seen. That narrowed it down to anyone on the *Trakis One*. Again. They were going to have to pay a visit there next, and she felt strangely reluctant.

There would be some trace of activity on the *Trakis One* logs. And, of course, the incoming code would have been recorded on the *Trakis Three* logs, but that was hardly of any help right now, with the ship in a million pieces.

Finally, the poison. She hated that more than the other two near-death experiences. It was so out of her control. She couldn't fight back; she'd just gone under. They had no clue what had been used—though Rico had the science officer analyzing everything from the cabin hoping to find some trace—or how it had been introduced. Nothing. She couldn't see how anything could have been introduced remotely, but Sardi had suggested that the air cleaning systems could have been messed with from the *Trakis One*.

It all came back to the *Trakis One*. But who on board would have any reason to commit murder?

It didn't make sense.

She needed more food.

Chapter Twenty-Three

The shuttle was only built for four, and there were five of them. It probably wouldn't even get off the ground—if they were lucky.

Dylan was flying, so he got the pilot's seat. Adam had grabbed the chair next to him. Layla stood staring at the empty seats for a moment. "This is against protocol," she muttered. "Only four passengers per shuttle."

"Would you like to stay behind?" Dylan asked.

She gave him a dirty look but then sat down abruptly in the seat behind him, which left one seat free. Logan gestured her to it.

"Isn't he a gentleman," Dylan muttered.

Katia accepted the offer, mainly because she didn't want to crush her party dress sitting on the floor. She smoothed it down as she sat. She wasn't a dress sort of person, couldn't remember the last time she had worn one, but Rico had outdone himself. She wondered how many suitcases he'd had to trawl through until he'd found one that would suit. It was dark red silk and fitted her to perfection, with a halter neck, and dipped low at the back, almost to her ass.

Logan's eyes had widened then heated up when he'd first caught sight of her. Whether he liked the idea or not—and she still had no clue—he wanted her. And while she was even less sure than ever that taking things further with him was a good idea, she wanted him right back. She couldn't remember a time when she'd even considered a repeat performance. Mostly she found it easy to walk away from the men she slept with, though obviously walking away was a little more difficult on a spaceship—nowhere to go. But Logan was different. And she couldn't put her finger on why.

Maybe because he was a loner like her. It made her feel special.

This was the first she'd seen of Layla since the poison incident. She'd eyed up the other woman as she came in, trying to see if she had any bite marks on her neck, but she wore a glittery scarf around her throat—probably a present from Rico. When Katia glanced across, she found Logan was doing the same thing—staring fixedly at Layla's neck. He'd caught her gaze and grinned. It was the first real smile she'd had out of him. She suspected he was suffering from a hangover of immense proportions.

He'd seated himself on the floor off to the side of the shuttle where she could still see him and he could see her. His legs were stretched out in front of him, his head leaning back against the wall, his eyes closed. He opened them as if sensing her gaze.

"Are you all right down there?" she asked.

"No. My head hurts. I'm trying not to move it too much or think too much or..." He gave a very small shrug. "How about you. Nervous?"

She'd been trying not to concentrate on the tight knot in her belly. But yeah, she was nervous. "I can't help but think of what could go wrong this time."

"Nothing will go wrong," Dylan said, looking at her over his shoulder. "Adam and I will look after you."

She snorted. "That makes me feel so much better."

"Really," Layla said, "the shuttles are super safe. There had never been a situation until Security Officer Caldwell was killed."

And that had hardly been down to the shuttle. All down to Rico.

"I've been thinking about it," Layla continued. "The shuttle explosion—it was obviously due to the terrorist as well. Stuart was no doubt about to uncover their existence, so they had to kill him before he could tell us what was going on."

Katia turned so she could see Logan's response to this theory. He caught her gaze and rolled his eyes.

"I'm so glad it was all settled." Layla gave a bright smile to the room. "And while it's a tragedy what happened to all those people on the *Trakis Three*, at least the matter is resolved. And the party will be good for morale."

They'd got the message this morning from the *Trakis One*—the powers that be were running with the terrorist theory, and as far as they were concerned, the investigation was officially closed and the embargo on inter-ship flights had been lifted. The party was on. Which was good news for her and Logan's hush-hush investigation. She hoped she would get the chance to find out some of the missing pieces.

If they got there alive.

• • •

"Welcome to the *Trakis Seven*." The robotic voice came over the comm system. "Your shuttle is in a queue. Please maintain your current orbit around the ship, and you will be given landing instructions shortly."

"Is something wrong?" Logan asked. They were so close. Just one shuttle ride without a catastrophe would be good. Without waiting for an answer, he pushed himself to his feet and came over to stand by Katia's chair where he could see the forward screen. It showed the huge bulk of the *Trakis Seven*. Identical to the other ships. They were slowly circling around her. Every muscle in his body had tensed up as they approached. Waiting for the explosion.

It never came. That didn't mean it still wouldn't.

"No," Dylan replied. "Just looks like there's a crowd coming to the party and they're bringing us in one at a time."

Logan lowered his gaze. If he moved a little to the left, he had a direct view right down the front of Katia's dress. The perfect image to take his mind off imminent explosions or the hangover that refused to be dislodged from his head. Or vampires or werewolves or things that go bump in the night.

Hard to forget that he was sharing this small space with two werewolves and a werecat. Once again, he was an outsider. Would always be an outsider with these people. Was it only a couple of days ago that he'd been thinking maybe they could have something between them?

A lot had changed since they'd made love.

She could shift into a cat.

She was complicit in the probable murder of five thousand Chosen Ones.

He liked her. A lot.

And he thought she liked him at least a little bit.

He had been so drunk last night. He couldn't ever remember being that inebriated. It probably wasn't the most sensible thing to let his guard down like that. But on the other hand, he was certain that if Rico wanted him dead, then there wasn't a lot he could do about it, drunk or sober. What was the point in worrying?

He'd woken up that morning alone in the small cot in

the cell but with Katia's scent still lingering. And with no memory of how he had gotten there. But she'd clearly let him in and stayed with him. He just wished he could remember. He had an idea that his nights were limited, and he didn't want to forget the good ones.

He still wanted her. Maybe he should get what he could, while he could, and not worry about a future that probably wasn't going to happen anyway.

She looked up then and caught him staring at her breasts. She raised an eyebrow. "You're staring, soldier."

He smirked. "It's a great view from here. You know, you clean up pretty well, detective. And nice dress, by the way."

"A present from Rico."

"That man sure has resources. Whiskey, bodyguards..." He did remember meeting their two babysitters last night. "Now fancy dresses."

"He's a resourceful man."

"Isn't he just. I'm surprised he didn't want to come to the party himself."

Dylan snorted. "Yeah, a real party guy. Not."

"I did ask him," Layla said. "He told me he would have loved to come, but he had things to do on the ship. He's so dedicated."

Dylan snorted again but didn't say anything.

"Come sit with me?" Logan said quietly. He wanted to talk to her without the others listening in. Who knew if they would get a moment alone today? He wanted to find out how much of an ass he'd been last night. She was still talking to him at least.

She studied him for a moment and then nodded and unfastened her harness. He went to the back of the shuttle and lowered himself to the floor again, sat with his legs stretched out, his back against the wall. She gave a small shrug, smoothed down her dress, and sank to the floor beside him. "I was trying not to crush my dress," she said. "But this whole dressy thing is just too high maintenance."

"You look beautiful," he murmured.

"Thank you."

"When I saw you, you actually made me forget my head was going to explode."

"You were pretty drunk last night."

"I don't remember much. Actually, I don't remember anything. Was I a complete asshole?"

"You were sweet."

"I was?" That had to be a first.

"Yeah, you told me you liked cats, then you passed out."

Well, he supposed it could have been worse. "I do like cats. One of my foster parents got me a kitten. I loved that kitten."

"What happened to it?"

It was his turn to shrug. "Who knows? But it didn't come with me when they sent me back."

"That's so sad."

At the time, it had nearly broken him. He was used to saying good-bye to foster parents; they came and went. But he'd fucking loved that cat. Had begged them to let him take it with him. "Probably liked the next kid as much as me."

She raised a brow, amusement flashing in her eyes. "Are you saying cats are fickle?"

Balls. "Hell no, I—"

She patted his leg. "Just kidding you, Logan. Actually, cats are pretty fickle creatures."

Was she warning him off? Preparing him so he wouldn't be a nuisance when she told him it was over? He moved around a little so he could see her face while he asked the next question. "What happens after the investigation is over?"

She looked definitely shifty. "What do you mean?"

He scrubbed a hand through his hair then around the

back of his neck, kneading his fingers into the tense muscles. "What do you think I mean? Am I going to survive this? How can you trust me not to go blabbing about what you are? What you did?"

She pressed a finger to the spot between her eyes. At least she was thinking about her answer, not just giving him a few platitudes to make him feel better. "I think you'll survive," she said. "Rico can be a total tosser. And he's ruthless to anything he perceives as a threat. But he's accepted you, and usually he doesn't kill people for no reason once he's accepted you."

"Well, that makes me feel all nice and safe."

A smile flashed across her face. "I've been thinking about it. I mean about what happens when this is over. To both of us. I think maybe they'll put us back in cryo. Worry about the problem later."

"I don't want to go back in cryo." How much his thoughts had changed since he'd woken up from the cryo sleep only days ago. Back then, he hadn't been sure he wanted to be awake. Now he knew he didn't want to go to sleep again.

It was unlikely Rico would insist *she* go back into cryo— they came across as, if not friends, then at least equals. He'd gotten the impression the vampire respected Katia.

"Neither do I," she said. "Not the least because I don't think any of them will be waking up. We haven't found anywhere even remotely life-supporting in five hundred years. The ships are falling apart."

"Except for the *Trakis Two*. Why is that?"

"I asked Rico that very same thing. He told me good management."

Logan laughed. He actually liked the vampire.

"He's probably not far off," Katia continued. "He's only kept a minimum of crew awake, so the resources have lasted longer. He's done a lot of the work himself—spent the first few decades learning everything from the original crew rotation. I think he's gone years when he was the only person conscious on the ship. I'm amazed by how he kept that from the rest of the fleet."

It was impressive, though Logan was guessing that the amount of to and fro happening between ships at the moment was unusual. Under normal circumstances, there could be years between visits.

That explained why Rico still had coffee while everyone else had run out. Did vampires drink coffee? Something occurred to him, and he wasn't sure he should go there but couldn't resist asking. "What does he eat?" Maybe the question should have been: who does he eat?

Her lips twitched. "I did ask. There are apparently plenty of Chosen Ones, if not willing to donate for a good cause then unaware they were doing it."

"He killed them?"

"I doubt it. I told you—he doesn't kill for no reason, and there would be no reason. Vampires don't need to kill their victims. In fact, they rarely do. At least these days." She frowned. "Well, not *these* days, but the years before we left Earth. Killing people tends to get you noticed, and that's the last thing any of us want."

Her use of the word "us" came as a shock. Although he'd seen what she was, what she could turn into, it hadn't actually sunk in. She wasn't human. She had more in common with a vampire than with him.

"But," she continued, "Dylan told me Rico occasionally wakes up a pretty woman and makes her an offer she can refuse if she wants, though apparently they very rarely do. He keeps them around for a while then wipes their memories and puts them back to sleep."

"That's sort of sick."

"Maybe." She looked him in the eye. "That would be

another option if you don't want to go back into cryo."

Ugh. "He'd have to feed on me."

"It doesn't hurt."

"He's done that to you?" He wasn't sure how he felt about that. Actually, that wasn't true. He hated the idea. The fucking vampire could keep his hands and his teeth off Katia.

"A long time ago, when we first met. He offered his protection, and blood was the only currency I had to pay with. Back then, I wouldn't have survived alone. I knew nothing. Rico taught me a lot. And vamps like were-blood."

Christ, it was a whole different world. One he would never belong in. "But you and he never…"

"Had sex? No. I never wanted him like that, and Rico likes his women willing."

"Thank God for that."

"There are worse people."

He was sure there were. "I don't want to forget."

"You wouldn't remember that you'd forgotten."

"I still don't want to." He didn't want to forget Katia and their one time together, which looked increasingly like it wasn't going to be repeated, and that made something ache deep in his chest. He shifted a little closer and lowered his voice. "What about you and me?"

Her eyes widened. She hadn't expected that question. Probably it hadn't even occurred to her that there was a "you and me" situation. "I thought you didn't do relationships?"

"I don't. I didn't." Hell, maybe that was why he was making such a fuckup of this one. Did he and Katia have a relationship? Did he want a relationship? With a woman who could turn into a cat? Who was at home with the monsters and talked about vampires like she knew them well? "What about you?"

She gave a small shrug. "I tried. But most weres are assholes and humans grow old and it never lasts and that hurts. So..." Another shrug. "Did you know in the wild, jaguars live alone? Not like lions, who have family groups. They come together for mating and that's about it."

"And is that who you are?"

"I always thought so."

But they'd definitely connected. He wasn't imagining that. Maybe he needed to find a means to make her remember how good it had been between them. But was that what he really wanted? All his life he'd longed to belong, to fit in. He would never fit into her world. Did he want to try, only to fail?

She reached across and rested her palm on his thigh. "Let's get this investigation over with and then we'll...talk."

If he had time before they put him back to sleep or zapped his memories. Would he be given the choice? He didn't know which he'd choose—he wanted neither and his head hurt. "What the hell is happening out there?" he muttered. He needed to do something.

Adam turned in his seat and grinned. "Not a lot. We're still waiting, but fascinating conversation."

They'd been keeping their voices low, but obviously werewolves had better than normal hearing. Something to remember.

The comm unit crackled to life. "Shuttle two-zero-two, you are cleared for docking."

"Looks like we're going in," Dylan said.

"About fucking time."

He thought Katia might get up, go back to her seat, but she stayed where she was. And a second later, he felt her hand slide across his thigh, and she tangled her fingers with his. He squeezed. "Our first shuttle ride together without a disaster," he said.

"We're not down yet."

Chapter Twenty-Four

The shuttle landed smoothly without anything going wrong at all. Amazing.

Katia sat for a minute, not willing to release her grip on Logan.

Dylan had unstrapped himself and stood up, stretching. He glanced to the back of the shuttle where she sat close to Logan, and he lifted one eyebrow.

Werewolves frowned upon relationships outside their small world. But then she wasn't a werewolf. They were pack animals with close ties to others of their kind. She was a werejaguar with no werecat friends.

The only other werejaguars she'd met had not appealed to her in any way. Rico had tried to set her up with a few over the years. Adam got up and wandered over then stood looking down at the two of them. "Isn't that sweet?"

"You're just jealous," she replied. But she pulled free of Logan's grip and pushed herself to her feet, smoothing the wrinkles from her dress.

Adam ran his gaze up and down her body. "Nice dress."

She was quite aware that Adam would have stretched his own relationship rules for her. He'd been trying to get into her pants for years. Never going to happen.

"Can we get off this thing?" she asked.

"Waiting for permission to disembark," he said. Reaching into his pocket, he pulled out a bar and tossed it to her. "Keep cool, kitty-cat. You're giving off vibes." He was right. If she'd had a tail at that point, it would have been twitching. She wanted this done with, resolved. She wanted to know what Rico planned to do about Logan. What Logan wanted. She needed to get him alone for a little while. Hell, she wanted him again. Just once more. She had a strange feeling that everything was going to go to shit any moment now. She didn't know how, but something was going to happen. And it wasn't going to be anything good.

Logan got to his feet beside her. "Can we not just get off?"

He crossed to the door, pressed his hand to the panel. Nothing happened.

"Locked from outside," Dylan said.

"They're disembarking people shuttle by shuttle," Layla said. She was still in her seat. "I remember from last time."

"You've been to one of these things before?" Katia asked.

"Yes. The year I first woke up. Someone fell ill, and I was offered their place. It will be our turn soon."

Katia unwrapped the bar, took a bite, paced the length of the shuttle, another bite.

"We've got company," Adam said.

Katia swallowed the last of her protein bar and went to stand beside him where she could see the screen. Two men were walking across the docking bay floor, looking like they were heading straight for their shuttle.

She would have recognized the man in front even without his green shirt. Captain Callum Meridian. Hero fighter pilot.

Tall and lean with close-cropped dark red hair, he moved with the purpose of a born leader, his hand resting on the pistol at his waist. Did he think someone was going to shoot him at his party? Slightly behind him was a man in a yellow shirt, which meant he was second in command. They were getting a welcome committee.

What made them special?

The two men disappeared from the screen as they got close to the shuttle, and a few seconds later, the door slid open.

Up close, Callum Meridian was stunning. He had a presence about him that was hard to define but instantly recognizable. He paused just inside, looked around, assessing the situation, then smiled at Layla, who had risen to her feet as the two men entered.

Logan had stood up straight but hadn't actually saluted. He was picking up bad habits.

"I was expecting three of you," the captain said. "Who are the other two?"

"That would be us." Dylan waved a hand to include Adam. "We've been assigned as security to Sergeant Farrell and Detective Mendoza."

"And do they need security?"

Katia decided it was time to introduce herself. She stepped forward and held out her hand. Callum looked at it and then slid his palm into hers. Did he hold it longer than strictly necessary? Maybe. She cast a sideways glance at Logan. He was watching her with narrowed eyes.

"I'm Detective Mendoza," she said, tugging her hand free. "I was the lead detective on the investigation."

"Callum Meridian. Call me Callum."

"Katia," she said. "And this is Sergeant Logan Farrell, who has been assisting me with my inquiries." Dylan snorted at that. She ignored him. Logan saluted.

"At ease, sergeant." He glanced between the two of them. "That still doesn't explain why you need security, especially as I believe the investigation is now closed."

"There have been a number of attempts on the life of Detective Mendoza," Dylan said.

She shrugged. "A few systems malfunctions, nothing more."

Dylan ignored her again. "The captain decided it would be a good idea if someone kept an eye on her until she can be tucked safely back in her cryotube."

"Piss off, Dylan."

Callum's eyes widened at that. But he merely gave her a speculative look and turned to where Layla stood hovering. He held out his hand. "Layla, as beautiful as ever." He lowered his head and kissed the back of her hand.

Katia glanced up, caught Logan's gaze, and he rolled his eyes.

"It's wonderful to be here," Layla said.

He turned to the man at his side. "Layla, this is John Taylor, my second in command. He's going to escort you to the party."

"Oh, but I thought we could catch up on old times."

"And we will. Later. Right now, I want to have a word with Detective Mendoza and Sergeant Farrell."

Layla's brows drew together. "Why? The investigation is closed."

"It is. But I have some information for them to include in their report. It won't take long."

Layla opened her mouth then shut it again as John Taylor deftly maneuvered her from the shuttle. Very impressive. They must have arranged it beforehand.

"You could go with them, join the party," Callum said to Dylan and Adam. "I'll keep your charges safe."

"It's more than our lives are worth," Dylan said with a

shrug. "Sorry. But I'm more scared of our captain than I am of you."

Callum's brows rose. "I'd like to meet him. Is he coming to the party?"

"He's not the party type."

Callum blew out his breath, gave their small group a speculative look. "Okay, come along. We'll go somewhere a little more comfortable." He turned and exited the shuttle. She got the impression Callum wasn't used to people not doing what he wanted. She remembered reading about him. He'd been the youngest of the captains. A war hero. He'd led a charmed life. The only discord was his breakup with President Beauchamp's daughter, not long before they'd shipped out. They'd been a fairy-tale couple. Tamara Beauchamp was tall, blond, and skinny and always managed to look elegant and groomed. Everything Katia wasn't. She was also asleep somewhere on the *Trakis One*.

She followed him out of the shuttle, and Logan fell in beside her, with Dylan and Adam behind. "What do you think he wants to talk about?" Logan asked.

"I have no clue, but no doubt we'll find out soon."

"I don't like him," Logan added.

She cast him a smile. "I think he seems very nice."

"I noticed."

They arrived at the door to exit the docking bay and came to a halt while Callum placed his hand on the panel. Nothing happened. He tried again then punched the panel. "Fucking ship is falling apart," he said. When still nothing happened, he pulled his pistol from the holster at his waist and shot out the door lock. The door slid open. He pressed his comm unit. "Ian, can you send an engineer down to the docking bay? Door malfunction."

"You mean you've shot another one."

"Yeah. So?"

"Nothing, captain."

She looked at Logan and raised a brow. She quite liked this guy. He got things done.

Finally, he stopped outside a door, pressed his hand to the panel. This time, it opened, revealing a meeting room similar to her operations room on the *Trakis Two*. "Would you mind waiting outside?" he said to Dylan.

Dylan peered into the room. It was clearly empty, and he nodded. Though he didn't look particularly happy, but then, he was a nosy bastard. Callum gestured for her and Logan to enter and then waved them to sit down at the circular table in the center of the room.

He sat down with a sigh. "Fucking party," he said. "The *Trakis Three* blew up and we have no clue who was responsible or why." That was interesting. So Callum wasn't buying into the whole terrorist theory. "The crappy piece of shit ship is falling apart, we're running out of everything, and they decide to have a fucking party." He ran a hand around the back of his neck. "Jesus, I could do with a drink."

Strangely, that was something she could help with.

Reaching into her bag, she pulled out one of the bottles Rico had given her. "To help you get through the God-awful boring party," were his words as he'd handed them over. She placed it on the table between them.

Callum viewed it suspiciously. "What's that?"

"Whiskey."

His eyes lit up. "You're kidding me?"

"No, she's not," Logan replied. "We need glasses." He looked at Callum. "Glasses?"

He scratched his head. "I've never actually needed glasses. Never had a drink. Not in the ten years I've been awake."

"Try underneath the table," she said. Maybe all the ships had them.

He looked and came up with a grin and a trio of glasses in his hand. "I might have to keep you people around."

Maybe that was an option. They could stay here. Out of Rico's way. But she didn't want to be exiled from the *Trakis Two*. They were her people. Or as much her people as anyone was ever going to be.

Logan did the honors, unscrewing the top and pouring a hefty measure into each glass. He grinned at her. "Hair of the dog," he said and lifted his glass. Katia picked hers up, raised it to Callum, who appeared a little wary, but then gave an almost imperceptible lift of his shoulders and picked up his own. He thought for a moment. "To making it home. Wherever that might be." He swallowed the contents on one go.

Katia watched with interest as his eyes widened, he coughed, cleared his throat, and closed his eyes for a second, wheezing. "Jesus fucking Christ. Where the hell did you get this stuff?"

Katia took a sip of her own drink before answering. But she could see no reason to lie. "The captain of the *Trakis Two* makes it. He's set up a still in the engine room." Rico had shown her. "Uses anything they can grow in the agro-center."

Callum reached across and topped off his glass. "The captain on the *Trakis Two* makes this stuff? I think I want a transfer." He sipped the next glass, and Katia could see the tension draining out of him. He sat back. "I really must meet this guy."

"Probably not a good idea," Logan said. He'd emptied his own glass and refilled it. He looked better than he had all day as well. Maybe it was time to discover what the captain of the *Trakis Seven* wanted to talk about. They'd been delayed coming in; the party must be due to start or already underway. As the host, shouldn't Callum be there? He didn't seem to be in any rush.

"So what did you want to talk about?" Logan asked.

Callum sat up straight and put his glass on the table. "You were both assigned to the investigation." They both nodded. "You're not crew, and you were woken specially to take this duty?"

"Yeah," Logan said. "We're both qualified, and they needed someone. Why not?"

"I've just never heard of it happening before."

"There's never been a suspected murder case before."

"Is that what you were told? That you would be investigating a murder case?"

Logan frowned. "Actually, I was told it was likely a malfunction, considering the age of the ships. But, for the sake of morale, we had to look like we were considering all possibilities."

Callum turned his attention to her. "And you the same?"

What did she want to divulge? But she had a feeling that, unlike the crew of the *Trakis One*, Callum Meridian was not going along with the malfunction theory. Though she had no clue why. She shook her head slowly. Sometimes the truth was the best route forward. "No. I was told it was a murder investigation. If Rico had—"

"Rico?" Callum asked.

"The captain of the *Trakis Two*—he made the decision to wake me up. Before all this, back on Earth, I was a detective working homicide. If Rico had believed it was a malfunction, he would have woken up an engineer. He told me the Security Officer from the *Trakis One* had died mid-investigation"— she certainly wasn't telling the truth about that particular death—"and they had no one qualified to continue. So I was the logical choice."

"Hmm." Callum leaned across and refilled all their glasses. "So *Trakis One* believed the deaths to be down to malfunctions, whereas—"

"Actually, I'm not sure they believe it," Logan interrupted. "They just strongly intimated that they would like that to be the result I came up with."

"Interesting. But the *Trakis Two* believe they were murders."

"Rico's a suspicious guy," she said. "The investigation has been officially closed. The deaths were the work of the terrorist who destroyed the *Trakis Three*, conveniently blowing himself up and any evidence with it. So what's your interest in all this?"

Callum slammed his glass on the table, spilling amber liquid onto the metal surface. "Because I don't believe a fucking word of this terrorist crap, and I want to know what the fuck is going on before someone comes along and decides to blow up my fucking ship. With me on it."

Well, she could see his point. She glanced at Logan, and he raised an eyebrow. They had to decide whether to trust him or keep up the pretense that the investigation was over. But they would certainly get the information they needed quicker and easier with Callum Meridian's help. And she believed he was genuine. He seemed atypical of most military people she had met, not likely to toe the line. Logan was also atypical, but he went through the motions and pretended. She didn't think Callum would pretend; there was an arrogance about him, a sort of fuck you, take me or leave me, arrogance that was inbred. He'd come from a wealthy background, never questioned who or what he was or his place in the world. She found she liked him despite that. Usually, privileged assholes were among her least favorite people, but there were always exceptions to every rule.

On balance, she decided that telling him the truth and getting some assistance was worth the risk. But it had to be Logan's decision as well. He likely had more to lose if this all went tits-up. He was watching her, waiting for some signal, and she gave a small nod. He nodded in return.

"Well, that's interesting," he said. "Because we happen to think it's a load of balls as well."

"You're continuing with the investigation?"

"We are. But under the radar. Rico knows—we couldn't do this without some support to enable us to move around the fleet. But otherwise, to all intents and purposes, the investigation is closed and we're tying up loose ends so we can submit our report."

"What do you know so far?" Callum asked.

"Not enough," Logan replied. "Unfortunately, someone keeps trying to kill us, which has interfered a little with our investigation." He took them through what had happened since they'd woken.

Callum leaned forward in his seat, listening intently. When Logan finished, he sat back and thought for a moment. "No, you don't have a lot. But what you do have is someone who doesn't want you to get to the truth and is willing to blow up ten thousand innocent lives to stop you finding whatever evidence there was on the *Trakis Three*. And the attempt on your life clearly indicates that our murderer sees you as a threat, so you must have been on to something."

"I just wish I knew what."

"So how can I help?" Callum asked. "I presume you didn't come here just for the party."

"No, we were looking for some information." She gathered her thoughts. "First, the names of the victims on the *Trakis Seven*."

"You don't have that? Why?"

"We have the numbers but not the corresponding data behind those numbers. Some glitch in the central database wiped out a whole load of information. It wasn't seen as a major deal as the ships all have their own backups."

"Except if the ships are destroyed then those backups are

destroyed along with the ship."

"Exactly. Very convenient, and we're looking at things from that angle as well. Maybe someone tampered with the central database and left some sort of trail. So can you give us the names and details?"

"Of course." He pressed a few buttons on his comm unit, and a screen flashed up in front of him. He swiped through it. "There you are," he said, reaching out and turning the screen so she and Logan could read the information.

"Bingo," Logan murmured.

"What is it?" Callum asked. "I take it you've seen something interesting."

"So far, we only have information for the victims on the *Trakis Two,* and they were crew family."

"Just like these," Callum said. "Someone is killing the families of former crews? Some sort of grudge?"

Katia pulled out her file and wrote down the names on her report. Logan was inputting them onto his laptop.

JASON BRODIE 28
SARAH BRODIE 12
SUSAN BRODIE 10

They were the family of Angela Brodie, the Second in Command, third rotation, of the *Trakis Six.*

So not a captain, then. She could cross off one possible motive. "Why attack this woman's family now? What possible revenge can you have on a woman who's not even awake and hasn't been for centuries? God, none of this makes sense." She searched her mind for some connection. Some pattern. Yes, both sets of victims were crew families, but different ships and different time scales. What the hell was the connection? Agh!

"Did you keep the bodies?" Logan asked.

"Of course. We made up a makeshift morgue."

"Could we see them?"

"I don't see why not. Though they're not pretty. It's only been a few weeks, but they'd started the decomposition process. If the units hadn't been sealed, it would have stunk the place out and we would have picked it up without the audit. But it wasn't a good death. They took time to die."

She wasn't squeamish; she'd seen a lot of murder victims in her time with the Metropolitan police. But these were children, and that was always harder. All the same, maybe seeing the bodies would trigger something—though she had no clue what.

"Let's go."

Callum looked at her for a moment and then nodded. "Come with me. We'll have to be quick—I'm expected at the party, but the morgue is on the way."

He led them out of the meeting room, along another identical gray corridor, through the sick bay, and out of a door at the back. The room was cold, and she shivered. Thankfully, this wouldn't take long.

They already knew the cause of death, so she wasn't sure what she expected to get out of this. They were wasting their time. This whole thing was a waste of time. What did it matter if they solved the stupid mystery? They would all still die on these great big disintegrating cans in space. She tried to shake off the negative thoughts and get her brain to function.

Three cryotubes were lined up in the room.

"We decided that was the best method to preserve the bodies—the tubes are set to below freezing so decomposition has been halted—in case anyone wanted to carry out an autopsy. Though it's pretty obvious what killed them." He moved to the closest tube and pressed the keypad to open the lid. There was no stench of decay, and Katia stepped closer,

Logan at her shoulder.

She did a quick review of the body. It was dressed in shorts and a T-shirt. The skin was bluish except on the face, which was almost black, the eyes open, staring into nothingness. And the fingers were blackened with dried blood where the man—she presumed this was Jason Brodie, who'd been twenty-eight when he'd gone into his cryotube—had obviously clawed to get out.

There was nothing new to tell from the body, nothing to say why he had died or who had orchestrated that death.

But there was the crew connection. That was something to work with.

She moved on to the next tube. Logan was standing over it, hands in his pockets. He glanced at her as she came to stand beside him, a smile curving his lips. He nodded toward the cryotube and corpse number two. "You see anything wrong with this picture?" he asked.

She turned her attention to the body in the cryotube. It appeared similar to the first, and she searched for whatever it was had put that smile on his face. The hair was a deep brown and short. It was hard to make out the features; they were contorted in death.

Callum had come to stand on the other side of her. "If that's Susan Brodie, then I'm a ten-year-old girl."

"Shit," she muttered. He was right. Her brain wasn't working. She flicked through her folder to where she'd written the names on the victims, checked against the number on the cryotube. "Yup. This should be ten-year-old Susan Brodie." It looked like an adult male, at least six foot tall. Interesting. "Could they have mixed up the bodies?"

Though the last body should have belonged to Susan's twelve-year-old sister.

They moved as one to the final cryotube. Callum keyed in the code to open it, and she studied the body. Another adult male from the looks of things. So what was going on? It was fair to say that this was not the crew family it was supposed to be.

She turned to Callum. "How likely that your records are screwed up?"

"I'd say unlikely. It's not complicated. One number, one name."

She could see his point. She remembered the loading procedures when she had gone on board the *Trakis Two*. Everything had been checked and rechecked. The cryotubes were actually programmed to match the individual's DNA so there could be no mistakes. Who were these people?

"Do you have any more crew families on board?" Logan asked.

She had an idea Logan's brain was working a damn sight better than hers at the moment. It was a good question.

Callum nodded as if he, too, understood the significance of the question. He pressed his comm unit, and the screen appeared in front of him. He swiped through the data, found what he was looking for. "Let's go see."

They followed him out and down the corridor and into the cryotube storage area, which appeared identical to the one on the *Trakis Two*. Callum led them through the rows of tubes, seemingly endless sleeping bodies. He finally came to a halt. "These three are the family of a technician in the fourth rotation on the *Trakis Five*. It should be his wife, a brother, and his young son." According to the records, he was five years old. Katia stepped closer so she could see through the glass. A woman, probably in her thirties. She shifted to the next tube. A man. How were they to tell if they were who they were supposed to be? But then she moved to the final tube, which should have contained the boy. She grinned at Logan. "Bingo again." The cryotube held an adult male, certainly not a young child. "Looks like we have a pattern."

"But why?" Logan said. He was rubbing his scalp as though he could miraculously make his brain give up the answer. "Who are these people?"

"And, more importantly, where are the people who should be here?" Long dead, she was guessing. Christ, she knew better than anyone that it was possible to change the Chosen Ones. Rico had done it with over half the people on the *Trakis Two*. It wasn't easy, but it could be done. It looked like the victims were all crew families. Or at least she was guessing they were from the groups of threes.

"There was talk about the lottery being rigged," Callum said. "For years before we left Earth, the rumors were going around. It was said that the places were filled before they even started the lottery process. Max always denied it, but I wouldn't have put anything past the old bastard."

By Max, he had to mean Max Beauchamp, president of the Federation of Nations. He didn't sound as if he liked the man. "Wasn't he going to be your father-in-law?" she asked.

His eyes narrowed, then he grinned. "And one of the reasons I decided that it was not in my best interests to marry Tamara."

"Only one of the reasons?"

"There were a few more."

"So what are you thinking?"

"Maybe someone got greedy," Logan put in. "The Chosen Ones' places had already been sold off to the highest bidder."

"But what would anyone do with money where we were going? Why get more?"

"Money isn't the only commodity," Callum said. "Maybe they offered other things. The promise of support in the new world, perhaps."

"So no more Chosen Ones places for sale. What was left?"

"The crew family tubes. Balls. A brave new fucking world, all right." Logan sounded totally pissed off. She decided to stay quiet; she didn't exactly have a leg to stand on, having paid for her own place on the *Trakis Two* with a combination of money and the promise to support Rico by whatever means necessary when, or if, they arrived at their destination.

"It's all supposition right now," was all she said. "We still have no clue who was responsible."

"But we do have an idea of where to look next. You said it yourself—the first victims of a serial killer are usually connected to the killer. How about our murderer somehow discovered that their family wasn't where they were supposed to be? That, instead, they'd been replaced by someone else and were long dead?"

"So they decided to take a little revenge."

Logan grinned. "All we have to do to catch our killer is discover which active crew members had family on board the *Trakis Three*."

"Sounds too easy."

"Not if all the records went up with the ship."

There was that. "But we do know one person who had family on the *Trakis Three*," she said. "Jake, the tech guy." And the more she thought about it, the more the idea made sense. "Who better to mess with the central database?"

Callum's comm beeped, and he read something on the screen. "We need to go to a party."

Chapter Twenty-Five

Logan wanted to get back to the *Trakis One* and do a bit of digging into Jake, somehow get access to the backup files for the *Trakis One*.

Instead, he had to go to a goddamn party.

It was taking place on the bridge of the *Trakis Seven* and appeared to be in full swing by the time they stepped through the doors. There must have been about fifty people present, presumably most of the crew of the *Trakis Seven* plus a maximum of four people from each of the other ships. He looked around to see if he recognized anyone—Jake, maybe—and caught sight of Pryce standing close to Layla. They were talking intently, but then Layla turned around and stalked away. Clearly, she wasn't happy with whatever he'd said. Chatting her up most likely. The old lech.

Callum nodded to them. "I'll send you the crew information for the ship—who has family and where. Now, enjoy the party. We'll talk afterward."

Katia had been quiet since they'd left the cryotube storage area. Was she thinking about her own situation?

Is that what had happened? Someone had sold the cryotubes to the highest bidder and jettisoned the original owners. The family of the crew members. But who would have the access to do that?

Though Rico had done it on the *Trakis Two*. How?

"How did Rico manage it?" he asked Katia.

She glanced at him; she'd been watching the party. All the pretty people. Actually, most of them looked a little on the doddery side. "Manage what?" she asked.

"Replacing the Chosen Ones. It can't have been easy. He must have had someone on the inside. Otherwise, it could never have worked." She wrinkled her nose as she no doubt considered whether to tell him or not. He could see in her eyes that she knew the answer to his question. "Come on, Katia. It might give me some insight into what we're looking at."

She gave a small shrug. "I already told you all I know. He bribed the captain of the *Trakis Two*, turned him into a vampire, and he said it was the worst thing he had ever done."

That meant it was pretty fucking bad. "Anything else? Even the captain couldn't have done it alone."

"All I know is the money we paid for our places went in bribes to various people. Rico could probably tell you more. I wasn't involved in that side of things." She peered around the room. "Come on, let's go find something to eat. I'm starving."

He supposed she had gone a long time without food. Probably a record for her. "Over there," he said, spotting a long table that had been set up with food along the edge of the room. Placing his hand on the small of her back—he almost expected her to brush him off—he ushered her through the crowd. He liked touching her, could feel the warmth of her skin through the thin silk of the dress. What was she wearing underneath? Not a lot, at a guess. He was filled with an overwhelming urge to take her somewhere away from all the people and find out. But maybe he'd better feed her first.

He was aware of a lot of people's interest as they passed. Most of the men were in their crew dress uniforms, but many of the women, like Katia, wore dresses. His military uniform gave him away as someone apart. No doubt Pryce had spread the word that they'd been woken up to head up the investigation. No one tried to talk to them.

There seemed an air of…he couldn't quite put his finger on it. Maybe desperation. Like fiddling while the Titanic went down. And he could almost smell fear on the air. Were they worried that the ship might explode around them before it got a chance to fall apart on them first? They were too shrill, too bright.

They came to a halt in front of the food. It looked okay. Probably rations for a month. But did that matter at this point?

Katia piled up a plate, but Logan wasn't hungry. Not for food, anyway. He was filled with a feeling that his time was running out.

Spotting an empty chair, he pointed her in that direction then stood over her as she concentrated on the food. If he remembered rightly, from this vantage point, he could see right down the front of her dress, to the creamy, freckled skin of her breasts. His dick twitched. He was fed up with people; he'd never been a party person, anyway. He glanced around and found Dylan and Adam across the room, leaning against the wall, both their gazes fixed on him and Katia. Doing their bodyguarding thing. What were the chances of slipping away and getting some alone time? He wanted to talk to her even more than he wanted to fuck her. Okay, maybe it was equal.

As he turned his attention back to Katia, Layla came to a halt beside them and cleared her throat. He sighed, tore his gaze away. Layla appeared a little peeved, her lips tight, her brows drawn together. Her "nice" image seemed to be slipping a little. Maybe she was missing Rico. "What did Callum want to talk to you about?" she asked without preamble.

Katia's mouth was full, so he answered. "He just wanted an update on the investigation."

"Why would he want an update? The investigation is closed." Her frown deepened. "The *Trakis One* sent out a comm yesterday. Everyone knows that. A terrorist blew up the *Trakis Three*, and he died in the explosion."

"Very convenient," Katia muttered between mouthfuls.

"And that's exactly what we told Callum," Logan said soothingly. Why was she so worked up about this? Why did she care? Though she'd nearly died in the explosion that had destroyed the *Trakis Three*. Maybe she needed a rational answer. To close off the episode, to make herself believe it wouldn't happen again.

She studied them for a moment longer then whirled around and stalked away. She crossed the room, halted beside Pryce, and leaned in close to talk to him. Pryce looked their way, a scowl on his face.

"I don't think she likes you anymore," Katia murmured.

"Good." He couldn't resist touching her any longer. He stroked a finger across her shoulder, felt a shiver run through her skin, and she stared up into his face, heat flaring in her eyes.

Some of his tension relaxed. He had been in no way sure. But she wanted him; he could see it in her eyes. And hell, she could have him. He just wasn't sure how he could make it happen. He leaned in closer. "How the fuck do we get out of here? I need to get you alone. Badly. How are we going to slip our babysitters?"

"It won't be easy."

But at that moment, the lights flickered and died. At the same time, the screens around the walls went blank, leaving the room in absolute darkness. The sound of raised voices assaulted his ears, but most people stayed calm. "Sorry, ladies and gentleman," a voice came over the comm system. "Please stay where you are. This is a minor malfunction and will be fixed shortly."

Katia's hand slipped into his, and she got to her feet beside him.

"Divine intervention," she said, and her breath feathered against his skin. He couldn't see a thing, but he didn't care if he had to trample over the whole party. This was an opportunity he wasn't going to miss.

"Just don't trip over anything and knock yourself out," he said. "I really want you conscious."

She gave a soft laugh. "Luckily, I have cat's eyes," she whispered. "I can see in the dark." Her fingers tightened on his hand, and she tugged him along. He gave himself into her care and kept his body close against hers. They didn't crash into anything or anyone, and he sensed as they left the bridge. Katia increased their speed, and he stretched out a hand and touched the cool curved wall. Then the lights flickered on, and they went even faster, almost running. He glanced back over his shoulder, but the corridor behind them was empty.

Dylan was going to be pissed, and he laughed.

She glanced at him, but he just sped up. He had an idea where they were heading. They didn't want to go anywhere they had been before, as that would be the first place someone would look for them. But the ships were all designed the same. So up this corridor and a left turn and then a right and they were at one of the small meeting rooms. He pressed his palm to the panel and the door slid open.

He didn't know how much time he had, but he wasn't wasting a second of it.

As the door slid closed behind them, he spun her around in his arms, lowered his head, and kissed her.

They could talk later.

• • •

They were so on the same wavelength.

Katia sank into the kiss, parting her lips. His tongue thrust inside, filling her, and heat flowed through her veins. This felt so right. All day, she'd been looking at him, wanting him. That he'd clearly felt the same released some of her inner tension. He knew her deepest secrets, and he still wanted her.

He pushed her back until she hit the wall behind her then deepened the kiss, and she twined her hands around his neck, dragging him closer. Finally, he raised his head.

"Apologies up front because this is going to be fast. I have the strangest feeling we're going to be interrupted any moment now."

"Well, you're wasting time talking, then."

He grinned. "I've been studying this dress for hours," he said. "And I think all I need to do is…" Slipping his hand around the back of her neck, he tugged at the bow. It unraveled. He stepped back to put a little space between them, and the dress fell to the floor in a pool of silk at her feet.

"Christ," he murmured. "You are so goddamn beautiful." His hand skimmed down over her shoulder to cup her breast, and her nipple hardened, heat sinking into her belly, settling in her sex. She was hot and swollen with need, and she wanted him. She didn't care how fast as long as it was now.

He scraped a thumb over her swollen nipple, and every cell tingled. Then he slid his hand lower, over her stomach, pushing inside the tiny black panties that were all she wore. She held her breath as his fingers slid between her thighs, her whole body jolting with the force of her reaction as he found the swollen bud at her core, playing over it lightly with his fingertip. Then lower, sinking inside her.

"You are so wet."

He pressed up inside her, and a pulse started a steady throb between her legs, everything so sensitive, he'd only have to stroke her again, just there, and she'd be flying. Instead, he withdrew his hand, and she almost screamed.

He pushed her panties down her thighs, and she was naked and more than ready. Maybe she needed to move things on. They were on a schedule here. Reaching out, she unfastened the buttons on his uniform jacket and pushed it off his shoulders. He shrugged out of it, and it fell to the floor. She examined him for a moment, her gaze snagging on the impressive bulge in his pants. She trailed her hand over his stomach to the waistband. Holding his dark gaze, she tugged open the belt, fumbled with the button. He was breathing hard—she liked that—as she slipped her hand inside, wrapped it around his erection. Hot and silky smooth and so goddamn big.

As he stepped back, she released her hold reluctantly. His hands gripped her ass, and he lifted her, backing her against the wall, balancing her there with one hand while he shoved his pants down with the other. He parted her thighs, and she wrapped her legs around his waist, felt him position himself. She took a deep breath as he pushed inside, filling her with one hard lunge. For a second, they remained motionless, simply enjoying the sensation, so much power held in check. It felt like coming home. Like where she belonged. Like the best freaking feeling in the world, and it would make everything worthwhile if only she could have this.

Except she didn't want the power in check. She wanted him out of control. As out of control as she felt. She bucked her hips against him, growling and lowering her head to the curve of his throat, biting down hard, and his hands tightened on her ass, his cock swelling inside her. He liked that. Good, she had been known to bite and scratch just a little.

He shifted her, holding her weight easily, pulling out of her exquisitely slow, the drag of his flesh sending tingles through her entire body. Then he pushed back in, entering her easily this time. She widened her legs, trying to get him closer, and he pulled her tighter, grinding against her, the pleasure building and building until she hovered on the edge of the stars.

He was moving faster now, sweat beading his forehead, and she buried her face against him, clung on for all she was worth, her whole being concentrated on the place where their bodies connected. She'd never experienced this sense of togetherness. Always in the past, she'd been totally her and them. Now she felt as if her very identity was merging, changing, blending with his. Becoming one.

For a second, the thought terrified her, and she must have gone still. He sensed the change and raised his head. His eyes were dark with desire, but something in them calmed her fears. Perhaps that he looked as shell-shocked as she felt.

"Kitten." The word was half groan.

He didn't say anything more, just lowered his head and took her mouth in a drugging kiss while he moved inside her, against her. She stopped thinking and let sensation take over. Felt the exact moment when she tipped over the edge and into the abyss. Pleasure pulsated through her, and she threw back her head and tightened her legs, squeezing him to her as he released the last hold on his control and came with her.

He rolled his hips, grinding against her, and she came again as though the pleasure would never end.

At last, he went still, and for a minute, they clung together. When he pulled out, she wanted to protest, but she clamped her lips together to keep the words inside. Logan shifted her in his arms, turned around, and slid down the wall so he sat legs stretched out, with her cradled in his lap, stroking her hair that had somehow come loose.

She thought about saying something but didn't trust the words that might slip out of her mouth.

Everything felt weird, different. Scary.

Maybe he felt the same, because they sat in silence for what seemed an age. But good silence. While he stroked her hair. Traced patterns on her skin until she purred with pleasure. But the horrible niggling feeling that their time was limited was nudging at her, and finally, she cleared her throat.

"I don't know what's happening."

"Me, either," he said. "All I do know is it's never happened before."

"Are you going to go all mushy on me?"

A chuckle rumbled through him. "I think I might."

There were those jumbled emotions again, fear and hope and something she was too afraid to identify. Maybe Logan was braver than her. Maybe he'd have the courage to say it out loud. Did she want that? It would change everything.

But if they were going to get deep and meaningful, then she wanted to see his face while they were doing it. She wriggled in his lap so he loosened his hold, then she twisted so she sat, straddling his thighs, his cock half hard between them.

She cupped his face, looked into those beautiful eyes, kissed his mouth, then sat back on her heels. She took a deep breath. She could do this. She just needed a moment.

He smiled. "I like you, Detective Mendoza."

Hmm. That wasn't what she'd expected.

He reached up and smoothed the line between her brows. "Hey, I'm building up to this. But it's important, the liking thing. I mean, how shitty would it be if you fell—" He broke off, shook his head. "Balls." Took a deep breath. "I can do this. Really, I can."

"You can, Logan. You're brave. You're a hero. You have medals to prove it."

He grinned, then the smile faded, and his face settled into a serious expression. His hands slid around her waist to hold her, as though he suspected she might bolt. She wasn't going anywhere. She was on edge, excitement shimmering just below the surface. Willing him to say the words.

"Katia Mendoza, I love you."

Her eyes pricked. She lowered her head to his and kissed him slowly, her tongue pushing inside, tasting him. His cock stiffened between them. Raising her head, she stared into his eyes, opened her mouth—

Someone banged on the door, and a voice came over the comm system. "Katia, you have ten seconds to put your clothes on and then we're coming in."

"Well, that sucks," she muttered. Not what she'd been planning on saying. "I should have shot out the door lock."

Should she say it quickly? But it didn't seem right with Dylan hovering outside the door. She gave Logan a last peck on the cheek, and then she jumped up and grabbed her dress, pulled it up, and tied a quick knot at the back of her neck. She glanced around for her panties but couldn't see them anywhere. Logan was still seated on the floor, a dazed expression on his face. "Pull up your pants, soldier."

He shook his head, pushed himself to his feet, and pulled up his pants as the door opened. She noticed something black on the floor, her panties; Logan swooped down and picked them up as Dylan appeared in the doorway, Adam behind him.

They took in the view with narrow-eyed disapproval.

"I can't believe you did that," Dylan growled. "Fucking inconsiderate. Do you know what Rico would have done to us if anything had happened to you?"

She shrugged.

Logan reached down and picked up his jacket, put it on.

He loved her. Or at least he'd said he loved her. Logan

wouldn't lie. *He loved her.* She needed to tell him she loved him, too. They might all die any moment, but for now, it was enough.

"Stop grinning like a fucking Cheshire cat." Dylan glared at her.

She wiped the expression from her face. "I'm not."

"You are. He must be a fucking good lay."

He was, but that wasn't why she had to concentrate on keeping the smile from curving her lips. Suddenly, she wished she'd told him. She wasn't ashamed. And who knew what might happen next? Someone had already tried to kill them three times. You couldn't guarantee anything. Coming to a decision, she crossed to where he stood, came to a halt in front of him, gave him a lingering kiss on the mouth, then whispered in his ear. "I love you, too."

"Jesus," Dylan muttered. "I'm going to puke."

Logan ignored the other man, wrapped his arms around her, and kissed her back, and she forgot everything for long moments. Finally, he sighed against her lips and put her away from him. "Let's get back to work."

Chapter Twenty-Six

She loved him.

It might mean nothing. Hell, it would probably mean nothing—there could be no future for them together when she wasn't even human. She might even be immortal.

And maybe no future apart, either, if the whole world crashed and burned around them.

But hell, actually, it meant everything.

She loved him.

He didn't think anyone had ever loved him before. Certainly no one had ever said the words.

It made his insides all sort of—

"Get that gormless expression of your face," Dylan said, glancing over his shoulder.

Instead, Logan reached out his hand and found Katia's. He didn't think he'd ever voluntarily walked hand in hand with a woman, either. Christ, he was repressed.

Dylan was walking in front of them, Adam behind, no doubt to prevent them from making a run for it. But where was there to run? They had to decide what to do next. He wished they could return to the *Trakis Two*. Hide away.

But he was still a soldier in the army. He had no choice but to follow orders. He should probably head back to base, report in, which meant the *Trakis One*. But he didn't want to go. Except a little part of him did. Because he was beginning to believe that the answers to everything were on the *Trakis One*.

They'd come to a halt outside the bridge, and he forced himself to say the words. "I think we should go back to the *Trakis One*."

He was hoping she'd argue with him. But nope. "I was thinking the same," she said. She tugged her hand free and reached into her bag, pulled out a bottle, and took a long swallow. She handed it to him. He took a mouthful and waited for her to continue. Dylan cleared his throat, and Logan reluctantly handed him the bottle. Dylan wasn't his favorite person right now. If he hadn't turned up when he did, there was a good chance that Logan's dick would have been deep inside Katia again at this point. Bastard.

"The answers are there if we can work out where to look," she continued. "I think we have to assume that the central information center is well and truly gone—whether by accident or design. So we can't get the information we need, but there must be other stuff we can get. I think we need to examine the ship's logs and look for someone who visited the *Trakis Three* shortly before the first deaths."

He blew out his breath, grabbed the bottle from Adam, took another gulp, and handed it on to Katia. "Maybe you should go back to the *Trakis Two* with Dylan and Adam," he suggested.

"You mean where it's safe?" Katia replied, tossing him a narrow-eyed look.

Dylan snorted. "You've got a lot to learn, soldier."

"I was just thinking—"

She patted his arm and gave him a smile that didn't reach her eyes. "Well, don't. I don't need you thinking about my safety. I have these two assholes to do that. We both go—"

"We all go," Dylan said. "Bodyguards, remember?"

She patted his arm again. "Looks like you're stuck with us."

He was glad and worried. And worried and glad and...

Love was a hard thing to navigate.

At that moment, someone approached them from behind, and they all turned, Dylan and Adam moving subtly so they stood between them and the newcomer. It was Callum, and he had the most enormous grin on his face. He looked happy, but maybe he was just enjoying his party.

"Hey, guys, what are you doing loitering out here?"

"Just heading back in."

He caught sight of the bottle in Katia's hand and held out his own. She handed it over, and he emptied it in one swallow. The grin was back. Definitely suspicious. "What's going on?" Logan asked.

"Come inside, and I'll tell you. I'm about to make a very important announcement." He waved them into the room, and they all shuffled inside. The party was going well, though there was a definite manic feel to it now, as if everyone was trying a little too hard. Callum left them by the door and weaved his way through the room to where his second in command stood. They spoke for a moment. What was going on?

"Sergeant Farrell?"

He turned to find Pryce standing at his side, a glower on his face. Beside him stood another member of the *Trakis One* crew, a woman in a blue shirt—Anna, the Tech supervisor they'd met the first day of the investigation.

"Layla appears to believe that you are continuing the investigation," Pryce said.

Logan glanced at Katia, and she gave an almost imperceptible shrug. No help there.

"She must have misunderstood," he said. "We're merely finishing up the report. We should be able to submit it very soon, and then the investigation can be officially closed."

"Good. That's probably it. Make sure I get a copy of that report ASAP." He gave them both a nod and walked away, heading toward where Layla stood across the room.

Anna gave them an uncomfortable smile. "Layla's a good officer, but she's likely not feeling herself right now."

"Why's that?" She'd seemed okay to him. Maybe a little less friendly than she'd originally appeared, but then there were probably good reasons for that.

Anna raised an eyebrow. "You didn't know? Layla's family members were on the *Trakis Three*. Her daughters, they all died in the explosion. So cut her some slack? She's hurting right now and trying not to show it. To do her duty." She nodded to them all. "Enjoy the rest of the party."

Logan stared after her, shock holding him immobile, the words swirling in his head. As she disappeared into the crowd, he turned to Katia. "What the fuck?"

"Let's not jump to conclusions. So she lost her family and never said anything. That doesn't mean anything. Does it?" She thought for a moment. "Though she did lose it straight after the explosion. She was screaming. I thought I was going to have to slap her. But then she pulled herself together. That doesn't make sense. Unless she screamed at the explosion and then went quiet with…shock? But she didn't act shocked."

No, she certainly hadn't acted like a woman who had recently lost her children.

Maybe she had already known they were dead.

Was he jumping to conclusions? It didn't seem possible. And he was sure there were plenty of others who would feel the same way. They needed proof, and fast. "We need the backup files for the *Trakis One*. Not only the crew information but also the shuttle movements. If we go to Pryce and the captain without evidence, they'll likely lock us up."

There was something else hovering at the back of his mind, something Layla had told him, but he couldn't remember what. Then a loud ringing filled the room. Logan shook his head and glanced across to where Callum stood in the center of the bridge.

The ringing stopped, and he raised his hands. "I have an announcement to make," he said, his voice coming over the comm unit and filling the room. "The day is finally here that we've all been waiting for." He paused, no doubt for dramatic effect. "We have received confirmation that we are approaching a system that appears to have everything required to support human life. Ladies and gentlemen, let me show you the Trakis System." The lights went out, and the screens around the room lit up. At first, Logan could make out nothing, just the vastness of space, darkness lit up by pinpricks of starlight. But all the screens were zooming in on one particular patch of space.

Shapes were taking form. Two suns close together, and around them orbited a number of planets.

Katia's hand slipped into his, and he squeezed her fingers. He was finding it hard to take in. He'd sort of accepted that the end was coming, that they had no real future, and now it lay before him.

A new home.

This changed everything. Katia appeared as dazed as he was.

Something red hovered on the edge of the system. A third star? As they closed in, he could make out a gaping hole of blackness surrounded by orange and red flames. It didn't look very inviting. "What the fuck is that?"

"Well, every Eden has its serpent," Callum said from

beside him. "That's a black hole, according to the analysis, but it apparently only affects one of the planets. We should be able to land on the others. Just tell me one thing…"

Logan dragged his attention from the screens to look at the captain. "What's that?"

"That no one is going to blow up my ship before I get there."

He searched the room for Layla, but she was nowhere to be seen. "Wish I could, captain. Maybe you should pray."

"I prefer to rely on other methods."

He wasn't alone there. They needed to catch their murderer, and maybe what was left of the fleet could reach safety. The future of mankind was in their hands.

He almost laughed.

"How long until we reach the system?" Katia asked.

"Forty-eight hours."

Two days and they would be home.

If they didn't blow up first.

Chapter Twenty-Seven

Katia paced the small space. Backward and forward, round and round.

The party had ended hours ago, but they'd been stuck in the freaking docking bay of the *Trakis Seven* for most of that time while the engineers sorted out some malfunction with the airlock. Now they were on their way back to the *Trakis One*.

Layla was not on the shuttle with them. Katia wasn't sure whether that was good or bad. Presumably she'd gotten a lift back with Pryce.

Could she be the murderer? Sweet, nice Layla? Except the nice thing seemed to be slipping. Had it all been an act?

If not, why hadn't she mentioned she had family on the *Trakis Three*? It was such a huge deal for them to get this far and then... It must be even more heartbreaking with a new home on the horizon. While Katia had never contemplated children, hadn't believed they were an option for her, she could see how devastating it must be to lose them.

She certainly wouldn't have felt like going to a party. But

Logan was right. They needed evidence.

If it was Layla, she'd tried to kill them three times already. She'd almost died herself in one of those attempts. Or had she? Maybe she'd timed it just right. Anyway, she was clearly not stable.

The thought made sweat break out on her skin, and she tugged at the silk of her dress.

Why hadn't she brought something to change into? Because she'd thought they would be heading back to the *Trakis Two* and it hadn't occurred to her. Now she was stuck in this stupid dress. At least she'd managed to retrieve her panties from Logan's pocket and they were back where they belonged.

Logan leaned against the wall of the shuttle, hands in his pockets, a frown between his eyes. Was he thinking of her or the case?

He'd said he loved her.

That was huge. She got the impression that speaking those particular words was a first for him. That made two of them. But it had seemed like the right thing to say at the time. Because it was true. When she'd said it, though, she'd thought they had only a limited time left. Now there was the possibility of a new home. The chance that they weren't going to die imminently.

Did that change things?

She snorted. Hell, it changed everything.

Would she have to live on only to see Logan grow old and die? Would she even get to see it? Even if they survived this, Logan was a serving soldier. He'd probably not be allowed to go where he liked or do what he liked. They'd probably end up on different planets, and she'd never see him again. Her insides tied up in knots at the thought.

Suddenly, he straightened, his eyes widening. He came across and stood in front of her. "I remembered what was bothering me."

"And that is…?"

"Layla told me she had no family. This was shortly after I was woken. She said she was an orphan like me."

Katia stopped her pacing. She tried to wrap her brain around the implications. "So she already knew her family was not on board the *Trakis Three*." It wasn't proof, but it was enough to convince her they'd found their killer. Right beside them all along. Mad bitch. And she'd seemed so nice. "We need to get that proof."

"As soon as we reach the *Trakis One*."

"If she doesn't blow us up first."

Dylan popped his head over the seat in front. "We're not going to blow up. I've checked. No bombs. Systems are all good. Nothing is going to happen."

"Good. Make sure it doesn't." She sighed. "So talk to me. We've found a new home. That's pretty momentous. What do you think happens next?"

He squeezed her shoulder. "I was talking to Callum about it while you disappeared to put your panties back on."

She jabbed him in the ribs. "And?"

"Well, apparently, they're still awaiting the results to confirm a match, but it all looks positive. They've sent out probes that should get there a few hours ahead of us, and once the readings come back from those, we're good to go."

"But go where?"

"There are at least twenty planets in the system. The idea is that each ship will land on a different planet. I suppose in case we meet hostile aliens on some of them, or poisonous gases, or man-eating plants or…"

"Okay, enough. I get the picture. So we'll be on different planets."

"You could stay on the *Trakis One*."

It just wasn't possible. While she wouldn't say they were

her people, on the *Trakis Two* at least they understood what she was. She didn't have to hide her true nature all the time as she would if she chose a life among humans.

"Or you could come back to the *Trakis Two*," she suggested.

He sighed. "I'd have to go AWOL. They'd probably come and get me. Besides, you're…" He trailed off as if unsure how to continue without offending her. Then he shook his head. "You know, all I ever wanted, for as long as I can remember, was to fit in. To belong somewhere."

And he clearly didn't think he belonged with her. And could she blame him? "I don't want to lose you," she said.

"You'll lose me anyway. You said it yourself. You'll live a long time and I won't." He pulled her closer against him. "Let's not think about it right now. Let's get this done with and then we'll see what the options are, whether we have any. I won't let you go without a fight."

But maybe it was a fight they'd lost before they started.

"Take your seats," Dylan said. "We're about to dock on the *Trakis One*. And we're all still alive."

"Super."

• • •

The shuttle landed, and the engine sound died to nothing.

Two rides without a catastrophe.

Logan concentrated on that. Otherwise, he didn't know what he was thinking. Everything was all muddled up. He didn't want to lose Katia but couldn't see how he could keep her. He'd told her he wouldn't go AWOL. But maybe he'd been lying. Maybe with Rico's help, he could disappear. But why would the vampire help him? He was only still alive because Katia had made Rico promise not to kill him.

At that moment, a voice came over the comm unit.

"Please keep your seats until you are given permission to leave the shuttle."

That was new. He sank back down again. What the hell was going on?

"This doesn't look good," Adam said.

Logan got up and crossed the small space to stand beside Adam's chair. The other man waved a hand at the screen, which showed a view of the docking bay.

"Balls," Logan muttered. A group of around fifteen men were heading toward the shuttle. What the hell was going on?

"What is it?" Katia asked, peering around him. "Are they soldiers?"

"Obviously." The men were in uniform. Not dress uniform like Logan but combat ready. And they were all armed. He recognized them—they'd trained together before they left Earth—though they weren't in his unit. They must have been woken up. But why? As they drew closer, they fanned out around the shuttle, drawing their weapons. Behind them, he caught sight of Major Pryce and Captain Stevens and, behind *them*, Layla.

Shit.

Could she be working with someone?

The comm crackled to life again. "We would like you to remove any weapons you may be carrying and leave the shuttle in single file with your hands in the air."

"Not going to happen," Dylan muttered. "I knew this was a bad idea."

"Well, nice of you to wait until now to share that little insight," Katia snapped. "What do we do? Can we turn around and fly away?"

"Not a chance. The doors closed behind us. They have to be opened by ship's controls."

"Can we shoot our way out?" she asked. "Don't these things have blasters or something?"

"Ballsy," Dylan said. "I like it. But unfortunately no—we don't have blasters."

"How many weapons do we have between us?"

Was she crazy? Was she seriously contemplating fighting their way out? They didn't even know what was going on. This might merely be a precaution. Though he couldn't see why. It made no sense. Nothing since he'd woken up made any sense.

He was getting a bad feeling about this. But it wasn't like they had a choice.

"Come out in the next minute or the shuttle will be gassed. On your feet or carried out. It's up to you."

Adam made to draw his weapon, but Dylan shook his head. "We're not going to win this one. Crap, Rico is going to be pissed." He stood up and unbuckled the weapons belt at his waist and dropped it onto the chair behind him. Adam did the same. Logan wasn't armed. Neither was Katia—not a lot of places to hide a weapon with a dress like that.

Logan leaned down and kissed her on the mouth. "Whatever you do, don't piss them off."

"Ha. He knows her so well," Dylan muttered.

Katia scowled but didn't respond.

"They're likely to shoot first and ask questions later. We'll get this sorted." He kissed her again because he did have a bad feeling, and he wasn't so sure they would get this sorted. There was a good chance Layla was way ahead of them.

He put his hand on Katia's waist and ushered her toward the door. She resisted for a second then gave in to the gentle pressure.

As she stood in the doorway, she raised her hands then made her way slowly down the ramp. Logan stood for a second, gazing down into the docking bay. The place was crowded. All the men had their weapons trained on them. He glanced down and saw a red dot on his chest. Shit, they meant business. His skin prickled as he walked slowly down the ramp, expecting to feel the bite of a bullet any moment, all his senses trained on Katia in front of him. There was no reason to hurt her, but every cell was screaming to protect her. And there was nothing he could do. Yet. Except maybe talk his way out of this.

He came to a halt at the bottom of the ramp. Katia was a couple of feet away to his left, Dylan and Adam to his right.

He searched the group, but Layla had disappeared.

Pryce came through the armed men and stopped in front of them. Should he talk to Pryce now? But what if he was working with Layla? There was definitely something going on between the two of them.

"What's this about, sir?" Logan asked.

Pryce looked him up and down. His face was expressionless, but Logan had an idea the other man was enjoying himself. Bastard probably hadn't had this much fun in decades.

"We have been given information that the terrorist survived the explosion on the *Trakis Three* and is now hiding out on the *Trakis Two*. Furthermore, we have reason to believe that the captain of the *Trakis Two* is in fact an impostor and is aiding and abetting the terrorist."

"That's bollocks," Katia snapped.

He wished she'd keep quiet.

Pryce smiled now as he looked at her. "And we have further reason to believe that Detective Mendoza was sent here with the intent to sabotage the investigation and make sure the truth never came out."

"And that's *total* bollocks," Katia yelled.

The captain spoke for the first time. "We're not holding you responsible, son." Christ, he hated it when officers called him son. It made him want to punch them on the fucking nose. "We understand you were duped by this woman, but at this point, with the end in sight, we can't take any chances. You'll be incarcerated until we have time to investigate fully and question the captain of the *Trakis Two*."

"Good luck with that," Dylan muttered.

"We have to be seen to be doing everything in our powers to keep the fleet safe and ensure the future of mankind. We are doing God's work."

Pompous ass. Logan looked around, searching for a way out of this. Once he was locked up, he couldn't do anything.

A prickle ran down his spine. Something made him glance to the side, some sixth sense that had always held true in combat. He honed in on the soldier to the far right. The man's finger was tightening on the trigger of his weapon. Logan saw the intent in his eyes. The gun wasn't trained on him, but on Katia.

He didn't even think. He was flying toward her. He knocked her to the floor as a searing pain punched him in the side. He went down, landed on top of her. Had one brief glimpse of her wide eyes staring up at him, filled with panic. He wanted to say something, but his vision was blurring, going dark at the outside, his mind numbing.

He tried to open his mouth, but the world was fading, and he wanted to stay.

And everything went black.

Chapter Twenty-Eight

Okay, so he wasn't dead.

Or maybe he was dead, and he was in hell. Suffering some sort of eternal punishment that would explain the pain pulsing through his head.

Someone slapped him across the face, and he growled.

"He's coming around." He recognized Adam's voice.

"About fucking time," Dylan said. Another slap, and Logan forced his eyes open. He blinked, trying to focus, but the room was swimming around him. Dylan appeared in front of him, coming in and out of focus. Hand raised.

"Slap me again and I'll rip your fucking hand off," Logan muttered.

"Ha. You could try." He lowered his arm. "How do you feel?"

Christ, his brain hurt. "Like I've been hit over the head with something heavy."

"You struck your head when you went down."

It was becoming a habit. He'd gone down? He tried to force his brain to work, but it wasn't cooperating. Closing his eyes to stop the swimming, he concentrated hard. It started to come back to him. He'd pushed Katia out of the way so they wouldn't shoot her. He'd been shot instead. In the side. Except he couldn't feel anything in his side, and every other time he'd been shot, it had hurt like hell.

He pushed himself up so he was sitting, a groan escaping him.

Looking around, he found Dylan and Adam, but no Katia. Pain gripped his chest, squeezing his heart. His head swam. Had they shot her after all? After he'd gone down? "Katia?" he forced the question out.

"Still alive as far as we know. They put her in the other cell. There are only two, so we got to share."

Logan patted his hand over his body, trying to find where the bullet had hit, but there was nothing. "I was shot."

"Tranquilizer dart. Meant for your girlfriend."

"I thought..." He'd thought she was about to die, and he'd jumped in like an idiot. Just responded to an impulse to save her, whatever the cost.

"It was adorable, really. Though, for a moment, I thought we were all dead. Lot of trigger-happy soldiers out there."

"Why were they taking out Katia?"

"Apparently, they've discovered some evidence that implicates her in the terrorist attack. She's in league with the terrorist, who is now alive and well on the *Trakis Two*. With Rico."

He remembered now. "Except there is no fucking terrorist." He rubbed at the back of his neck where an impressive lump was forming. Another.

"Not according to the captain. He's real and he's in league with Satan and he's hiding out on the *Trakis Two*. Katia was sent to mess up the investigation. And she did a great job of it. Apparently, she's a modern day Mata Hari, using her delectable little body to lure the poor, susceptible soldier—that's you, by the way—astray. And she could very well have the ability to blow us all up, which is why they were knocking her out."

"Was she conscious?"

"Och aye," Adam said. "She surrendered when you went down. She was quite distraught. There might have even been a few tears. Until they showed her that you were just taking a nap. Then she looked a wee bit pissed off. They searched her, handcuffed her, and threw her in the cell. She'll be fine."

No, none of them would be fine. He had a really bad feeling about this. Another bad feeling—something else that was becoming a habit. He was getting fed up with them, but he couldn't shake the idea that Layla wasn't finished. That right now she was in control. And—more than ever—he didn't want to die.

That was a first. Not that he'd ever actively courted death, but neither had he looked to the future. Now he did. He wanted to live and go exploring this new world, and he wanted Katia beside him while he did it. For however long she would put up with him. Until he was too old and decrepit to keep up with her.

So they had a murderer to stop. Maybe more than one. Did Layla have an accomplice?

How the hell was he supposed to find out from inside a cell?

He closed his eyes and cleared his mind.

"Are you going to sleep again?" Dylan asked. "Because we have things to do."

What things? They were locked in a cell. "Just give me a minute. I need to think."

Layla had said that she sometimes visited the other ships.

She must have made a trip to the *Trakis Three*, hadn't been able to resist going and taking a look at her children, and they hadn't been there. How had she reacted? He could only imagine.

So she'd killed the interlopers.

And, after that, she'd dug a little deeper. Found out that other crew families had also been replaced. So she'd killed again and again. Maybe out of genuine outrage, but also to muddy the waters. So if the deaths did come to light, the finger wouldn't be pointed directly at her.

She'd been on the shuttle before they had taken off for the *Trakis Three* the first time. She could have easily disabled the guidance systems and overridden the auto controls.

She'd nearly died with them when the *Trakis Three* had exploded. Except she would have known the timing. She might have even detonated the explosives from on board the shuttle. As she sat behind them, fiddling with her bag. Could she really be that ruthless? And still come across so nice? He could understand her killing the people who had taken her daughters' lives. He could even understand the others. But to kill over ten thousand people?

If he was right, then she'd also tried to kill him and Katia with poisoned gas on the *Trakis Two*. She couldn't have known he would go off in search of food. If he hadn't, they would have both died that day. Had they been getting too close?

"You finished thinking yet?" Dylan asked.

He opened his eyes. "Yeah." He had to talk to the captain. Because he was guessing Layla wasn't finished.

Dylan was seated on the cot bed. Adam leaned against the wall by the door. They were both looking at him, speculation in their eyes and something else. "What?" he asked.

Dylan ran his hands through his hair, rose to his feet, took the few steps so he was standing over Logan. "There's something we need to do."

"What?" Was he going to die after all? Had that been their plan all along? Part of Rico's orders. If that was the case, why hadn't they finished him off while he was out cold? Whatever, he wasn't going to take it sitting down. He pushed himself to his feet, staggered, balanced himself with a hand on the wall while his legs steadied under him. He glanced between the two men. Except they weren't men. If they were, then he might have had a chance to take them down. But they were werewolves. Katia had told him that even in human form they were much faster and stronger than any human.

"Are you going to kill me?" he asked.

Dylan studied him for a moment then gave a small shrug. "That's up to you."

Well, that was a no-brainer. "Then I vote a no."

Dylan laughed. "Not that easy, I'm afraid."

Balls.

Suddenly, he was fed up with all the playing around. If he was going to die, then get it the fuck over with. Except he wasn't just going to stand here. He might have no chance in a fight against two werewolves, but that didn't mean he was going to roll over and let them kill him.

He tensed his muscles, his gaze flicking between the two men, balancing on the balls of his feet, waiting to see who would make the first move.

"Stand down, soldier," Dylan said. "You need to listen to what we have to say before you come out fighting."

"Then get the fuck on with it."

Dylan paced the room a couple of times; it didn't take long. He came back to stand in front of Logan. "Rico told us we had to make the decision before we came back to the *Trakis Two.*"

"What decision?" Was he being slow? Probably, but he had just been knocked out, so he was allowed a little sluggishness in the brain department.

"Whether you live or die."

He wasn't sure he liked the idea of these two fuckers

MALFUNCTION

deciding on his right to live. What gave *them* the right? He scowled, shoved his hands in his pockets, and waited for Dylan to continue. Obviously, it wasn't a straightforward decision or he was guessing he'd already be dead. Something occurred to him. "Does Katia know?" His chest ached at the idea that she could have made love to him, knowing that his life hung in the balance, and not told him.

"Are you kidding me? She would have ripped our hearts out."

He could feel a goofy grin tugging up the corners of his mouth.

Dylan shook his head. "But we don't take orders from Katia. We take our orders from Rico, and he's not going to risk the whole ship for the sake of Katia's fuck buddy."

They weren't fuck buddies. She loved him. But he decided to keep quiet about that.

"So do I live or die? The suspense is killing me."

"It was touch and go for a while. We weren't sure even if we changed you where your loyalties would lie."

His brain caught on that one word. "What do you mean 'changed'?"

Dylan smiled. He raised his arm so it was between them, and while Logan watched, it *changed*. Something shivered through the air, prickling over his skin. The arm elongated, black fur sprouting, vicious claws growing where the tips of Dylan's fingers had been. It took only seconds. Logan couldn't drag his gaze away. A primordial fear ran through him. This was the stuff of nightmares. The monsters were *really* real and locked in a small cell with him. He would have backed away, but he was already up against the wall.

Instead, he forced himself to look into Dylan's face. His eyes had changed, glowing amber and feral, some of the humanity bleeding away.

"We don't change people who don't want to be changed,"

he said. "It's pack law. So you get the choice."

He opened his mouth. Swallowed. Tried again. "Choice?" he croaked. Dylan raised an eyebrow, and Logan knew without asking again what the choice was. He could let them turn him into one of the monsters or they would kill him. "What made you decide to offer me life?" he asked.

"You saved Katia. You thought you were taking a bullet for her, and you didn't hesitate. I think that proves where your loyalties lie."

Yeah. His loyalties lay with Katia. Not with these guys or with Rico or the crew of the *Trakis One* or President Max Beauchamp. Just Katia.

"Do I get to think about it?" he asked, even though he didn't actually need to think about it.

Dylan laughed again. "No."

He wished he knew a little more about what was going to happen. He hated going in blind. And he hated the fact that his future was being taken from his hands. But it really wasn't a choice.

He glanced at the razor-sharp claws and took a deep breath. "Do it."

Dylan nodded. "This is going to hurt like shit," he said, seeming quite pleased by the idea. He stripped off his clothes then sank to all fours. His spine twisted and bent, the bones cracking as they realigned, black fur flowing over his skin. And within seconds, the biggest goddamn wolf Logan had ever seen stood before him. It raised its lip, revealing a sharp white fang, and a low growl rumbled from its throat.

"Holy shit," Logan muttered. Then the wolf leaped for him, and he went down under the force of the blow. Hot breath in his face. He tried not to fight. What was the point? But it was instinctive. And he pressed his hands into the thick coat, trying to keep the snapping jaws from his throat. The thing was strong, and he felt the scrape of fangs across his skin. His nostrils filled with the metallic scent of his own blood. Teeth sank into his flesh, and burning agony shot through his nerves, filling his body. He threw back his head and screamed.

And for the second time that day, everything went black.

He woke up once again with his head throbbing, but this time his mind was clear.

His throat and neck were on fire, and he raised his hand to touch the skin, expecting to find torn and bleeding flesh. Instead, he encountered some sort of bandage. He must have been out for a while. He rolled his head and found that he could actually move.

Adam was seated on the cot bed, arms resting on his thighs, watching him. He looked a little further and found Dylan still in wolf form.

He was huge, black-furred, but with an almost human intelligence in his yellow eyes.

He searched inside himself for changes and could sense a slumbering power. Waiting to awaken. "When will I...shift?" he asked, his voice sounding hoarse and his throat feeling raw—too much screaming.

"We're not sure," Adam replied. "Back on Earth, the first shift always took place at the first full moon after the bite."

"Er...there are no full moons on a spaceship."

"No. And no one has been changed since we set off from Earth. Out here, we can shift at will. We're no longer controlled by the moon. Though sometimes stress can bring it on—especially when you're still new. The first time can be...interesting. Feels like your whole body is on fire," Adam continued. "It's not recommended in an enclosed space. So let's hope we find a planet to land on before you can't hold it off any longer."

"Sounds fun. Any idea how long that will take?"

"None whatsoever. Everyone is different, and this is a whole new situation. But if you feel anything weird, you might mention it."

Weird… Nothing about this *wasn't* weird.

"You're already stronger," Adam said. "The wound in your neck is healing nicely."

"How long was I out?"

"Twenty-four long and boring hours."

Balls. What must Katia be thinking all this time? "So what next?"

"We need to get out of this cell and off this ship."

"Actually, we need to stop the murderer before they kill again or it might be us they blow up next. How do we get out of here? I take it there's a plan."

"You call them up—tell them you have information about Katia. They come here. Dylan will do the rest. Just be ready."

He blew out his breath. "I'm ready."

Chapter Twenty-Nine

Katia lay on her back on the cot and stared at the ceiling. It was gray like the walls.

Why the hell hadn't they seen this coming?

Layla was one step ahead of them.

She had to get out of here. She'd tried the comm unit on the wall, but either it wasn't working or they were ignoring her. Probably the latter. Though they'd want to question her about her terrorist friends at some point.

How was Logan? Had he woken up yet? It seemed like she'd been in here for days, not hours. Her heart skipped a beat as she relived the moment Logan had crashed into her. She'd heard the crack of some sort of weapon, and he'd gone down. She'd thought he was dead. And she might have gone a little crazy. Someone, or likely more than one, had taken hold of her, cuffed her hands behind her back. She'd not been functioning.

Only Dylan shouting at her that Logan wasn't dead had brought her out of it, but by then, she was tied and helpless. There had been too many of them anyway and all armed.

They wouldn't have stood a chance.

The last sight she'd had of Logan was him being dragged away, unconscious, between two soldiers. They'd tossed her in the cell still in handcuffs. She'd managed to slide them down behind her, step over them so at least her hands were in front of her instead of behind, which was marginally more comfortable.

Then she'd had to wait. She just wasn't sure for what. Something to happen.

For the ship to blow up?

Or Layla to poison her in her cell?

Finally, she heard the click of the door lock. She jumped to her feet, every muscle tensing. The door slid open, and Logan stood there, Adam at his back, Dylan in wolf form at his side.

She grinned. "About time. Let's go find that bitch." But as she closed in on him, she sensed a difference. Halting, she sniffed the air then studied him for a moment. A blood-stained bandage was tied at his throat. His scent had subtly changed, held a hint of musk beneath the metallic taint of blood.

She glanced at Dylan. If a wolf could shrug, then that's what he did.

Shock blasted her in the chest, and she gritted her teeth.

They'd freaking changed him.

Why?

She caught Logan's gaze, and he also gave a shrug. Way too much shrugging going on. She turned to Adam. "You turned him into a freaking dog," she snapped. "What the hell?"

Adam grinned. "Just following orders."

Her eyes narrowed. "Rico?" Adam nodded. She'd kill the vampire. He'd promised not to harm Logan. He was such a sneaky bastard. She turned to Logan. "You let them?"

"I didn't actually have a lot of choice."

"Hey," Adam said, "we gave you a choice."

"Yeah. They did. This"—he waved a hand toward his throat—"or death. I decided I wasn't ready to die. This seemed the better option."

She sort of saw his point, but she couldn't cope with this right now. He was a freaking dog. Didn't he know about the whole cats and dogs thing? It probably hadn't occurred to him. And really, would she rather he'd chosen death? Of course not. But Jesus, a dog? She shook her head then stalked toward the door. She stopped in front of Adam and rattled her cuffs in his face. "Can you get these off me?"

"Aye. It just so happens I liberated a key from one of the guards we knocked out. Say 'please.'"

"Piss off," she growled, sticking her hands under his nose.

He grinned but fished into his pocket and came out a moment later with a key. A few seconds later, she dropped the cuffs on the floor and rubbed her wrists.

She headed out of the door and down the corridor. Logan fell into step beside her. "So you don't like dogs?" he asked.

She cast him a look of disbelief. "I'm a goddamn cat. Of course I don't like dogs."

"You'd rather I was dead?"

"Of course not." She shook her head. "Let's get through this and we'll worry about the furry thing later." It wasn't as though he could take it back. It was irreversible. *Later.* "How do we do this? How do we find the bitch?"

"They killed her family. Her daughters."

Was he feeling sorry for Layla? Unbelievable. "Then she should have gone after those responsible. You don't blow up ten thousand innocent people."

"Don't you think you're being a little...hypocritical? You all"—he waved a hand to encompass her and the two werewolves—"were guilty of killing off at least five thousand

Chosen Ones. What makes you any different? Maybe nobody is innocent. Maybe Layla realized that."

"She tried to kill us both. Three times. That makes it personal. And who knows what she's up to now? I don't want to die."

"Good point. Let's go find her. I have a bad feeling about this."

"Me, too."

They'd come to a halt. Where did they start?

"We've got to involve Pryce," Logan said. "There's a chance he might be working with Layla, but I think we have to take the risk. We need to find her and fast, and right now we have no clue where to look."

"Shit," she growled. "I really hate that guy."

"Me, too. But he's our best chance. The captain cares too much for appearances. She's never going to admit she's wrong."

Katia glanced around them, found a comm unit on the wall, and headed over. "You'd better do the honors," she said to Logan. "I don't think he likes me very much."

"That's because you're a terrorist."

"Ha ha."

She leaned against the wall, arms folded across her chest, and watched as he pressed the comm unit, found Pryce from the list, and pressed to open the communication.

"Sir? It's Sergeant Farrell."

"Hand yourself in, sergeant. This can only end badly for you. If you surrender now, then we will not have to use lethal force."

Logan ignored the words. "It's Layla," he said.

"What's Layla?"

"She's the murderer."

"Are you crazy?"

"She found out that her family never made it on board.

Their places were taken by somebody who paid to get on. So she killed them. If you check the shuttle logs, I'm betting you'll find she made a trip to the *Trakis Three* shortly before the first murders."

There was silence on the other end, presumably while Pryce checked the logs and the corresponding dates of the murders.

"It doesn't prove anything," Pryce said.

"She disabled the guidance system in our shuttle to prevent the investigation taking place. She was with you on board before we took off. She had the time and the opportunity."

"That could have been a malfunction." Christ, the guy was persistent. He obviously didn't like the Layla theory. He clearly had a soft spot for the scientific officer, and it wasn't hard to guess why.

"She blew up the *Trakis Three* to prevent us finding the identities of the first murders, because they would have pointed directly to her."

Another silence, though she could hear the man breathing.

"We need to find her," Logan pressed. "She's got to be desperate, and she was hardly stable before. She could be planning anything. Do you want to blow up when we finally have a new home within reach?"

"She's in the docking bay. I left her there only a few minutes ago. Bugger. If this is just to get your girlfriend off, then you're making a huge mistake. Where are you now?"

Logan glanced around. "Corridor eight, section three."

"Well, wait there. We'll be with you in five minutes. Do not go in without us."

The comm went silent, and Logan turned to her. "Do we wait?"

"Hell, no."

She headed off at a run in the direction of the docking bay. Logan fell into step beside her, Adam behind her, Dylan padding along at the rear.

She skidded to a halt at the doors, pressed her hand to the panel, and fuck-all happened.

"Shit."

"Stand back," Logan said. She stepped away as he pulled a pistol that had been pushed down the back of his pants, likely another offering from the guards they had taken down. He aimed at the lock and fired a continual burst. The door slid open.

Inside, she could hear the roar of an engine. It looked like someone was about to take off. She ran toward the noise. The shuttle was still on the ground but was readying for takeoff.

"How do we stop it?" she asked.

Somehow, she didn't think a pistol would be enough.

• • •

Logan searched the docking bay, looking for some means to stop the shuttle. He had a feeling that if Layla escaped, then things would not end well for the rest of them on the *Trakis One*. She had to be stopped. They had to find out what else she'd set in motion. She'd blown up the *Trakis Three*. She could have explosives set throughout the fleet for all they knew. She was clearly not thinking with a level head.

His eyes settled on the tanks parked off to the right, and despite the direness of the situation, a grin tugged at his lips.

He goddamn loved tanks.

If he could move one between the shuttle and the external doors, then he could stop her from leaving. He ran across, studied the machine. Where would *he* hide the keys? He reached into the turret basket and found them then jumped up onto the top and swiped over the opening mechanism, and the hatch rose.

He dropped down inside, and the machine activated. He swiped the key over the pad. The tank awoke beneath him, rumbling to life. He slid it into forward, and they were moving. Through the viewer, he could see the shuttle rising, hovering. He increased the speed and headed for the external doors. Stopped in front of them. Turned so he was facing the shuttle.

He opened the comm unit.

"Give up, Layla. You're not going anywhere."

For a minute, he thought she wasn't going to answer. Then her voice came over the docking bay comm.

"Do you know what they did?"

"I know."

"They killed my babies. I gave up everything so my girls could have a chance at life. And they stole that from me."

Somehow, he had to talk her down. "But you killed them, Layla. You killed the people responsible."

A shrill laugh filled the room. "Are you kidding? Do you actually know who's responsible? Because I do. I know who killed my babies. President Max Beauchamp. Sold their cryotubes to the highest bidder. You think we're heading to a brave new world. All we're heading for is more of the same old shit."

Well, hadn't he suspected that all along? It made no difference. "Come on, Layla. You have nowhere to go."

"Just away from here will work for me."

"That's not going to happen."

"I think it will. I think you'll let me go."

Balls. There was that bad feeling again. "What have you done?"

"You have ten minutes, and then the *Trakis One* blows, with all of us on it. So you have a choice. You can let me go, and then you might have time to find the bomb and disable it—I know you're good at that. Or you can stay there and we all blow up."

He gritted his teeth. His life was full of crappy choices right now. "Why don't I leave the tank here and go defuse the bomb?"

Could he shoot the shuttle down, blast her to pieces? But these tanks weren't designed for shooting inside a spaceship. There was a good chance they'd breach the hull, and they'd all be sucked into space. Which would hardly help matters.

"If you're a good boy and get out of my way, then I'll give you a head start and tell you where the bomb is. You'll never find it in time otherwise."

"Why should I believe you?"

"I never wanted to kill you, Logan. I don't want you to die now. I like you. But time is running out."

More balls.

He shifted the tank into reverse and rolled it out of the way. Then he was up and out of the hatch, jumping to the floor of the docking bay. "Where's the bomb, Layla?"

Chapter Thirty

Logan held his breath as the shuttle's engines roared.

Was she telling the truth? Would she tell him where the bomb was? Was there even a bomb at all?

Damned if he knew. She'd clearly lost her sanity somewhere along the way. But he was guessing yes, at least to the latter. The door to the airlock was already sliding open. Soon she'd be gone. The shuttle moved slowly out of the docking bay, into the airlock, and the doors were sliding shut. As the shuttle disappeared from sight, Layla's voice came over the comm unit.

"Engine room. You'd better run."

He released his breath, and his shoulders slumped. For a second, his mind was blank, and he couldn't work out what he was supposed to be doing. Engine room. Fast.

Katia ran up, skidding to a halt in front of him. "We have to get out of here."

He wished. But he shook his head. "I can't."

For a second, she closed her eyes. When they opened, her expression was resigned. "Why the hell did I fall for a goddamn hero?"

"Just bad luck, I guess."

She didn't move.

"Go."

Her eyes narrowed. "You're kidding, right?"

"Hell, no. Take the other shuttle and get out of here."

"Not happening," she growled.

"*We'll* take the other shuttle and get out of here," Adam said, coming up beside them. "You have thirty seconds to join us or...not. You owe these people nothing."

That was beside the point. He couldn't turn his back on this. He was trained—perhaps the only person in the fleet who could stop this bomb. Maybe they weren't *his* people, but that made no difference.

"Have you got through to Rico?" Katia asked Adam.

"No. We can't get a signal out. She must have jammed it. Once we're away from here, we'll try again. Good luck. You'll need it." Adam hurried away to where Dylan waited still in wolf form on the ramp of the last shuttle. He paused at the door and turned back to them. "We'll send the shuttle back—if there's anything left to send it back to." They both disappeared inside.

Logan touched Katia lightly on the arm. "You should go." He wanted her to go, and at the same time he couldn't bear to see her leave. Looked like it wasn't his choice anyway. She wasn't budging. And he had to move. He had no time for this. But he couldn't make himself turn away.

"We'll go together or not at all," she said. "I have faith in you. But if you don't stop arguing, we're all going to go boom."

He sighed, but she was right. Then he turned and ran for the door, Katia behind him. Which way was the goddamn engine room?

"Turn left," Katia shouted.

They were running flat out when someone called out from behind. "Surrender."

Balls.

He cast a glance over his shoulder. Six guys in military uniform were coming up on them fast. He turned a corner and skidded to a halt, drew his weapon.

"Surrender or we open fire."

"Double balls," he muttered.

"Give me your pistol," Katia said. "I'll hold them off." He looked at her. "You've got to stop that bomb or I'll be dead anyway."

She was right, but he hated it. He handed her the pistol. "Just delay them for a couple of minutes. That's all I need. And don't take any stupid risks. Whatever you fucking do, don't die." He leaned in and kissed her briefly then turned and sped off. He forced himself not to look back as he heard the first shots blast out.

He paused just inside the engine room. The place was huge and circular but almost empty. The engine, inside a silver casing, gave out a muted hum. It seemed impossible that it could be powering this ship, could have kept her moving for five hundred years. There were few places to hide a bomb, and he moved methodically through the room. A cabinet ran around the far wall, and he opened the doors one by one. At the third one, he found his bomb—a rectangle of some sort of plastic explosive—enough to blow a huge hole in the engine room—with a detonator and a timer. He had less than four minutes.

"Don't move."

For all of one second, he remained motionless. But time had nearly run out, and he turned slowly. Pryce stood in the doorway, his weapon drawn and aimed straight at Logan.

Time seemed to stand still. Pryce's finger tightened on the trigger. Logan could almost feel the bullet ripping into him. This wasn't happening.

Panic clawed inside him. Something shifted in his head, and he swayed, fighting for balance. What the hell?

Concentrate.

Breathe.

"Did you know there's a bomb in here?" His voice came out rusty, and he cleared his throat.

Pryce ignored the comment. "Have you seen Layla?"

The question took him unawares. What did Pryce know? He decided the truth was his only option. "She's gone."

Pryce's eyes widened. He stepped through the door, looking around him as though Logan might have Layla hidden away somewhere in the room. "What do you mean 'gone'?"

"Got in a shuttle and flown away. But she has left us a little present."

Pryce shook his head. The hand with the gun wavered slightly. "She wouldn't go. We were supposed to…" He shook his head again. "You're lying."

"Nope. Not about Layla and not about the bomb." Though he had a funny idea Pryce knew about the bomb. "You and Layla, you're…" He wasn't sure how to word the question, and the timer was running down. He had three minutes before the whole ship would blow.

His skin prickled, and sharp pains shot through his arms and legs. The air around him shimmered, and black spots danced in front of his eyes. Concussion?

"She loves me," Pryce said.

No fool like an old fool. A red fog filled his brain, blurring his vision. And he was hot. So hot. He shook his head, forcing his thoughts to focus. What was his best option: to go along with it or try and get through to the other man? "She's played you for a fool, Pryce. She told me you gave her the creeps. That you were an old tosser. She came on to me from the moment she met me. Said that she hated being surrounded by old guys."

"No, she was playing you. It was the plan. That was all. It was me she wanted. Me she turned to when her family was gone and she was alone."

"You knew?"

"She told me. She told me my family was dead as well. My brother and his children. Gone. Replaced by strangers. She killed them for me. We were going to have a life together. She can't be gone."

Christ. "Why don't you go check the docking bay? Maybe she's not gone after all. Or maybe she's come back for you. She probably does love you." Steeling himself, waiting for the bullet.

Pain was building inside him now, flames streaking along his limbs, a ball of fire roiling in his belly, burning him from the inside. And Adam's words came back to him… *Feels like your whole body is on fire.*

No!

Not happening. Not now.

His vision blurred as he stared at the bomb then sharpened so he could see everything more clearly. No more time. He had to stop it. He couldn't do this. But he crashed to his knees, out of control. The crack of bones was loud in his ears. His spine arched, snapped, and he threw back his head and screamed.

• • •

Katia was out of bullets. Any moment now they would realize she wasn't shooting back, and she'd be overrun. Then the shooting stopped. Just like that. She peered around the corner. They were all disappearing in the opposite direction.

What the hell?

She pivoted and raced after Logan. Hopefully, he would have dealt with the bomb, but just in case…

She was almost at the engine room when a piercing scream tore through the air. A second later, the scream turned to a howl.

Holy hell, no.

Skidding to a halt at the door, she peered inside. A huge dark blond wolf lay on its side, panting. It raised its head and stared at her out of purple eyes.

Not good. In fact, very, very bad.

Pryce was standing over him, a pistol in his hand, eyes wide, jaw slack. He must have heard her because his gaze shifted to her, and he slowly raised the gun and aimed it at her chest. His finger tightened on the trigger. She was going to die. Then the bomb would explode and Logan would die. Not happening.

Willing the change over herself, she leaped toward Pryce while still shifting, crashed into him. The roar of the gun filled her ears. Ignoring the pain that sliced through her side, she ripped at his throat, her mouth filling with the warm, metallic taste of blood.

Without checking if he was dead, she shifted back, scrambled to her feet, and crashed to her knees besides Logan. His wolf's eyes were wide, staring at something behind her. She twisted, followed his gaze. An open cupboard. The bomb. Ticking down. Less than a minute. No off switch.

For a moment, panic clouded her mind, her heart hammering, blood pounding. Then she turned back to Logan, dug her hands into his thick fur of his neck. "Logan, I know you're in there. Come back. I don't know how to stop it." Nothing. She shook him. "God damnit. I'll freaking die if you don't come back right now. We'll all die. There's a freaking bomb about to go off."

Yup. They were going to die.

Then the air shimmered around her, and a moment later, he was back.

He dragged himself up, almost falling against the wall.

The timer showed they had fifteen seconds. They weren't going to make it.

Sweat rolled down Logan's forehead as he studied the device. She hoped he knew what he was doing.

He had only one chance at this. He reached out a hand then dropped it to his side again.

Do it!

She held her breath as he reached out again, pulled out the red wire...and the timer stopped. One second to go.

She blew out her breath as Logan rested his arms against the wall then his head against his arms. He was naked. His clothes were in shreds on the floor where he'd shifted. She was still in the red dress, though it was ripped down one side.

But they'd done it. She'd honestly thought they were dead. She'd never known a new shifter with any sort of control.

Finally, he turned to face her. "Well, that was interesting."

"You did it. That's all that matters. We're safe."

"Thank God."

She heard a short, harsh laugh. Pryce. Not dead after all. It looked like she'd missed his jugular, but his throat was a bloody mess.

Logan crossed the room to stand over him. "What do you know?"

The bad feeling that had been an almost constant companion was back again and stronger than ever. Blood bubbled from Pryce's crimson lips. She was pretty sure the man was dying, and she couldn't feel sad about that. He was clearly one of the bad guys here. But how? Why? Had he been working with Layla all along?

"It's too late," Pryce whispered, his voice hoarse, his breath labored. "Even if you stopped the bomb, it was already too late. Don't you see? The people who did this have to be punished. They have to die. Layla knew that."

"Do you know what he means?" she asked Logan.

"I have no clue. But, apparently, he's in love," Logan said.

"With Layla?" She couldn't seem to get her brain working, was finding it hard to come back from that place of certain death. "We need to find out what the hell he's talking about."

"Too late. He's dead." His frown deepened. "What about the ones following you? Where are they?"

"I don't know. Something happened and they disappeared."

Then the shrill buzz of an alarm filled her ears.

Chapter Thirty-One

What the fuck now?

Logan couldn't cope with this. He'd changed into a goddamn wolf. And it had hurt. A lot.

Now he was naked. Searching the room, he identified the remains of his pants. He picked them up, pulled them on. The fastener was gone, and he tied them together with a strip from his torn shirt. It would have to do. Now he could cope.

The alarm was cut abruptly.

Logan stared at Katia.

What was their next move? He'd defused the bomb, done his duty, saved the goddamn ship, and now he wanted off it. Even if it meant he was going AWOL. He'd worry about that once he was down on firm land. Pryce's last words were churning in his mind. It was too late. That was a load of balls. But too late for what? Did he want to stay and find out? Hell no! Unfortunately, there were no shuttles left.

How long would it take for Adam and Dylan to return to the *Trakis Two* and send the shuttle back? About an hour and a half at a guess. They'd only been gone about twenty minutes. *Just don't panic and stay alive.*

He looked at Katia. She appeared dazed. "Any ideas?"

Before she could answer, the shrill of the alarm started up again, and the main lights went out, replaced by a flashing red light. Something was happening, and he was guessing it wasn't anything good. A booming voice filled the engine room, and he heard it echoing through the corridor outside.

"All personnel return to your quarters. This is an order from your captain. All personnel to your quarters."

Like that was going to happen.

He headed across to where Pryce lay, his eyes open and staring, blood staining his mouth. Crouching down, he released the comms unit from his wrist. But who to call?

He tried to get a link out, but nothing was happening, and he shoved the comm unit in his pocket. Next, he grabbed Pryce's pistol, which he shoved into his waistband at the back. Now they needed to find out exactly what was going on. "Come on," he said.

He headed out of the room and along the corridor. Then he stopped at a junction. The corridors all looked the same to him. He glanced at Katia beside him. "The bridge?" he said.

She gave a nod and ran off up the corridor to the left. He followed at a jog. The alarms were still ringing.

The doors to the bridge were shut, and there was no response when he pressed his palm to the panel. He didn't even hesitate, just drew Pryce's pistol and shot at the lock. Except the pistol was empty. Fuck. He turned it in his hand and smashed the panel with the grip. Sparks flew and the doors slid open. Inside, he could see the same dull red light flashing. It was as annoying as hell. He glanced at Katia. "Stay here."

"Yeah, right," she muttered.

At first, he thought the bridge was empty. He squinted into the dim light then spotted Stevens in the big captain's chair. Hunched and shrunken, she glanced up, her eyes narrowing on Logan. "All crew are to stay in their quarters."

Logan thought about pointing out that he was not crew and he didn't actually have any quarters but decided it was a pointless exercise. There was a strange expression in Stevens' eyes. The woman looked manic, her white hair on end. "What's happening?" he asked.

"You should go to your quarters. Make your peace with God."

"Balls to that." He moved farther into the room, keeping his eyes on Stevens.

"There's nothing we can do. This is divine retribution."

Okay. So the captain had lost it. Totally. "What. Is. Happening?" He spoke the words slowly, enunciating each one in the hope they would get through.

The captain gave a small smile. "The guidance system has been locked, and we're heading straight to Hell." She reached down and pressed a button on the arm of the chair, and around the room, the screens came to life.

It took Logan a moment to work out what he was seeing. He stood in the center of the room and stared at the images on the screens. The same image on each one. It was official—they were heading into Hell.

His eyes were drawn to the whirling mass of flames that filled the screens.

"Holy crap," Katia said from behind him.

In the center was a black hole. Stygian black. He remembered Callum mentioning there was a black hole at the edge of the system they were heading for and that they would need to avoid it. Except it looked like they were making a direct route right for the center. Logan couldn't drag his eyes from the darkness filling the monitors. In a strange way, it was beautiful, a vision of whirling iridescent gases surrounding a gaping maw of blackness. The hole didn't quite fill the screen, and off to the left he could see a planet—extremely inhospitable looking, ocher with rings shading from palest yellow to blood crimson circling it, and a single moon in orbit. And every second, the black hole loomed closer as though all the brightness was being sucked from the world.

He dragged his gaze away and back to Stevens. "Maybe it might be a good idea to change course," he suggested in what he thought was a reasonable tone considering the circumstances.

Stevens turned her manic smile on him, seeming satanic in the glow of the red flashing lights. "I can't. The guidance system is not responding. God is guiding us now."

Christ.

He wished he knew how to fly a goddamn spaceship. Why hadn't he taken a course?

He hurried across to the console and searched it for something that made sense. Something like a big button saying *press me.* Or maybe a steering wheel.

"Don't touch that. You can't stop this now."

Stevens had risen to her feet, a pistol in her hand. And it was aimed at Logan. He drew his own and then remembered he'd run out of bullets. He aimed it anyway, but Stevens ignored him, took a step closer, and Logan threw the pistol at her. It hit her forehead, deflecting her to the side, but she was still coming, her finger tightening on the trigger.

Logan backed away, but there was nowhere to go and no cover. He was well and truly fucked. Changing into a wolf would be good right now. Except he had no clue how to shift. Last time, he'd had no control.

Then a dark blur flew across the bridge, crashed into Stevens, and she went down. She was screaming, a high-pitched sound more of anger than fear, her hands scrabbling for purchase.

The great cat lunged, tearing at her throat, and blood

spurted from the wound, turning the scream into a gurgle as she drowned in her own blood. She went limp, arms collapsing, the pistol falling to the floor by her head. Logan snatched it up and backed away.

The huge cat stared at the body for a second then leaped off, landing in front of Logan. A second later, it was gone, and Katia stood before him naked. Blood was smeared across her face, and she wiped it with the back of her hand then gave him a slow smile.

"Having problems?"

He shook his head. "You could say that. And, unfortunately, they're not over yet." He crossed the room and picked up her dress from the floor, handed it to her. Though maybe he should just keep her naked. She might distract him from the whole diving headfirst into a black hole scenario.

Though he wasn't ready to give up yet. There had to be something he could do. He cast a last look at Stevens then back to Katia. "Hey, do you ever…you know…eat people?"

She frowned. Maybe it wasn't good shifter etiquette to ask, but he was curious.

"It has been known. But not her. Too stringy and tough."

Thing was he had no clue if she was having him on or telling the truth. It would have to wait until later.

A voice came over the comm unit. Layla.

"To the people of the *Trakis One*: I'm sorry it has come to this, but the corruption inherent in our system has followed us from Earth. Our leaders must die for what they have done."

Logan crossed to the captain's chair. There must be some way to stop her, to get her to give this up. Except he couldn't work out how to even talk to her. He stared at the array of buttons. He didn't want to make things worse, but *could* they be worse? The black hole nearly filled the screens now. Probably his imagination, but he could feel himself getting warmer. He didn't want to burn.

And how close could they get before they were sucked in?

Katia came up beside him, reached across, and pressed a green button.

"Layla?" he said. "Layla, it's Logan. I didn't kill your family, and I'm not ready to die, so could you please fucking tell me how to steer this fucking ship?"

"Logan, I'm sorry. But you're collateral damage. And besides, you're the enemy. Have you ever asked yourself why we need an army in the new world? What do you think would happen when people wake up and realize that their families have been murdered? Replaced by the president's cronies?"

He hadn't thought of that. But he was guessing there would be a few unhappy people. "What about the crew on board? They're innocent, Layla."

"No one is innocent."

He blew out his breath. "Pryce was upset you left without him. He thought the two of you were the real thing."

"He was wrong." The comm line went dead.

"Crazy freaking bitch," Katia said. She gritted her teeth. "I do not want to die. I have not come all this way just to get sucked into a big black hole. We need to know how to fly this thing." She thought for a moment, brows drawn together. Then she sat down in the chair and pressed a few buttons, but absolutely nothing happened. She growled.

Pryce's comm unit beeped from his pocket. He pulled it out and stared at it. Opened the link.

"Pryce? What the hell is going on? I've been trying to get through to Captain Stevens for the last half hour. Are you a-fucking-ware you're heading into a fucking black hole?"

It was Callum Meridian. Katia reached across and grabbed the unit. "Callum?"

"Katia? What the fuck is going on? We're heading for the black hole, and there's nothing we can do about it from this end. We're locked into the guidance system on the *Trakis*

One. And I can't get hold of Captain Stevens."

"Stevens is…incapacitated right now."

There was silence for a second. "What are you doing with his second-in-command's comm unit? Where's Pryce? We need someone with the authority to release the fleet."

"Pryce is incapacitated as well. Look, you're going to have to talk us through it. Just tell us what we need to do."

Another moment of silence. "You've got to switch off the automatic guidance system and turn the ship."

He took a deep breath. "Then tell us how."

"Where are you?"

"The bridge."

"There's a pad on the top right of the captain's chair. The console is activated by thumbprint. You need Stevens, and I'm guessing that's a problem."

Logan glanced over to where Stevens lay in a pool of blood. "No problem." He hurried over, crouched down, and grabbed the body under the armpits, dragged it across, and heaved it up onto the chair. Taking the dead woman's hand, he pressed her thumb to the panel.

Captain's Console Activated.

So far so good. "Now what?"

"I'm not even going to ask how you did that. Now you need to access the automated guidance control and switch it off. That should give you manual control. Swipe the screen, and a number keypad should come up."

He did, and it did. "I've got it."

"Key in, 10451."

He did and then stared at the screen, his teeth gritted.

Guidance system malfunction.

Fucking hell.

"I don't believe this," Katia said.

"What's the problem?" Callum sounded rattled now.

"We have a guidance system malfunction." The man on

the other end was silent. Again. That wasn't good. "Callum? What next?"

"There's no way we can fix it remotely."

Logan ran a hand over his face then scrubbed it through his hair. "There has to be a way."

"Look, Logan, you need to break the link. Free the other ships from the *Trakis One*."

He pressed a finger to the spot between his eyes. "If you say the fate of humanity is in our hands, I might just switch off this comm unit."

Callum let out a snort of laughter. Logan liked a man who could laugh in the face of death. "How about my fate?"

That wasn't going to do him and Katia a lot of good. "Not much better." He glanced at Katia, saw the understanding in her eyes, but she caught his gaze and gave a small nod. He blew out his breath. "Okay, what do I need to do?"

"Break the uplink between the ships. There's a signal that goes out—close it down. Go back to the keypad. Type in 25487."

He typed.

Uplink system Malfunction.

He kicked the chair and swore again. *Balls, balls, and more fucking balls.* "Malfunction."

"Fuck."

"Where does this link originate from? There must be somewhere physical."

"To your right, you'll see a console. That's the uplink generator."

Logan crossed the room and tapped the console. *Malfunction.* What a surprise.

He looked around then crossed the room and picked up Stevens' pistol from the floor, came back. He took a deep breath, and before he could give himself time to think, he shot out the uplink console. An alarm sounded then cut out.

"Anything happened?" he asked.

"Wait a minute…we're free. What the hell did you do?"

"I shot the fucking console."

"Thank you. The other ships are unlinked. You did good. Humanity owes you a debt of gratitude."

"Fuck off."

Callum was silent for a moment. "There's no way we can reach you in time. I'm sorry."

Logan was sorry as well. "Yeah, well, I guess this is good-bye."

"Good-bye."

And the comm unit went dead.

He breathed out slowly then held out his hand to Katia. She slipped her fingers into his and rested her head on his shoulder. "Do you really hate dogs?" he asked.

"No. Actually, I always wanted a puppy."

He stared into the screens. They were filled with the black hole now, like peering into Hell.

How long did they have? Minutes, he was guessing.

A message flashed up on the main screen.

Emergency mode initiated. All systems malfunction. Activate cooling systems.

Turning to face her, he lowered his head and took her mouth in a slow, drugging kiss. She tasted of…blood. He tried not to think of it as Stevens' blood; he wanted to enjoy this last kiss.

He curled his hand around the back of her neck, beneath the long silky strands of her hair, and pulled her closer. Kissed her some more.

Finally, he raised his head. "I love you."

She smiled. "You're only saying that because we're about to die."

"No, I'm not."

"I love you, too. You're the only man I've ever said that

to."

He turned her in his arms so she could see the screens and pulled her back against him, wrapping his arms around her waist. She was so short she tucked in beneath his chin. "Are you scared?"

She gripped his arms and squeezed. "Terrified. It's weird, but for so long I didn't care if I lived or died. Now I want to live so much it hurts."

"Me, too." He stared at the screen. "It's beautiful in a way. Beautiful and terrible. But at least we got to go into space."

"And save humanity."

Yeah, there was that. Only one problem. "I'm not sure humanity is worth saving."

"Maybe not. Too late now. You're a hero. They'll no doubt sing songs about you around campfires on the new world."

"Hah. And we solved the case. I wonder what will happen to Layla."

"If there's any justice in the world, something very, very bad." She sighed. "No regrets?"

"Loads of regrets. For one, I'm totally pissed that I never got to land on a new planet. We were so close."

It was no longer his imagination; he could actually feel the heat now. Would it hurt? Probably not. He kissed the top of Katia's head and tightened his hold. Closed his eyes.

A moment later, she thumped him on the shoulder. He didn't want to look, but she thumped him harder this time, and he opened his eyes. The screen was flashing again.

Docking bay airlock opened for shuttle approach.

All the other screens showed the black hole, so close now he could see the individual flames. Wiping the sweat from his forehead, he tried to make sense of the words in front of him. "We won't make it. It's too far. We'll never get to the docking bay in time."

"We will if we shift."

"I don't know how."

"Yes, you do. Just reach inside yourself and find your wolf. Do it or we both die."

He reached. And nothing.

In front of him, Katia gritted her teeth. Then she extended her hand toward him. Black fur sprouted. Fingers turning to wicked claws. And she raked them down over his bare chest.

Pain flared. His nostrils filled with the scent of fresh blood. And deep inside him, his wolf awoke and howled.

This time the shift came over him like magic, smooth and easy.

And the world was changed. Beside him, the huge black panther growled. Then they were off and racing down the corridors. The heat almost singed his fur, but he felt alive, reveled in the stretch of muscle, the strength of his wolf body. They were in the docking bay as the shuttle touched down. Up the ramp. Katia was human again, and she slammed her hand against the door panel, and he hurled himself after her, hit the back wall of the shuttle, crashed to the floor.

Were they too late? Once within the gravitational pull of the black hole, they would never get out. They'd be sucked in with the *Trakis One*.

And then they were flying, the speed pressing him against the wall.

Arms enfolded him. A face buried in the fur of his throat. Warm breath. Katia.

If this was the end, he wanted to hold her, and he found his human form deep inside himself. A moment later, he was back. Wrapping his arms around her, he held on tight. He lost track of time, unsure whether they were heading away from the black hole or straight into its fiery depths.

Finally, after what seemed like an age, they slowed. Katia wriggled in his arms, and he loosened his grip. She opened her eyes and looked straight into his. "Hi."

"Hi," he said back.

"I love you."

"I love you, too. And this time, hopefully, I'm not about to die." Logan took a deep breath. He cleared his throat. "Are we okay?"

"Let's go take a look."

He pushed himself to his feet and held out a hand for Katia, pulled her up. They moved to stand in front of the screen.

"Holy shit."

"That about sums it up."

Katia gripped his hand. The black hole filled the screen, and against the circling burning gases he could see the silhouette of the *Trakis One* as she was pulled inexorably toward her death. All those people, who had come so far across the universe, and to end like this.

He'd saved the other ships, done his best, and that was all he could ever do.

They watched until the ship got smaller and finally disappeared into the darkness. Maybe there was something on the other side. No one really knew how black holes worked. Perhaps the *Trakis One* would find herself in a different dimension. A new world. A better one. Hell, it could hardly be worse.

Then he breathed out and turned away. "That was close," he said.

"It was indeed."

"I turned into a wolf. Twice. That was pretty surreal."

"You did good."

All his life, he'd looked for somewhere to belong. And never found it until now. He'd survived against all the odds, and now the future stretched ahead of him. For the first time in his life, he felt a sense of optimism. Excitement. Maybe it wasn't paradise waiting for them out there. Who knew what this new world would offer? But now he had the time to find out. And he wouldn't be alone.

He had to pick his side, and he'd picked Katia.

"*We* did good." He grinned. "I guess I'm one of the monsters now."

Epilogue

Something woke her.

Katia didn't want to be woken; she was having this wonderful dream. "Piss off," she mumbled. But the dream was fading and reality taking its place.

For a moment, she was disorientated. Where was she?

Soft lips kissed the back of her neck, and a shiver of pleasure ran through her. A hand cupped her breast; it felt so good, and a groan escaped her lips.

Warm breath teased her ear. "Wakey, wakey, kitten."

"Don't call me kitten." But the protest was half hearted, and she rolled onto her back and pulled Logan to her, kissed his mouth, her tongue pushing inside, sliding against his, tasting the sharp sweetness of him.

His erection nudged at her belly.

Oh yeah, she could wake up like this every morning.

"We have to get up," he whispered. Not words she wanted to hear.

"Oh no, we don't."

They were in the cabin Rico had originally assigned her.

Exhaustion had hit as soon as they had landed back on the *Trakis Two*, and she'd grabbed Logan and disappeared. She knew Rico wanted to hear everything. But he'd have to wait. And once alone, they'd made sweet love and then fallen into a deep sleep wrapped in each other's arms.

"Rico just commed. He said he's the captain and to get our asses to the bridge pronto or we'd be court-marshaled."

"That vampire has delusions of grandeur. But I suppose we could humor him."

She gave him one last kiss and rolled out of bed. They'd both lost their clothes in that last shift. But they'd wrapped themselves in the silver space blankets on board the shuttle so as to not give everyone an eyeful when they'd disembarked on the *Trakis Two*. Now the blankets lay in a pool of silver foil on the floor. Her bag was still on the chair where she'd left it, and she dug out a pair of jeans and a T-shirt.

Logan wrapped one of the blankets around his waist, and she bit back a grin. They'd have to find him some new clothes, maybe raid a few cryotubes before they woke up the Chosen Ones.

The bridge was crowded when they arrived. She recognized most of the people there, and she nodded to Dylan and Adam.

She was getting over her aversion to werewolves. Being in love would do that. She found herself smiling.

"Okay, children," Rico said. "I got you all here today to show you your new home. This, people, is the Trakis System."

He pressed a switch, and the screens came to life. She took a step closer, Logan rustling at her side.

All the screens showed the same thing. The system they'd been approaching. Closest to them, she could see the black hole and its accompanying planet. But beyond that, she saw other suns and planets orbiting them.

Then the monitors were closing in on the system, past

the black hole, past other planets, finally homing in on one particular sphere that orbited a small orange sun. There was something odd about it, and she realized that it wasn't rotating on its axis like the others. Instead, it appeared to be half in darkness, half in light.

"Welcome to the planet that never sleeps," Rico said. "Half is eternal day and half forever night. I thought it would suit some of us just fine. We'll be landing within hours. Get your stuff together."

She'd gone into this not expecting to ever wake up. Then she'd woken, and she hadn't expected to survive. They'd come so close to dying so many times. And she'd fallen in love. She'd been a loner for so long she didn't know how she was going to take to being a loner no longer. She was about to embark on a new life. With a goddamn dog. A small laugh escaped her.

"What is it?" Logan asked.

"Just thinking how weird everything has turned out. Did you ever expect this when you went to sleep on the *Trakis One*?"

"You mean that I'd be standing on the bridge of a spaceship, in a crowd of werewolves, vampires, demons—"

"And werecats. Well, one, anyway."

"Yeah. And the weirdest thing of all—that I'd fall in love. Hell, no, I never expected that." He lowered his head and kissed her. "But you know what, it doesn't really matter. All that matters is that you'll be beside me. I never had a home, ever, in my whole life. Now as long as you're with me, wherever we are will be home."

Rico was circling the room, pouring out glasses of whiskey, handing them around. Today was a day for celebrations. They were alive, together, and had a future. She raised her glass, clinked it with Logan's. "To coming home."

Acknowledgments

Thank you so much to my fabulous publisher, Liz Pelletier, for suggesting I write this series and revisit my Dark Desires world, albeit a few hundred years before *Break Out*, book 1 in that series, begins. And thanks to everyone at Entangled Publishing for all the support and the amazing cover, and especially my editors, Liz and Lydia Sharp, for their great work and advice.

Thanks to my marvellous critique group, Passionate Critters, for reading my stories and telling me what they really think.

And finally, thanks to Rob, my other and better half, for putting up with me constantly disappearing into worlds of my own making.

About the Author

Growing up, Nina Croft spent her time dreaming of faraway sunnier places and ponies. When she discovered both, and much more, could be found between the covers of a book, her life changed forever.

Later, she headed south, picked up a husband on the way, and together they discovered a love of travel and a dislike of 9 to 5 work. Eventually they stumbled upon the small almond farm in Spain they now call home.

Nina spends her days reading, writing, and riding under the blue Spanish skies—sunshine and ponies. Proof that dreams can come true if you want them enough.

If you'd like to learn about new releases, sign up for Nina's newsletter here.

www.ninacroft.com

Discover more Amara titles...

STEEL COYOTE
a novel by Beth Williamson

The universe is a tough place for a female captain. A sketchy deal goes south, and Remington is forced to accept help from Max Fletcher. He's hot. And he's trouble. But every crooked cartel is on her tail. Max Fletcher has spent his life running from his past and has no idea what makes him bail out sassy Remy when she needs a pilot to get her illegal cargo to its destination—the last place in the universe he ever wants to land.

RED ZONE
a *Red Zone* novel by Janet Elizabeth Henderson

In a world where everything you see and hear is recorded by an implant in your brain, Friday Jones has seen something she shouldn't. And now everyone either wants her dead or to steal what's locked in her memory banks. The last thing Striker wants to do is draw attention to his team and their special abilities. Helping Friday will do exactly that. She's hard-headed, smart, and a walking dead woman. But when he discovers what's in her head, there's no way he's going to leave her behind.

SHIFTER PLANET: THE RETURN
a novel by D.B. Reynolds

Scientist Rachel Fortier thinks she'd on the tiny planet of Harp to study the planet's wild cats. But her shipmates have a darker purpose. And when they capture a gorgeous golden panther, she discovers they intend to keep it--for experimentation! Rachel has to free him. But when she does, she learns two things... One, her cat is a shifter. And two, he's the most beautiful man she's ever met.